"Look at that moon, Sloan," Paris said in awe as she caught a glimpse of the huge golden globe. "Have you ever seen so beautiful a summer night?" The moon had risen off the horizon and cast a brilliant light over the swimmers, glistening on the surface of the water like tiny twinkling lights. Paris had been drifting and walking further away from the bridge where the water was shallower.

She was so engrossed with the moon's spectacle she didn't realize her breasts were now fully above the water's surface.

"Yes, very beautiful," Sloan replied quietly, noticing Paris's breasts and erect nipples glistening in the moonlight. She tried to will her attention away from Paris's supple whiteness, but it was not to be. She had never seen a woman with such extraordinary beauty before. She told herself it was the romantic setting, the moonlight, the water droplets on Paris's perfect skin, the warm summer night all conspiring against her. But she couldn't help it.

Paris was beautiful. Sloan had always thought Paris was beautiful, even as a skinny, gap-toothed six-year-old . . .

"Look over there," Paris pointed at the island. "Look at the fireflies under the willow." Paris had turned around, her shimmering shoulders toward Sloan.

"Uh-huh." Sloan blinked and looked in the direction of the willow as if coming out of a trance.

Beneath the WILLOW

Kenna White

Bella
BOOKS

Bella Books, Inc.
P.O. Box 10543
Tallahassee, FL 32302

Printed in the United States of America

Editor: Anna Chinappi
Cover designer: LA Callaghan

ISBN 978-0-7394-7046-6

This book is dedicated to all those who loved and lost on
September 11, 2001.

In Loving Memory of Jan,
Amis de l'ame.
You will be missed.

Acknowledgments

A big thank you to Craig, Beth, Annie, Kristi, Cameron, Haley and Ann. You don't know how special you are to me and my work. May angels smile upon you and lighten your load.

CHAPTER 1

The door to exam room number two opened, and a woman strode out. She jotted some notes in the patient's folder before handing it to the nurse who met her in the hall. She then took the folder from the pocket on the door to exam room three and read the lab report clipped to the front. The thirty-eight-year-old woman wore a pair of black slacks and a peach-colored silk blouse under her white lab coat. A stethoscope was draped around her neck, and her name was embroidered in script letters over the breast pocket, Doctor Paris E. DeMont. Her shoulder length blond hair was artistically French-braided and held by tortoise shell clips on either side. Her makeup was thin and nearly unnecessary over a clear but pale complexion and pleasingly full lips. She had strict posture to accompany her professional demeanor softened only by her pale blue eyes. Her forehead furrowed as she studied the lab report and unfolded the EKG readout. After leafing through several pages, she opened the door and disappeared inside. Ten minutes later she reappeared and closed the door behind her.

"Carly, can you reschedule Mrs. Stecklinburg's CT for sometime next month?" Paris asked as she made a note in the folder then added it to the stack at the nurse's station.

"I practically had to promise my firstborn child just to get the one she has," the nurse scowled. "Is there a problem with the fourteenth?"

"She will be out of the country," Paris replied. "She's taking a cruise. I guess her palpitations are better. See if you can schedule it for sometime after the first of the month. In fact, see if you can swap appointments with Mr. Patrino. I didn't like the looks of his echo this time."

"Angiography suite two won't be available tomorrow. The hospital called and said they moved you to suite four at six thirty in the morning. Something about a leak in the ceiling."

"Did you call Mrs. Romano to let her know her appointment is earlier?"

"Yes," Carly reported.

"Paris?" A gray-haired man in a lab coat and thick glasses stepped out of an exam room at the end of the hall. "Do you remember the name of that doctor we met at the conference a few months ago? The cardiologist from Seattle?"

"Osborn," she replied still studying a stack of lab reports. "And Bill, he was from Tacoma, not Seattle."

"Thanks," he replied ducking inside his office and closing the door.

"Mr. Burns?" she asked Carly, nodding her head toward the exam room Bill had just left.

"Yes," she whispered. "His CT just came back." Carly shook her head sympathetically. "And he's being transferred to Seattle in two weeks."

Paris turned her attention back to the stack of lab reports. When she finished with them she looked up at Carly and raised her eyebrows.

"Who's next?"

"Believe it or not, you are officially finished for the day."

"You're kidding." Paris checked her watch. "It is only five fifteen. Are you sure you don't have someone hidden in an exam room somewhere? Someone with a big stack of lab reports and X-rays to read? Someone who has been waiting since noon?"

"Nope. Not a one." Carly took a message from her desk and handed it to Paris. "You do have a phone message from someone named Malcolm Vetch. He said he is your property manager and was calling about your house in Banyon, somewhere or other."

"Missouri," Paris inserted, reading over the message.

"Yeah, Missouri. Do you know him?" Carly asked cautiously.

"Yes. Malcolm and I know each other." Paris grimaced as she continued to read.

"He was very insistent you return his call before the weekend. Something about repairs that couldn't wait."

"So what's new?" Paris mumbled to herself.

"Is it something I could help you with, Doctor DeMont?" Carly asked with concern. "I'll be glad to handle it if you tell me what you want me to say."

"Thanks, Carly. But I can handle it." Paris patted the nurse's hand and gave an understanding smile. Paris knew her nurse was trying to help. It was something she had been doing since 9/11. Something all the nurses and doctors in Paris's office had been doing since the World Trade Center collapsed and turned Paris's life into an empty, sterile existence. It had been over five years but her friends and colleagues continued to stand guard over Paris's life until they felt she was ready to handle it alone. She appreciated their concern, their friendship, but she had learned to carry on, in spite of the huge void Gabby's death left in her life.

Gabriella Buttichi had been Paris's own personal spark plug. A woman who had talked, smiled, laughed, jogged, danced, worked, teased and loved her way through thirty-five years of life until the insanity of that horrifying day snuffed out her enormous energy. Their eight years together had barely scratched the surface of their life's potential.

Paris pocketed the message and headed for her office. She spent

3

the next two hours dictating her charts and reviewing tests results for tomorrow's patients. She didn't mind spending her evenings at the office. It was something she had found herself doing more and more. More hours at work meant fewer hours at home or out on the streets where people lived in vibrant and enthusiastic New York City. Paris had never liked the rush hour traffic or the congestion. She had always preferred the more quiet hours before or after the normal rush hour commutes. Since 9/11 she subconsciously avoided lower Manhattan or any of the streets and highways that offered a view of the vacant Battery Park skyline. Paris was thankful for her hectic and busy work schedule.

Her office door opened slowly after a knock. "Hey, Paris. You still at it?" Bill asked, his tie now loosened and his shirt collar open. "Getting late."

"Almost finished. Last chart."

"You're putting in a lot of time, Paris. You need to pace yourself. You can't keep coming in first and leaving last and still be on top of your game. Who's on call this weekend?"

"You are." Paris gave a small grin.

"Oh yeah, I am, aren't I?"

"As a matter of fact, after tomorrow, I have four days off."

"Well God damn! Paris DeMont, doctor of cardiology to Manhattan's elite is actually taking four whole days off? I don't believe it. It must be a mistake. Alert the *Times*." Bill waved his hands dramatically across the air as if this news was worthy of print.

"Fine, have your little joke. Make fun of me." Paris leaned back in her leather desk chair and crossed her hands in her lap. "But who is the one who handled that collapsed stent at three in the morning for you last month? And who cut short a meeting in Dallas to cover your patients so you could attend Marianne's midterm graduation? And who put in a twenty-four hour shift covering two hospitals over Christmas so you and Joe could take your wives to Atlantic City to overeat and over-imbibe?"

Bill removed his glasses and cleaned them on his tie. "Four days does not a vacation make, my dear doctor."

"I'm fine, but thanks for the concern."

"If you need some time off, just let me know, okay?" he offered.

"I will, Bill."

"How long have I been telling you that?"

"Oh, about five years."

"Go home, Paris. Go out to dinner. Go to the movies. Go to the beach. Go on a trip that has absolutely nothing to do with medicine."

"Go home, Bill. Vera has your dinner ready."

He returned her smile and closed the door behind him, leaving Paris with an empty clinic and her lonely ride home. She hung her white lab coat on the brass coat rack behind the office door. She retrieved the telephone messages and her pager from the pockets before turning off the lights and closing the door. She walked the long hall of exam rooms, navigated the route through the lab, the nurse's station, and the waiting room, turning off lights and closing doors until she was locking the clinic door imprinted with the names Doctor Paris DeMont, Doctor William Hays and Doctor Joseph Corelli, Manhattan Cardiology Associates.

"Good evening, Doctor DeMont," offered a small black man with graying hair. His navy blue uniform shirt and matching pants were neatly pressed, the shirt buttoned to the neck and his black work shoes polished to a brilliant shine.

"Hello, Mr. Williams," she replied fondly. "How's your wife doing?"

"She's much better, thank you. That's nice of you to ask." He stopped his janitorial cart outside her office door. "You're looking lovely this evening, Doctor D."

"Thank you, Mr. Williams." Paris patted his shoulder. "You're looking pretty dapper yourself."

He smiled shyly as he unlocked her office, then pushed his cart through her door.

"Good night, Mr. Williams." Paris waved as she headed for the elevator.

"Good night, Doctor. You take care of yourself now."

A taxi pulled up in front of a white granite-fronted apartment building on West Seventy-Fourth Street where a doorman opened the back door and offered Paris a hand.

"Good evening, Doctor DeMont," the doorman acknowledged.

"Hello, Mike." Paris hurried through the front door and into the elevator. Inside her ninth floor two-bedroom corner apartment she stepped out of her shoes and pressed the button on the answering machine. As it chirped and beeped through its playback cycle, she set her briefcase on the end table and draped her jacket over the back of the couch.

"Hello, Paris dear. This is your mother. Why haven't you called me this week? Are you all right, sweetheart? Do you need some of my chicken soup? Call me. I'll be home after seven thirty. I'm going to visit Madeline Hunter in the hospital. She had a knee replacement yesterday, and I told her I would come by this afternoon. Thank you, sweetheart, for the DVD player you sent me for my birthday. The gals are all jealous. I'm sure I can figure out how to use it. Give your mother a call. 'Bye."

Paris smiled at her mother's voice. Liz DeMont telephoned Paris once a week as regular as clockwork. She and Paris's father had moved to Florida the year after Paris graduated from medical school so he could play golf year round. When he died from pancreatic cancer two years later, Liz decided the Florida climate was more to her liking than New York's weather so she stayed. She now had a circle of friends, mostly widows, who played bridge, shopped the malls, ate long lunches at every café within twenty miles of Vero Beach and gossiped about each other's families.

The machine beeped again.

"Hello, Miss DeMont. This is Malcolm Vetch. I've been trying to get a hold of you about your house in Banyon. It's vacant again and before I can make it available for rent, there are some repairs we need to make. The kitchen sink needs a new faucet, a couple light fixtures need replacing, several of the balusters are dangerously weak and need replacing, and there isn't any hot water coming from the hot water tank. It probably has a rusted tank, and we'll need to get a new one. There are some subflooring problems in the back of the house also. I have to do a thorough inspection tomorrow, and there may be more. Looks like the old house is showing its age, but I'm sure I can get it back in shape."

Paris changed into a robe and went into the kitchen to make a salad for dinner. Before she could finish eating the telephone rang, Liz DeMont's name flashing across the caller ID.

"Hello, Mother," Paris said and quickly swallowed her bite.

"Paris dear. How are you? How's New York? How's the practice?" Liz didn't seem to need answers to her questions. To ask them seemed sufficient.

"Fine, mother. Everything's fine. How are you? How's your cold?"

"Oh, you know me. A cold one minute, fine the next. Everyone in the bridge club has something. We just pass it around." She laughed and coughed. "But I'll be better when my daughter tells me she's coming to Vero Beach to see her mother. It has been ages and ages, you know."

"It's been three months. I came down for Christmas and for your birthday."

"Three months is ages for an old woman like me." She coughed again then blew her nose.

"You aren't old, mother."

"If you say so, dear. Let's talk about you. How have you been Paris, really? Have you been taking care of yourself?"

"I'm fine, mother. Bill sends his best. He always asks about you."

"He is a very nice man. His wife is a lovely woman."

"Yes, he is. They both are very kind."

There was a silence. Each of them knew that Bill Hays and his wife being kind people was a direct reference to their selfless concern for Paris after 9/11 and Gabby's death.

"So dear, have you been seeing anyone?" Liz asked.

"No, mother," Paris said quietly.

"But sweetheart, it has been—"

"Mother, please."

"Okay. Not another word about it from me."

"I got a call from Malcolm Vetch," Paris offered.

"Malcolm Vetch? Who's Malcolm Vetch?"

"He owns the property management company that is handling the house in Banyon for me."

"Do you still own that old thing? I thought you got rid of it years ago when mother passed away."

"No, I kept it for a tax shelter. He has been handling the renters for me. It has been costing me quite a bit in repairs over the past few years."

"Sell it, honey. Cut your losses and dump the old place for whatever you can get out of it. When mother left that place to you she didn't do you any favors. It didn't even have a dishwasher or air conditioning. It was nothing more than a big barn of a place with drafty windows and high ceilings. And there is nothing in Banyon worth crossing the street to see. Sell it, Paris. Sell it right away." There was a cold detachment in her mother's voice as if the old house held no fond memories for her.

"I don't remember it being that bad."

"I know, honey. You had a great time visiting as a little girl but that was thirty years ago." Her voice softened, knowing Paris had treasured memories of her visits with her grandmother. "I remember the first time we let you stay with mother. You were six. I was so worried you would be homesick, but you weren't. You had your suitcase and Floppy under your arm."

"Who was Floppy?" Paris asked with a chuckle.

"Don't you remember that old brown stuffed dog you had, a cocker spaniel or some such thing?"

"You mean Flag. Yes, I remember."

"Yes, Flag. Anyway, we dropped you off in Banyon and hoped you wouldn't cry the whole time you were there. Mother said you watched us drive down the road then skipped off to play, never cried a tear. When we came back to pick you up, you cried for hours over leaving."

They both laughed.

"You had your hair braided when we got there. Something you had never had before. It looked so cute. Mother said you insisted on her braiding your hair. You said a little girl you met showed you how to braid. You were so proud you had learned to do that."

"Yes. Her name was Sloan." Paris smiled at the cobweb-covered memory. "I played with her every summer. We were the same age."

"You insisted on wearing your hair braided for weeks after that."

"I still braid my hair. French braids," Paris added.

"You were such a smart little girl. You could read the newspaper by the time you were five." Liz hummed with a proud mother's contentment.

"Now I don't have time to read the newspaper," Paris advised.

"You work so hard, honey. You should take some time off. Take a nice vacation. Go somewhere. Forget about work."

"As a matter of fact I do have four days off."

"Four days? That isn't time off. That's a long weekend, Paris. I meant a few weeks or months. That isn't enough time to catch up on your laundry and housework."

Paris smiled to herself. Her mother must be able to see through the telephone.

"Well, do something fun with your four days, dear. And take care of yourself, Paris. Do you hear me?" Liz had taken on the mantel of protective mother.

"Yes, Mother. I will." Paris had learned years ago every conversation with her mother would eventually include these comments broadcast like an emotional antiseptic. It was best to nod politely and agree. They were more frequent in long distance telephone conversations than in their face-to-face meetings. It was as if Liz had trouble expressing her feelings in person but found more profound mothering skills when there were hundreds of miles between them.

"You call me next week and tell me all the things you did with your time off."

"Okay, but you take care of yourself, Mother. Call if you need me."

"I will. I have to go, dear. The *Golden Girls* is on now, and you know how I love to watch the reruns of that show. That Rose just tickles the heck out of me. I love you, Paris."

"I love you too, Mother. Talk to you." The line had gone dead before she could finish.

Paris hung up and went to make a cup of tea. She checked her watch and decided it was too late to call Malcolm. Since she hadn't fully decided what to do about the house and the repairs, another day wouldn't matter.

CHAPTER 2

"Good Friday morning, Doctor DeMont."

"Good morning, Margaret," Paris said, making her way down the hall to her office.

Margaret was a short woman with a pair of glasses perpetually hung on a chain around her neck but seldom worn. She was hurrying up the hall carrying a coffee mug with cats on it and trying to sip as she walked. She had a full bouncy figure, a big nose and a pen behind each ear. Margaret had been Paris's office manager since she started her practice ten years ago. As loyal as a cocker spaniel, she was habitually happy and as efficient as a Cuisinart. She had accepted early in her employment that her duties were widespread. They included everything from employee management to travel agent. She followed Paris into her office.

Paris exchanged her jacket for the white coat on the coat rack as Margaret placed some mail on her desk.

"Anything important?" Paris asked, looking down at the envelopes.

"Did you need car insurance for a fleet of vehicles or season tickets to NYU's music concerts?" Margaret asked cheerfully.

"No."

"Then you don't have any mail." She smiled broadly. "I, on the other hand, have tons."

"Good. That's the way I like it. Delegate authority. By the way, how is Ziti this morning?" Paris felt obliged to ask about her cat since it was like a child to Margaret.

"Much better, thank you. She hacked up a hairball the size of a matzo last night." Margaret seemed proud of her cat's accomplishment, like a grandmother reporting a new addition to the family.

Paris smiled, almost sorry she had asked. "Good."

"Did you want me to check out the details for that Squibb conference in Detroit?"

"When is it?"

"July something or other, toward the end of the month," she related.

"Get the particulars then I'll decide. Last one I attended in Detroit was a lush-fest. Squibb pulled out when no one would attend the meetings. There is something else I need you to check on for me, while you're looking up airfares," Paris said, draping her stethoscope around her neck. "I need to fly to Missouri to see about my rental house."

"I thought you had a property management company to handle that?" Margaret asked with a frown.

"I do, but I need to run out there and take a look. Can you see what you can do with my four days off?"

"Sure. Banyon, isn't it?"

"Yes. But you'll have to check flights to Springfield or Joplin. There's an airport in northwest Arkansas, too."

"Hotel, too?"

"Yes. Get one as close to Banyon as you can find that isn't one of those rent by the hour places. Maybe a Marriott or a Sheridan."

"You're scheduled for rounds Wednesday morning, right?" Margaret asked, making mental notes.

"Yes. Doctor Hays is on call Tuesday night."

"I'll let you know what I can find." Margaret hurried out the door.

"Doctor DeMont," Carly said, sticking her head in Paris's office. "Doctor Crayler from Boston is returning your call."

"I'll take it here," Paris replied, and picked up the telephone. Her day had begun and like most days, it would be long and busy for her and her associates.

Paris had carefully selected the doctors to join her practice when she realized it was growing faster than she could cover by herself. Bill Hays was a brilliant doctor whose abilities were being wasted in a small hospital in Queens. For years he had been stuck in the monotonous rut of paper pushing after each patient rather than freeing himself to do what he did best, diagnose. Doctor Joseph Corelli was fresh out of the military. His gung-ho attitude camouflaged the deep concern he carried for each of his patients. They all worked well together, Bill's insight, Joe's military efficiency and Paris's outstanding medical prowess. Margaret handled the business end of things, something Paris gladly relegated to her abilities. Three RNs, two LPNs, an X-ray technician, a medical technologist for the laboratory, an insurance clerk, a file clerk and a receptionist completed the staff. There were fourteen employees in the practice, but everyone knew it was Paris's baby through and through. She had invested one hundred percent of herself to make it successful, even more since Gabby's death. With steeled dedication, she put her practice above all else as if the pain of Gabby's loss could be obscured by a work ethic second to none. Now it was second nature to her. What else was there but work? Going home late and exhausted insured Paris could sleep without lonely tears staining her pillow.

"Nine twenty a.m., United out of LaGuardia to St. Louis, then three forty p.m. to Springfield," Margaret said in a quiet voice as she caught Paris in the hall between patients.

"Great. Hotel?" Paris replied, giving the patient's chart a quick look before entering the exam room.

"Still working on that. How do you feel about Coleman tents?" she said with a glint in her eye.

Paris lowered her chin and gave a sideways glance.

"Right. Tents are out." Margaret continued down the hall, humming cheerfully.

Paris finished her last patient at five thirty and went to her office to take care of telephone messages and finish patient charts before calling it a day.

Margaret tapped on the door and opened it. "You're all set." She handed Paris an envelope with printouts of her e-tickets and hotel confirmation. "There's a map in there for the hotel. Comfort Inn Suites for Saturday, Sunday and Monday. You get back just before nine Tuesday night. Rental car confirmation is with Avis. I requested something bigger than a skateboard but no guarantees."

"That'll be fine. Thank you, Margaret. Give Bill the hotel number, and I'll have my cell phone with me if there's any emergency."

"Don't worry about us, doctor. Just go and have a good time. Rest for a couple days." She patted Paris on the hand. "Doctor Hays can handle everything on this end."

"I know," she said looking through the e-mails in the envelope. "You just never know." Her voice trailed off.

Margaret saw something in her eyes that meant Paris had gone to that empty place where people go when they have lost someone close to them.

"I'll tell him," she said, then smiled and left Paris with her thoughts. "Have a safe trip," she added as she closed the door.

Paris finished the charts and last details on her desk then headed home to pack. She had her suitcase nearly filled when she realized she was packing as if she was going to a medical conference. Silk suit, wool slacks, Cashmere sweater, matching shoes and accessories for each outfit was hardly what she needed for a trip to Banyon, Missouri. It was a rural town nestled in Barry County, doorstep to the Ozarks. She sat down on the bed and laughed out loud at the thought of stomping across the pasture in heels, spearing meadow muffins with each step. She emptied the suitcase and began again with slacks, oxford shirts, a fleece pullover, a pair of sensible walking shoes and a pair of Nikes. She set out a pair of gray slacks with a matching blazer and pink blouse to wear on the plane. She found the large envelope where she kept all her papers and receipts about the Banyon house and dropped it in her carry-on.

Paris treated this trip like she did every other job, with crisp efficiency and a detailed itinerary. She would fly in, meet with Malcolm, assess the repairs then fly back to Manhattan satisfied she had dotted every i and crossed every t. It didn't matter that she didn't know anything about home repairs. In New York City if the sink leaked or the balusters were loose, you called the super. The only repair Paris had accomplished was the wooden silverware divider she had slipped into the kitchen drawer. She and Gabby had installed window locks in their apartment but that was mostly Paris reading the instructions while Gabby did the installation, one step ahead of Paris's reading.

It wasn't that Paris didn't know about being a handyman, it was more a lack of time to learn. Besides, Gabby did it. She could cut a board, install a shelf or repair a lamp faster than Paris could look up a repairman in the yellow pages. She admired the way Gabby would fearlessly tackle any job. On their first Christmas together, Paris gave Gabby a leather tool belt with her initials on the buckle. The next Christmas Gabby gave Paris a Fisher Price toy tool belt with PD written on each of the plastic tools. God, how Paris wished Gabby was there to go with her to Banyon. She would know what needed fixing.

The flight was a blur. Paris spent it reading a medical journal and leafing through the papers on the house in Banyon. She had the letter her grandmother had written explaining why she had left her Maybelline, the name her grandmother had jokingly given her large Victorian farmhouse.

"Big Victorian houses are called painted ladies, Paris," she had told the little girl on her first summer in Banyon. "It's because of all the different colors of paint. It makes them look like they are wearing makeup. So I call the house Maybelline."

Paris had loved the summers she spent as a child running, playing and learning in the fresh country air. That was why her grandmother said she left it to her, to someone who loved it as much as she did. Paris's mother had never been a country girl at heart. She fled to the big city as soon as she graduated from high school. She wanted more than Banyon could offer. She wanted bright lights. She wanted a city man who worked in an office and drove a big city car, not a farmer with a pickup truck and a trailer hitch.

Paris's father, Marcus DeMont, was tall, dark and handsome. He also had a shiny new business degree from the University of Illinois. Liz West was beautiful, personable and deeply in love. They married after only six weeks of courtship and against her parent's wishes. They moved to Chicago then on to Watertown, New York, where they began an all-American picket fence dream. Paris came along four years later. It had been a shock to Liz how much a child interfered with her plans for husband, home and social interaction. She had been a good mother, or as good a mother as a woman who belonged to the Woman's Literary Guild, Friends of the Opera, New York Democratic Women's Society and Welcome Wagons can be. Marcus was equally active in the community. He was coerced into running for city council and won handily.

Paris was busy growing up in the presence of a babysitter. By the time she was six, her parents decided she was old enough to spend a month or two each summer with her grandmother in Banyon. Grandpa West had died when Paris was just a baby and Grandmother West was overjoyed with the chance to spend time with her only grandchild. They developed a bond reserved for mothers and daughters. The winter after Paris's fourteenth birthday, Grandmother West had a stroke and a wicked fall that shattered her hip. The realization that she would live out her years in a nursing home was like a knife through Paris's heart. It was far more than just losing a place to go every summer. It was losing her pal, her confidant, her mentor, her friend. Grandmother West said in the letter that she was confident Paris understood what was important about the house and the acreage.

"Maybelline is in your soul, Paris. It isn't the house; it's the way of life. Never give it up. Never forget how it makes you feel."

Paris closed the letter and slipped it back in the envelope. Sometimes she wished Grandmother hadn't given her the house. Sometimes she wished she didn't feel so attached to it. Perhaps everyone was right. Perhaps she should just sell it and be done with it. Let someone else have the headaches of keeping up an old ten-room Victorian farmhouse. Paris leaned back against the headrest and closed her eyes.

Paris claimed her luggage at the Springfield Airport and checked in at the Avis rental counter. All the sedans were checked out. If she wanted a large vehicle, the lady behind the counter suggested a pickup truck or an SUV. Paris settled for an economy coupe with an automatic transmission, a radio with limited range and a moon roof that didn't open. She headed west on U.S. 44 to state highway 39 south. The first thing Paris noticed was the traffic, or the lack of it. She reminded herself this was Missouri, not New York City.

It took just over an hour for Paris to make it to Banyon and the road to her grandmother's house. She slowed to a crawl as she pulled into the drive that led around the house and stopped at the back porch. The house had been painted white with yellow shutters. The multi-colored trim that Paris remembered from her childhood was all the same color. The front porch still stretched around the corner with pilasters and fretwork at the top, but it looked tacky and in need of repair. The frames around the tall living room and dining room windows needed painting. The rose garden outside the kitchen window was long gone, replaced by a picnic table and dilapidated barbecue grill.

She tried her key in the front door, but it didn't open. She walked around to the back door and tried it in the lock, but it didn't work there either. She peered in the back door, but all she could see was the mudroom wall. She frowned with disappointment and took out her cell phone. She punched in Malcolm's office number and left a message for him to call her. She tried the key in the front door one more time.

"Damn," she muttered and gave it a shove.

She walked across the yard to the pasture gate and looked down the slope. One thing hadn't changed. The pond was still there and so was the big weeping willow tree standing majestically on the little island. There was a new bridge over to the island. It was bright white with whimsical Victorian railings on either side of the arched walkway. The view of her island and the tree instantly brought a smile to her face—and a flood of memories. It was just as she remembered it. The moments and events of her childhood settled over her like flower petals, soft and pleasing to the senses.

Paris was happily reliving her summers in Banyon when she saw someone standing in her pond on the far side. She opened the gate and started down the hill.

"Excuse me," Paris called to the woman standing thigh deep in the water.

The woman looked up from her crouching position. She had been poking long sticks into the muddy bottom where the pond narrowed before leading off into the woods as a babbling stream. She didn't reply but watched as Paris descended the slope to the pond.

"May I help you?" Paris asked, fighting the urge to perch her hands on her hips and scowl at the intruder.

The woman wiped the back of her hand across her forehead, leaving a muddy smear. "Sure you can help," she replied, broadcasting a bright smile through a muddy face and matted hair. Her jean shorts were wet to her waist, and her pale blue T-shirt was stained with mud, pond scum and sweat. "Wade on in."

"No, I meant what are you doing there?" Paris said with a measure of exasperation.

"I'm planting *Betula nigra* saplings in the pond bottom." The woman took another stick from the bucket on the bank and nestled

18

it into the muddy ooze beneath her feet. "Can I help you with something?" she added.

Paris had begun walking around to where the strange woman was standing in her pond.

"I'm looking over the property," Paris offered.

"Nice place, huh?" The woman continued to plant the saplings. "If you are interested in renting it, you have to contact Ozark Property Management over in Aurora. Malcolm Vetch is handling it for the owner."

"Yes, I know."

"You going to rent it?" she asked, finishing the last planting and rinsing her hands in the water.

"No," Paris stated, looking back up at the large house on the top of the hill. "I'm the owner."

Paris watched as the woman slowly straightened up and fixed her with a studious gaze. The woman raised a hand to shade her eyes against the evening sunlight.

"You're the owner?" She sounded surprised and doubtful.

"Yes. And who are you?"

"I'm just a neighbor," she replied defensively. "From over the hill back that way." She waved over her shoulder beyond a grove of trees.

"And why is a neighbor planting . . ."

"*Betula nigra,*" the woman supplied.

"Yes, *Betula nigra,*" Paris repeated. "Does my pond require these plantings?"

"It's River Birch. No, not really. But I'm the one who pays to plant and harvest in your pond. I've been doing it for six years now. Malcolm has the agreement I signed."

"Oh really?" Paris didn't remember if Malcolm had ever mentioned it.

"Yeah, I've been paying five hundred dollars a year to plant and harvest from your pond and the surrounding woods. I plant saplings when the pond level is up like this so they get a good start then I harvest mature ones. I also thin the trees in the woods. My land doesn't supply enough, and my pond is too small for my needs. And I explained to Malcolm that thinning the woods occasionally would keep it healthier. I keep the vines under control and clear out the dead and decaying trees. Actually you should be paying me for all I do. But thanks for letting me harvest from your land. It keeps me from driving all over creation to find what I need."

"What do you do with what you cut down?"

"I don't cut down, usually. I trim or separate or thin. If I cut down every tree I harvest from I'd be out of stock in no time. It would be like killing the golden goose."

"So what do you do with what you harvest?" Paris clarified.

"I make furniture and accessories." She splashed some water on her legs to rinse off the mud then climbed up the bank.

"Accessories? What kind of accessories?" Paris watched as the woman wrung out the hem of her T-shirt and stepped into a pair of dirty sneakers.

"I make twig furniture and household items like picture frames, plant stands, lamps, anything cabin rustic."

"Like the tables and chairs in the mountain lodges in the Adirondacks?"

"Exactly."

"So twigs from my trees are decorating some cabin in the woods?"

The woman thought a moment, then nodded.

"Probably." She picked up her tools and dropped them into the bucket.

"That sounds like a fun hobby."

The woman scowled at Paris as if her pride had been wounded by suggesting it was merely a hobby.

"What is it you do?" she asked with a challenging air.

"I work at a hospital," Paris replied with the same cosmetic defense of her profession she always used when traveling. She found it easier to avoid admitting she was a doctor than to listen to strangers relay a long list of ailments and expect an instant diagnosis.

"Oh really? Where?"

"Back east."

The woman raised her eyebrows at Paris's vague answers.

"New York City," Paris heard herself say.

"I have a retailer in Albany who handles my furniture."

"That's in the heart of the Adirondacks. Lots of retreats and lodges up there."

"I didn't catch your name," the woman inquired cautiously.

"DeMont," Paris replied.

"DeMont? Is that first or last?" she asked nonchalantly as she picked up the bucket, ready to start up the hill for home.

"Paris DeMont," Paris added.

The woman stopped in her tracks and snapped a look at Paris. Her eyes did a slow survey of her from head to toe then back up again. She slowly ran her fingers through her reddish-brown hair. Her emerald green eyes fixed Paris with a plaintive stare. One corner of her mouth pulled an ever so slight smile.

Paris watched this filthy woman with strange interest. Her muscular legs and trim figure seemed curiously attractive, as if the layers of pond scum and dirt were invisible. The early summer evening seemed to hang heavily between them. The breeze that had floated around them was suddenly still. Both women found it difficult to blink, much less turn away from the gaze they shared. The shocking scream of Paris's cell phone made them both jump.

"Hello," Paris said as she fumbled the phone from her pocket, her eyes still stuck on the woman.

"Miss DeMont?" the man on the other end asked skeptically.

"Yes."

"This is Malcolm Vetch. I got a message to call this number."

"Yes. I'm at the house in Banyon and my key doesn't work." As she turned her attention to Malcolm and the house, the woman started up the hill toward her property. By the time Paris had finalized a meeting with Malcolm to look over the needed repairs the woman had reached the top of the ridge. Silhouetted against the waning evening light, she stopped and looked back at Paris. She nodded a salutation then disappeared through the stand of trees.

Paris stood alone, wondering what had just happened and who that woman was. She realized she hadn't asked her name. All she knew was that she was a neighbor, made rustic furniture and harvested tree branches from her property. A tingling curiosity floated across Paris's subconscious telling her she wanted to know more, a feeling she tried desperately hard to ignore.

CHAPTER 3

Paris returned to her rental car and checked the map. The hotel reservation Margaret had made for her was in Purdy, at least twenty minutes away. There was nothing else she could do at the house this evening, and it suddenly dawned on her she hadn't had a meal since breakfast in New York. The stale peanuts and flavorless coffee on the flight were a poor excuse for lunch. Surely there would be some place to grab a light dinner in Purdy. The pleasing memory of her grandmother's cooking that ran across her mind was almost real enough to be waiting for her on the kitchen table. The memory of her grandmother's voice from the back steps seemed to split the evening and warm her down to her soul.

"Paris! Dinner's ready. Come a running, youngin'."

A long-legged blond girl ran the path from the pasture gate to the back porch, her hair flagging behind her, her long strides graceful and innocent.

"I'm coming Grandma," she called breathlessly.

"Wipe your feet and wash your hands, Paris." Grandmother held the screen door open until she was inside. The heavenly aroma of fried chicken and apple pie dueled for control of the big kitchen. The table was set for two with blue willow dishes and blue-checkered place mats with matching cotton napkins folded under the forks. A glass of milk for Paris and a glass of iced tea for Grandmother marked the places. Grandmother served the plates with fried chicken, mashed potatoes dotted with butter and a sprig of parsley, steamed green beans from the garden, biscuits made from scratch and homemade apple butter. There was a ten-inch apple pie waiting on the counter for dessert. Dinner fit for a king. And tomorrow breakfast would be mashed potato pancakes from the leftovers with a dollop of apple butter on top. Lunch would be cold fried chicken and biscuits, maybe with clover honey. Grandmother's meals were predictable and delicious. Food to feed the stomach and the soul. The skinny girl from upstate New York always went home a few pounds heavier after her summer visits with Grandmother. Paris's mother would make well-intentioned efforts to re-create those winning recipes, but nothing was quite the same. Grandmother had a special way with breaded pork chops, garden fresh vegetables and anything needing gravy.

Paris instinctively checked her rearview mirror to see if a blond child was running across the meadow. She smiled and closed her eyes, listening to the breeze gently flutter through the trees. A soft tapping of a loose shutter on the second floor disturbed her serenity. She started the car and slowly pulled away, mad at Malcolm that she couldn't go inside.

She turned onto the road that meandered down the hill, over the iron bridge and through the three s-curves that wound past fields and pastures on the way back to the highway. The road seemed narrower, and the canopy of trees seemed denser than she remembered as a child. The round barn just beyond the creek had a new roof. There was a bigger stop sign where the country road emptied onto the highway. Spits and flicks of childhood memories, like slowly rising fog, drifted through the half-hour drive to Purdy and the hotel.

Paris checked in and deposited her luggage in the room before walking across the street to the cafe to quiet the grumbling in her stomach. It was after nine o'clock when she locked her hotel door and slid the safety chain. She showered off the traveler's dust and slid into bed. Just as she was about to drift off to sleep, Paris remembered the woman she had seen standing in her pond. She chided herself again for not asking her name. It wasn't like her to overlook that detail. Whether it was her eyes or her smile, there was something about the woman that rang a bell. But Paris was too tired to think about it tonight.

Paris was up early, her body still clinging to East Coast time. She was dressed and in the hotel lobby for the continental breakfast by seven thirty. By nine she was back in front of the house, waiting for Malcolm to arrive with a key.

He arrived twenty minutes late and roared into the drive, waving at Paris as she sat waiting on the front steps.

"Shall we take a look, Malcolm?" Paris said as he approached, anxious to see inside.

"Sure," he said after a deliberate hesitation. "I was a little surprised you came all the way out here to Banyon just for this. We could have handled it over the phone. You should have let me know you were coming." He fumbled with his key ring.

"You carry the keys to my house on your key ring all the time?" she asked with interest.

"It just makes it easier," he stammered, then swung the door open. "Here we are."

The air inside was heavy and musty. The house was empty except for a box of trash behind the front door. Empty pop cans, hamburger wrappers and empty cigarette packs littered the floor in the living room. Grandmother's green floral carpeting was long gone, replaced by out-of-date matted and worn shag carpeting in three ugly shades of brown. The lace curtains that once fluttered on an evening summer breeze had been replaced with mini-blinds, a few of the slats hanging bent and out of place. The wallpaper had been painted over and the ceiling had been sprayed with sparkly texture. Paris gritted her teeth and swallowed hard. Nothing was as she remembered it.

Malcolm went to the front bay window and tugged at the sash. After a grunt or two he was able to raise it a few inches.

"Let's get some fresh air in here," he said nervously. "When the house is closed up like this the air gets stale."

"It smells like someone has been smoking in here. I thought you knew I didn't want smokers in here." Paris smirked and rubbed her nose.

"Absolutely! I put it in the lease. No one was supposed to smoke in the house. I made that very clear."

"I see that," she said, kicking one of the empty packs with her toe.

"Must have been the movers," he quickly added.

Paris went to the fireplace and ran her fingers over the dusty mantel.

"Who painted the mantel, Malcolm?"

"Painted? Is that painted? I think it's just stained. The wood got pretty distressed over the years. I believe that is a stain, a nice rich mahogany to match the wood."

"The mantel was walnut. And this is paint, not stain." Paris studied the carved detailing.

"Let me show you the kitchen. I've made a list of repairs." He headed through the dining room and the swinging door into the kitchen.

Paris followed, making a mental list of her own. "Where is the dining room chandelier?"

"We had to replace it a couple of years ago. It shorted out and could have started a fire. It was a good thing we noticed it." He held the door for Paris.

"It couldn't be rewired?" she asked with a cutting tone.

"It would have cost a fortune. That old thing was a fire hazard."

Paris gave the simple three-bulb replacement fixture a last look. Malcolm opened the cabinet under the kitchen sink. A dishpan was catching a slow drip from the faucet and was in need of emptying. A mousetrap was set, but there was no bait in it. Paris gave Malcolm a bristled look and waited to see if he would empty the pan. When he made no move to touch any of the disgusting chores under the sink, she did. She carefully poured the stale water into the sink then quickly replaced the pan as the drip again came to life. Malcolm watched with little interest, as if Paris was doing the women's work, and he need not be concerned.

"Not only does the plumbing leak but," he said, turning on the faucet. Water sprayed in every direction except into the sink. "This faucet is shot, too." He quickly turned it off once he had made his point and sprayed them both as well as the wall, ceiling and counter.

Paris jumped back. "I would have taken your word for it."

"The half bath downstairs and the full bath upstairs both have leaks. The shower doesn't work, and some of the tiles have fallen off. I think the wallboard is water damaged and until we replace that, no tile is going to stick." Malcolm went to the mudroom door off the kitchen. He stood straddling the threshold rocking back and forth. The floor flexed and creaked each time he put his weight on the mudroom floor. "The subflooring is like a sponge. One of these days someone's going to fall through and break their neck." He pointed to the kitchen window over the sink and the one in the nook. "Both of those windows have broken sash cords. They won't stay open. There are four more around the house just the same. The wood framing around the master bedroom windows is swollen and warped so you can't open them at all. Gets pretty stuffy up there in the summer."

"I thought there was air conditioning?" Paris questioned.

"There used to be a couple of those window units, but they conked out years ago. Compressors. Cost more to fix them than they were worth. One of the renters had their own window units, but they took them when they moved out. I can check on prices if you are thinking about installing central air. Might be a good time to do it, what with the furnace needing some work. You might consider a heat pump with heat and air all in one unit. They are real efficient." Malcolm gave Paris an eager look. "I can get you a good deal on a three-ton unit. There's a heating company in Pierce City running a summer special. I can talk the guy down even more, I'm sure. He owes me a favor."

"I'll have to see what else we have to do." Paris peeked through the dirty mini-blinds to see the window.

"Come have a look down the hall." Malcolm led the way from the kitchen into a dark hallway that led back to the front entry and the heavy mahogany staircase.

"The hall light fixture needs to be replaced. Had to pull the breaker for the hall outlets and lights. It started sparking last month."

He then stood on the first step and wiggled the newel post. Paris noticed several of the balusters did not match the rich dark wood in either styling or color. The front of the steps were worn and splintered. The wallpaper she so vividly remembered as a child had long been painted over. The joint lines of the wallpaper were visible and slivers of paper had been picked off by curious fingers and bodies rubbing against it. She stroked her hand along the wall as if it were a forgiving remedy for the years of abuse and neglect. Malcolm had climbed the stairs, each worn tread creaking his progress. Paris followed, her hand clutching the smooth handrail, rubbed to a high gloss by a thousand hands.

Malcolm pointed into the large bathroom across the hall at the top of the stairs. A plywood cabinet and sink had been installed where the pedestal sink once stood. The ball and claw footed tub where Paris learned to wash her own hair at age six and where Grandmother had showed her how to "do a good job with the wash cloth" at age seven was now a pre-fab fiberglass tub and shower unit with a sliding door. The sink cabinet door stood open, a small plastic bucket catching a drip here as well. The bathtub's fill lever was missing and a large rubber stopper was dangling from a brown shoelace tied to the faucet. The shower dripped a slow reminder that it, too, had plumbing woes. Paris felt tears welling up in her eyes. Maybelline looked terrible. It had been a refuge, a castle, a fantasyland for her childhood. Now it was just an old house with poorly made repairs and a dismal future. It had lost the character that so proudly welcomed her when her grandmother had lived here. It had lost the mystique, the flavor of childhood and tea parties and laughter. It no longer smelled like fresh baked chocolate chip cookies and apple butter simmering on the stove. It smelled moldy. It smelled like an ashtray. It smelled disgusting.

Paris turned and hurried down the stairs. She flung open the front door and rushed out onto the front porch. Tears had begun to sting her eyes, tears she could not contain. She stood at the porch railing, closed her eyes and took a deep breath. She desperately wished when she opened her eyes, the house she remembered would somehow return, nestled in a warm summer day, with birds at Grandmother's bird feeder, the heavenly scent of her rose garden floating toward her, the sound of a little girl giggling and galloping down the front steps. Instead the heavy smell of Malcolm's cheap aftershave greeted her.

"Are you all right, Miss DeMont?" he asked with a puzzled stare.

"Yes, I'm fine," she replied, taking another cleansing breath and quickly wiping her eyes. "The moldy smell got to me. The house needs to be aired out."

"It sure does," he rolled his eyes and waved at his nose.

"Can I see your list of the repairs and cost estimates?" Paris asked, once again in control of her emotions.

"Sure. I can have it for you later today."

"I'll be here until Tuesday. I'd like to get an idea of what needs to be done before I leave. I have some decisions to make."

"Say five o'clock?"

"That'll be fine. I am thinking about selling it. It seems to be costing more and more every year." Paris hated the way that sounded. Her grandmother's voice veritably screamed in her ear.

Malcolm's eyes widened. "Sell it? I thought you liked the depreciation and tax write off," he stated in surprise.

"That was the idea, but now," Paris became lost in thought as Malcolm rambled on about the pros and cons for selling it, adding he could act as her real estate agent when she was ready to list it.

"Call me this afternoon when you have the estimate ready. You have my cell number," she said returning to reality. "I'll be around town."

"I'll do that," he said locking the front door.

"Could I have the key, Malcolm?" Paris asked, following him to his car. "I might want to have another look around."

"Well, I," he stammered as he climbed in the car.

Paris held out her hand.

"Sure, I guess I can do without it for a couple days," he added after a short hesitation. He peeled it off his key ring and handed it to her. He pulled away slowly, a worried look on his thin face.

CHAPTER 4

Paris pocketed the key and headed for the barn. It was the one thing that seemed to be frozen in time. The weathered red paint and white trim made it look like it jumped right out of a Currier and Ives Christmas card. The big doors were slightly open, enough for a stray cat to sit in the opening, nonchalantly washing its face.

"Hey there," Paris said, looking down at the orange tabby. It immediately stopped washing, meowed a greeting then rubbed against her leg before wandering off.

Paris peeked through the opening then pushed the heavy door back. The barn was empty except for a stack of boxes that looked like party decorations. The ladder that led to the loft was missing most of its rungs. The dirt floor was littered with cigarette butts, beer cans and paper napkins. Paris dug in one of the boxes and took out a silver pleated tissue paper bell and a stack of matching silver cocktail napkins embossed "Kathy and Ryan" in burgundy script. There were also several plastic banquet-size tablecloths, a dozen silver and white pillar candles and several small baskets of silk flowers in shades of burgundy, mauve and white.

She thought it strange someone would have moved out and left these behind. She wondered if Kathy, whoever she was, had changed her mind about marrying Ryan or was so scatterbrained over the wedding plans that she forgot them.

Paris looked up toward the loft, a little disappointed she couldn't climb up and take a look. She remembered the first time she climbed the wooden ladder into her make-believe castle. The memory of her grandmother's helping hands as she took the first rung washed over her.

"You be careful, Paris. Hold on tight." Her grandmother stood at the bottom of the ladder, watching every step she took, her arms ready to catch Paris if she faltered.

"I can do it, Grandma. See. I can climb up all by myself." Paris replied confidently as she scrambled up the dozen rungs to the loft.

"I know you can," she said with an encouraging voice. "But you be careful. You stay back from the railing. No hanging over. Do you hear me missy?"

"I will Grandma." Paris stood at the top, a broad grin of accomplishment brightening her face. "Put something in the bucket, Grandma. I want to pull it up."

"I already did. Pull the rope."

Paris pulled the rope that was looped through a pulley attached to a galvanized bucket.

"Oh, boy! Cookies and milk," she squealed at the fruit jar filled with fresh milk and chocolate chip cookies wrapped in a paper napkin. "Can I have a tea party up here, Grandma. Can I?"

"Sure. And it is may I."

"Will you come up too, Grandma?" Paris urged.

Grandmother laughed at the thought and folded her hands over her stomach.

"Thank you, Paris. But this grandmother doesn't climb into the loft anymore. You have fun and remember what I said, no leaning over."

Grandmother gave a stern look then left the princess to enjoy her tea party in the castle tower.

Paris ran her hand along the remnants of the wooden ladder as she remembered that first climb. She looked around for the bucket and the rope that brought so many treasures up to her in the loft but it, too, was long gone. She stepped out into the warm morning sunshine and pushed the barn door closed. The cat was watching from a safe distance, perched on a tree stump. It meowed and tried to look noncommittal. Paris smiled at the cat and slid the barn door back to its open position.

"How's that?" she mused.

The cat yawned and stretched, seemingly satisfied with her benevolence. Paris strolled down the meadow to the bank of the pond where a pair of mallard ducks was serenely paddling across the far side. She stood quietly watching them as they headed around the island and passed out of sight.

The pond was shaped like a large lima bean that tapered to the left side and fed a meandering stream. The mouth of the stream was overgrown with cattails and saplings probably planted by that woman she had seen yesterday, Paris thought. The island was gently mounded and covered with a thick carpet of grass. The willow tree leaned gracefully out over the pond, draping its long branches down to touch the water. Paris studied the new footbridge. She remembered the narrow bridge from her childhood that was made from tree branches stuck in the mud supporting an unpainted barn board walkway. The old bridge was low to the water and disappeared when the pond flooded after a heavy rain. This new bridge arched high over the water with whimsical detailing on the newel posts and railings. It was a good four feet wide and inviting. Paris climbed to the middle of the bridge and looked down into the water; a few small fish swam lazily back and forth under her feet. A pair of dragonflies played tag across the surface of the water.

The cat had followed Paris at a safe distance and was making its way over the bridge to join her under the sweeping branches of the tree. Paris closed her eyes and took in a deep breath. The smells of grass, wild flowers, musty pond water and stray cat all blended together. Paris knew that the sense of smell was one of the greatest triggers for memory, but that one breath had set off a sensory explosion she hadn't expected.

"Great tree, huh?"

Paris opened her eyes to see the tree-planting woman standing on the bridge. At least the voice told her it was. But today she was clean and dressed smartly in a pair of jeans that fit her long legs and trim hips perfectly. She also wore a long sleeve blue chambray shirt with the cuffs turned back opened over a white T-shirt that was tucked into her jeans. Her hair was short and reddish brown, more red than brown and was stirred by the summer breeze. She stood watching Paris through a pair of sunglasses, her hands on the railing.

"Yes, it is," Paris finally replied after taking in the woman's appearance with attention to every detail. "It's lovely out here."

"This is the only thing that hasn't changed much over the years." The woman offered.

"How long have you lived in Banyon?" Paris asked with growing curiosity.

"I was born here. Actually born in St. John's Hospital in Springfield, but Banyon has been my family's home for four generations."

"Did you know my grandmother? This was her home until she died ten years ago. Her name was—"

"West," the woman interjected. "Yes, I knew her. She was a wonderful person." The woman had crossed the bridge and was wandering toward Paris under the willow tree. "She sure loved this place."

Paris studied the woman, hoping something would trigger recognition of who this woman was.

"Have you always lived over the hill?" Paris asked, her brain working overtime trying to identify her. She wished she could see her eyes. The sunglasses seemed to be hiding a key piece of the identification.

"No. I bought it a few years back. I needed a larger place for my shop. So, Paris, are you moving back to Banyon?"

"You have me at a disadvantage. You know my name, and you seem to know about me, but I don't know your name."

A teasing little smile curled one corner of the woman's mouth revealing a dimple in her cheek. Paris had seen that dimple before, but where, when? It had become torture for Paris as she rifled through her brain's Rolodex. The woman moved through the swaying willow branches, ducking and dodging the lazy tentacles. Paris watched her, a curious stare on her face.

"You might remember me. It's been a long time, but you might." She stopped and looked back at Paris. She then began slowly braiding three branches of the willow tree. Her eyes were fixed on Paris as if she was waiting for her to say something.

Paris frowned, growing impatient with the woman's secrecy and the distraction of her branch braiding. She watched the woman's long fingers artfully fold the long twigs over each other in slow but relentless motion, braiding and unbraiding the branches. Suddenly Paris's eyes widened. Her mouth dropped as she gasped and took one step backward as shock set in.

"Sloan? Sloan McKinley?" Paris gasped.

The woman smiled and looked over the top of her sunglasses. "Hi, Paris."

"Sloan McKinley. I can't believe it." Paris rushed over and hugged her warmly. Sloan hugged her back as they both giggled with delight. Their eyes were bright and welcoming as they looked at each other fondly. "After all these years. It's really you." Paris grinned so hard it hurt. "Look at you. All grown up."

"You grew up too, Paris." Sloan's eyes shone as they held hands and stepped back to admire how much the other had changed.

"I heard you had moved away," Paris said.

"I left for a few years. College. Then I spent a couple of years in Stockton as a teacher."

"So you became a teacher?" Paris asked warmly.

"Well, let's say I thought that's what I wanted to do."

"What was your major?"

35

Sloan laughed as she thought over her reply. "Would you believe art history and industrial trades applications?"

"Art history sounds very interesting. I'm impressed. But what are industrial trades applications?"

"Shop," Sloan said, raising her eyebrows.

"Shop? You majored in shop?" Paris didn't mean to sound condescending, but the idea of Sloan mixing the refined study of art history with the world of sawdust and grease surprised her.

"That was exactly the way my parents said it."

"So how did you get into making tree furniture?"

"Rustic furniture," Sloan corrected. "Or twig furniture. Well, I kind of found it by accident. I always liked building and creating things. I had a student who wanted to make a gypsy twig chair. You know, the ones with the bent wood arms and big fan shaped back. Well, I didn't know anything about making that stuff so we did some research on it and learned together. He gave up on it. It takes a lot of time and preparation. But I made one just for the fun of it. A lady offered me three hundred dollars for it and voila, a business was born."

"You made one chair and quit teaching?"

"No, it took a couple of years. But I realized pretty quickly this was for me. I could work outside, make what I wanted, work on special orders and I even get to travel occasionally. I have several distributors for my rustic pieces."

"That's great. I'd love to see some of you work sometime."

"Do you remember the first time I showed you how to braid the branches?" Sloan asked smiling with the memory.

"Yes. We were swinging on the branches."

"It was the first time you came to Banyon. How old were we? Six?"

"A long time ago. You have a terrific memory."

Sloan smiled. "Your grandmother let me play on the island when my mother came to visit Josephine Walker. The Walkers used to own the house I bought." Sloan pointed up the hill toward her property. I was on that old bridge the first time you walked down the meadow." Sloan laughed and sneered at Paris. "You were a little snot."

"I was not," Paris inserted defensively. "I was just a city girl." She laughed brightly. "Gosh, maybe I was," she added as she thought back.

"What are you doing on that bridge? My grandma said this is our bridge and our pond." Paris skipped down to the edge of the pond and frowned up at the girl on the battered footbridge. Paris was neatly dressed in a pair of white shorts with blue flower-shaped pockets and a matching blue flowered top. She wore white sandals. The little girl on the bridge wore a pair of cutoff jean shorts and a bright red T-shirt. She was barefoot.

"I can play here if I want to," she snapped back. "I even know how to swim."

"No, you can't. You might get hurt."

"My name is Sloan McKinley and your grandma said I can play here all I want. Go ask her." Sloan ran over the bridge onto the island and began climbing the willow tree. "What's your name?"

"Paris Elizabeth DeMont." Paris stood at the edge of the bridge, unsure if she should cross.

"Paris? That's a funny name."

"No it isn't. Sloan is a funny name. I've never heard anyone named Sloan before." Paris took one step onto the bridge and swallowed hard. She looked down between the boards to the green pond water. She knew how to swim, too, but the water looked nasty. She couldn't see how deep it was either.

"My great grandfather was named Sloan. He was a general or a soldier or something." Sloan jumped down from her low perch in the tree. "Wanna play with me?" she asked, watching Paris's tentative exploration of the bridge. "Just run across it. It's not scary if you run."

Paris did as she was told and was quickly safe under the tree with Sloan playing among the whip-like branches.

"Can you swing on the tree?" Sloan asked, grabbing up several branches in her hands.

"Sure I can." Paris replied defiantly. She grabbed as high up on a

single branch as she could reach. She backed up then ran forward picking up her feet, expecting to swing out gracefully. Instead the slender branch broke and she stumbled to the ground in an awkward heap, her eyes wide with surprise and embarrassment.

Sloan laughed at her accident, making Paris's humiliation even more painful. Tears welled up in Paris's eyes, and she scrambled to her feet ready to run for the house.

"Wait," Sloan said, realizing she should not have laughed. "Let me braid some for you. You can't swing until you braid the branches." Sloan quickly started to braid three of the thin branches into one strong one, her little fingers working feverishly. "Here, you can use this," she said, holding out the branches for Paris.

Paris looked at the braid skeptically, tears still threatening to spill out of her eyes.

Sloan grabbed the branch to demonstrate its integrity and her technique. She backed up as far as the branch would allow then picked up both feet and sailed past Paris, squealing with delight. She swung back and dropped her feet to stop her flight.

"Wanna try it?" Sloan held it out toward Paris. "It's fun."

"Okay," Paris replied cautiously, wiping her arm across her eyes. She backed up to the spot Sloan had used, grabbed onto the braiding with both hands as high and tight as she could, then picked up her feet. She, too, sailed out in a grand arc and back again. Her face brightened as she swung out again.

"See," Sloan said proudly. "I told you." She made herself a braiding on the other side of the tree.

Soon they were swinging, giggling and sharing their first warm summer day together.

"I remember that day." Paris smiled and pulled at a branch as the image of the two little girls skipped across her mind. "I think it would take considerably more than three branches to support us now."

"Oh, I don't know. You look pretty good to me," Sloan said, removing her sunglasses.

Paris smiled to herself. It had been a long time since anyone had given her a compliment.

"So you work at a hospital?" Sloan asked.

"Yes. In New York City." Paris realized she had just spent a half hour not thinking about her practice. She also realized she enjoyed it.

"Wow, big city."

"BIG city."

"So you are here to see about fixing up the old house?"

"Yes. Malcolm can't rent it out again until we get some things repaired. Plumbing, electrical, who knows what else. Age has played a lot of nasty tricks on the old place." Paris played with a tuft of grass with the toe of her shoe. "I hate to see it looking so—" Her voice trailed off.

"I know. Time does that to things. They change."

"This is more than change. It's deterioration. By the way, any suggestions where I might get a house key made?" She took the one Malcolm gave her out of her pocket.

"Sure. Dad's hardware store."

"That's right. I forgot. McKinley's Paint and Hardware, right?" Sloan nodded. "Still on the square, southwest corner."

"I have some errands to run in town so I think I'll go surprise him," she declared.

"I have some errands myself," Sloan replied, seemingly unable to take her eyes off of Paris. "Maybe I'll see you in town later."

Paris headed for town, her mind spinning with memories of Sloan and their childhood together. She circled the square and parked down the street from McKinley's Paint and Hardware store. The sign was new, but the store front looked like she remembered it. Corner building with double doors, paint signs in one window, chainsaws and garden tools in another and a row of charcoal grills out front lining the sidewalk.

Charlie McKinley was finishing up with a customer at the cash register so Paris strolled up and down the aisles. Paris knew it was Charlie. He hadn't changed in twenty years. He still had pudgy cheeks, salt and pepper hair, square shoulders and a dimple in his chin. He had a big laugh and a bright smile, just like Sloan's.

"May I help you, miss?" he said following her down the aisle.

Paris turned around and smiled at him warmly.

"Hello, Charlie," she said.

"Hello." He returned her smile, but it was obvious he had no idea who she was.

"I guess I have changed a bit, but I remember you. I used to play with Sloan at my grandmother's house," she offered as a hint.

"Paris!" he yelled. "Paris!" He clapped his hands. "Well, what do you know? Paris." He beamed brightly and offered her his hand. "How many years has it been? Twenty?"

"At least," she replied, ignoring his hand and giving him a warm hug.

"Have you seen Sloan? She'll be excited to see you, I'm sure."

"Yes, I saw her. She hasn't changed much either."

He gave her a long face, as if he didn't believe her.

"Well, maybe a little," she added, then chuckled.

"What are you doing in Banyon after all these years?"

"I still own my grandmother's house, and it needs some repairs before it can be rented out again so I came to take a look."

"That's right. I heard her house was a rental now. Nice piece of land you got there. Good pond and acreage."

"I hope I can get it back to being a nice place again. But your store hasn't changed. It's still just as warm and pleasant as I remember. You should be very proud of it."

"I don't know about that. Family run stores are a dying breed," he said with chagrin.

"I hate to hear it, Charlie. I love little town stores like this. They make you feel welcome."

"You want to know why I can't survive in this business? Storage."

"Storage?" Paris asked thoughtfully.

40

"Yes ma'am. Storage is the root of all evils for us family run businesses."

"But you offer something the super stores don't offer."

"What's that?"

"Friendly personalized service. That is one thing those huge box stores don't have and never will have."

"Don't tell me you're giving Paris the storage lecture?" Sloan asked from the doorway, smirking at her father. "Hello, Paris."

"He was explaining the high finances of retail storage."

"That's a new one. Last month it was door knob sets," Sloan said.

"Speaking of door knobs, I need to have a key made." Paris dug the key out of her pocket. "Do you make keys?"

"You betcha. Brass, color coded, rubber tipped. You name it, we make it." He leaned over to Paris and whispered. "Keys are small. They don't take a lot of room. Storage isn't a problem with keys." He then winked and took off to the back of the store to copy it.

"Don't use those flimsy colored aluminum keys, dad. They bend too easy," Sloan called to him.

"I threw the damn things out," he replied.

"Where's the glue?" Sloan asked loudly as she scanned the shelves behind the counter.

"On aisle six, halfway back, second shelf from the bottom. I moved it," Charlie replied over the grinding of the key machine.

Sloan retrieved a gallon of wood glue and a box of finish nails.

"He's right you know." Paris browsed through the paint folders. "He seems like a very smart business man."

"Oh, Lord, don't let him hear you say that. We won't be able to shut him up."

"I heard that," Charlie scoffed from the back. "Paris, you are welcome in McKinley's Paint and Hardware store anytime."

"Thank you, Charlie," Paris called then smiled at Sloan devilishly. "Ha, ha, he likes me better."

Sloan wrinkled her nose and wagged a finger at her playfully. Paris grabbed her finger and pretended to bite it.

"Behave you two. Just like when you were kids. Always misbehaving," he said with a chuckle as he returned to the front. He held the keys up to the light for comparison. "Here you go. Try it out and let me know if it sticks. I buffed it off, but sometimes they take a bit of persuasion."

Paris extended her Visa card as she took the keys. "Thank you."

Charlie scoffed and pushed the card back at her.

"There's no charge, Paris. It's for old time's sake."

"No, no, Charlie. For old time's sake, I want to pay you." She dug in her jacket pocket and pulled out a twenty. "If you prefer cash."

Charlie closed his eyes and held up his hands as if touching her money would give him the plague.

"Charlie!" she complained, trying to grab one of his waving hands.

"Oh, for God's sake," Sloan muttered. She took some change from her pocket and counted out eighty-nine cents. She reached over the counter, punched in the amount and cascaded the coins into the till. "There, an eighty-nine-cent sale." She shook her head and frowned at Paris and Charlie doing the I-don't-want-it-you-can-have-it dance.

Paris quickly turned to Sloan and fumbled in her pocket for some change.

"If you even think about giving me eighty-nine cents, I'm going to pour this glue right in your pocket," Sloan warned, holding up a threatening finger.

"I wouldn't dream of it," Paris said, momentarily frozen in Sloan's eyes.

"I'd listen to her if I were you, Paris." Charlie laughed robustly.

Sloan dropped some money on the counter and bagged her purchases. "Later, Pop." She headed for the front door.

"Nice to see you again, Paris," Charlie said.

"It was nice to see you, too, Charlie," Paris replied, and gave him a hug then hurried to catch up with Sloan.

"How about a cup of coffee?" Sloan asked, waiting for her on the sidewalk. "We have a place a couple blocks up. They have cappuccinos and great lattes. My treat."

"I haven't had a good latte in weeks," Paris replied brightly.

"You want to walk or ride?"

"Walk, silly. It's only a couple blocks."

"I thought you city girls were spoiled. I figured you'd want a taxi or a subway ride."

Paris smirked at her and stuck out her tongue. Sloan stuck her tongue out in return. They both laughed and started up the street, giggling at their antics. It was like old times.

CHAPTER 5

"Would you like a regular or a mocha latte?" Sloan asked after finding a table.

"Just regular, please."

"Be right back," Sloan said, leaving Paris at the table and taking her place in line.

Paris sat back and watched as Sloan ordered their drinks and waited for the girl behind the counter to make them. The heady aroma of the fresh ground coffee beans instantly brought back memories of New York City and Gabby. It had been a long time since she had thought of that afternoon at the hospital when Gabby introduced herself and presented her with a gift. Paris opened her mind and allowed the memory to crystallize.

It was after three before she had found time for lunch. Paris hurried through the hospital cafeteria line with a chef salad and a cup of coffee, anxious to sit down and slip out of her shoes for a few minutes. She found a table in the corner and hoped she could finish at least half her salad before her pager called her back upstairs. She was so preoccupied remov-

ing the brown lettuce and dabbing on the salad dressing she hadn't noticed the woman standing next to her table.

"Hi," the woman said cheerfully. She was dressed in navy blue uniform pants and shirt. The name tag over her pocket read G. Buttichi, Paramedic. She had curly dark brown hair with wispy bangs feathered over her forehead. Her eyes were large pools of brown with a mischievous twinkle about them. The baggy utility pockets of her pants didn't hide her athletic physique. She was tall with a smooth confidence in her demeanor. Her grin was infectious, invading Paris's body instantly and thoroughly all the way down to her soul.

"Hi," Paris replied after swallowing her bite. "I remember you. You're the paramedic I saw in the ER last week. You brought in one of my patients."

"Yeah. How is he?" she asked.

"He's doing much better."

"Good." The woman's eyes searched the room as if wondering what to say next. "Good," she repeated after clearing her throat.

"What's the G for?" Paris asked noticing the woman's nervousness.

"What G?"

Paris pointed to the woman's name tag as she washed down the bite with a gulp of coffee.

"Oh that G. Gabriella. Gabby."

"Hi Gabby," Paris declared. "Thanks for doing such a good job with Mr. Jacoby last week."

Gabby squinted at Paris's embroidered name over the pocket of her white coat. "Paris E. DeMont, MD. What's the E for?"

"Elizabeth."

"Hi, Paris Elizabeth DeMont." Gabby produced a small white sack with a bow on top from behind her back and set it on the table.

"What's that?"

"It's for you," Gabby said, sliding it toward Paris. "Open it."

"Why are you giving me a gift?" Paris asked cautiously.

"Because you deserve it, and I wanted to give it to you, that's why." She pointed to a chair across from Paris as if asking permission to sit down. Paris nodded.

"If I'm accepting a gift from you, I guess I can let you sit down for a

45

minute." She carefully opened the top of the sack and peeked in. "What are these?"

"You said you needed a lot of caffeine to get through the long days sometimes. So I got you some chocolate-covered espresso beans. They're better than stale coffee from a hospital coffee machine."

"Thank you." Paris smiled broadly. "I can't believe you remembered I said that," she admitted with a chuckle. "But I don't drink that much coffee."

Gabby took a sip from Paris's cup then narrowed her eyes skeptically.

"Uh-huh," she declared. "I bet you stay at the hospital far too late and drink coffee to keep you awake."

"Sometimes. Not always," Paris insisted. Paris took a sip from the cup, subconsciously putting her mouth where Gabby's had been on the rim.

Gabby gazed softly into Paris's eyes. "And sometimes you just go home and go to bed?" she asked quietly.

"Sometimes," Paris replied, feeling the breath tighten in her chest as she returned the woman's gaze.

Paris usually discounted such advances, but there was something innocent and childlike in this woman's bold demeanor. Her eyes were soft, and her smile gave Paris a strange sense of comfort and security. Even though she knew almost nothing about this Gabriella Buttichi, paramedic and gift-giver, Paris felt her curiosity growing by the second. They sat silently swimming in each other's eyes for a long moment until Paris's pager startled them back to reality.

"Thank you for the goodies," she said, before checking the message on the pager. "It was very thoughtful of you. Chocolate and coffee, two of my favorite things."

Gabby stood up and took Paris's tray from her.

"I'll take this for you. I've got to go that way anyway."

"Thank you," Paris replied.

A small contented smile pulled across Gabby's face. "Have a nice day, Doctor Paris Elizabeth DeMont."

"You, too, Gabriella Buttichi," Paris replied, and started across the cafeteria. She turned back to see the woman watching her. "Be careful out there, Gabby," she added.

"Here you are. Regular latte, single shot, and I brought the sugar so you can decide how much you want," Sloan announced, placing two cups on the table. "And chocolate dipped biscotti." She opened the napkin and showed off the pastries.

"Don't these look yummy?" Paris exclaimed, returning to the present and locking Gabby once again into the past. "Thanks."

Sloan sensed Paris had been daydreaming but allowed her to have her private moment without interfering.

"So," Sloan said sitting down across from Paris. She sounded as if she intended on asking Paris a question.

"Yes?" Paris looked over at her, waiting for the rest of what she wanted to say.

"So you're not married or anything, right?" Sloan asked carefully.

"No. I'm not married."

"Fiancé?" she asked after a moment of thought.

"No. No fiancé." Paris smiled to herself.

"Good," Sloan offered, trying to decide what to ask next. "No boyfriend?" she asked, trying to cover every possibility.

Paris shook her head. She knew where Sloan was heading and what she wanted to ask. She wanted to ask if she was a lesbian. It was one of those silent communications she had sensed the first time she met Gabby in the emergency room. Gabby had the same look in her eyes when she bought Paris a cup of stale coffee from the vending machine. Paris thought it was awkward but cute when she handed her the foam cup and asked her if any other woman had ever bought the gorgeous doctor a cup of tar before. Gabby was straightforward about it. Sloan was being more cautious and coy in her approach. Paris smiled to herself, deciding to let her struggle with it a bit longer.

Sloan's eyes narrowed as she waited for any additional information Paris might offer, but none was forthcoming. There was a short silence, then Sloan sat up straight and fixed Paris with an inquisitive stare.

"Are you a nun?" she asked seriously.

Paris laughed out loud and shook her head again.

"Not hardly, Sloan." Paris leaned closer and spoke quietly. "But men aren't my flavor of choice."

Sloan leaned back, contented with the news. "Well, well. I was right." She smiled at Paris.

"And how about you? Are you married?" Paris asked, then sipped at her coffee. "I don't see a ring on your finger."

"The only ring I wear is the one around my neck after working in the shop." Sloan studied Paris over the rim of her coffee cup. "How long have you known?"

"That I was gay?" Paris asked with a quiet confidence.

Sloan nodded, breaking off a piece of biscotti.

"Gosh, I don't know. High school, I guess." Paris hadn't given it much thought. She just knew her two dates with boys during her sophomore year were boring and uncomfortable. By her junior year she stuck to homework, debate club, science fair and photography club to keep herself busy. She learned the delicate art of saying no without sounding negative. Her senior year required three dates with boys, one to prom and one to homecoming since she was a queen candidate to both, and one to the National Honor Society dinner dance. All three were with Jeremy Henderson, the geekiest boy in her class. He was voted the most likely to wear a pocket protector in the shower. He was thrilled when Paris suggested they coexist at the events but with the strict understanding that after the dance it was right home. Jeremy agreed, practically steaming up his own glasses at the thought of going out with the attractive Paris DeMont. Her straight-A average had his complete attention. Paris assumed he had never even danced with a girl, let alone kissed one. She was right. He spent the three evenings discussing homework, college applications and his asthma. Paris's gender identity remained a secret. Jeremy's manhood was also saved since the three dates with Paris were the only ones he had had throughout high school.

"High school can be a rough time," Sloan said retrospectively.

"How about you, Sloan? Have you known for a long time? Any cute young things tickle your fancy in high school," Paris prodded.

"Junior high," Sloan corrected with a wry smile. "I was in seventh grade. Clarine Sternberger was in eighth grade." She smiled softly as her mind floated backward.

"Oh my, an older woman," Paris declared.

"Yes. And"—Sloan leaned in and whispered in her best school-girl tone—"she wore a bra that hooked in the front. And she shaved all the way up to her thigh." She flashed a knowing glance.

"No!" Paris declared, playing along. "All the way up?"

Sloan nodded sinisterly. They both laughed at the childish non-sense.

"She and I were on the volleyball team and she had a long, blond ponytail. Of course she didn't even know I existed. Or that I had a crush on her." Sloan chuckled as she thought of it. "How about you? Who was your first puppy love, Paris?" she asked.

"Paulette Kessinger," she replied, surprising herself at the memory. "I don't know if it was puppy love. She was the girl who made the dip cones at the Dairy Queen on Freemont Avenue. She was *way* older though. She was probably seventeen. I was almost fifteen." Paris snickered and rolled her eyes.

"Good dipper?"

"Great dipper. But alas, it wasn't to be. She left the Dairy Queen for a better job at Baskin-Robbins across town. I never saw her again." Paris made it sound as dramatic as possible.

"Oh, God. Lost out to a better ice cream store. I hate it when that happens."

"Who came next for you?" Paris asked.

"Let's see. There was Linda Cody in eighth grade. I told her she had cute ears. She told me I was boring. Holly Regar was freshman year in high school. She was class president, and she rode horses in barrel races. I think I liked her because she wore really tight-fitting jeans to school, the ones that went way up her butt. I was sure she didn't wear any underwear. Then there was Cheryl Craig. She was my sophomore locker partner. She had the most gorgeous eyes. And hands like a model's with long fingers and beautiful nails. She broke my heart when she started dating Josh Squires, quarterback of the football team."

"So she wasn't gay?" Paris asked tentatively.

"No. Only in my dreams. Then junior year there was Fred." Sloan nodded to herself as she resurrected the memory. "Fred Taylor was six feet tall, part Osage Indian and could run like being shot out of a cannon."

"Fred?" Paris asked with a frown.

"Yes, Fred. Frederica Eloise Marie Renee Taylor. She was named for every one of her aunts. She had this golden tan skin that glistened all over when she sweat. She's the reason I went out for the track team."

"You went out for track so you could watch Fred sweat?"

"Sure. That and watch her shower," Sloan said with a wink.

"What event did you run?"

"That was the only problem. I couldn't run to save my life. Coach had me throwing shot put and the discus."

"So you made the team."

"Yeah, but I was always putting the shot when Fred was running and glistening."

"That's too bad. All that effort, and you didn't get to see her sweat," Paris teased.

"But there was always the shower," Sloan whispered.

"So she and you . . . ," Paris started.

"It wasn't she and I. The only thing I got up enough courage to say to her was nice gym bag."

"You didn't date anyone in high school?" Paris asked watching Sloan drift up and down memory lane.

"No, not really. I went to the movies a few times with one girl from Cassville. But she was way too clingy and possessive."

"When did you find your first true love?" Paris asked dreamily, expecting Sloan to confess some dark secret.

"First true love?" Sloan thought a moment. "When I was six," she declared finally. "Her name was Paris Elizabeth DeMont." She looked deeply into Paris's eyes. Sloan tried to make the confession sound innocent, but her expression betrayed her. She felt powerless to control the flood of adoration that filled her eyes.

"Thank you, Sloan. That is nice of you to say. We did have

great times together when we were kids, didn't we?" Paris replied, uncertain how to accept Sloan's confession or her gaze. "But aren't you dating anyone now?"

Sloan began stacking the creamer cups into a pyramid. The question had brought on a pensive look, as if she didn't know how to answer it.

"Not really. You know me, love 'em and leave 'em," she joked.

"Actually I don't know you, Sloan. We were so close as kids, but we haven't even talked to each other in years. We hardly know anything about each other now," Paris said almost apologetically. "We have a lot of catching up to do." Paris reached across and patted her hand. "It'll be just like old times. We can eat cookies and milk on the back porch and laugh about the funny things we used to do."

"How long are you going to be here?"

"I fly home on Tuesday."

"Damn, Paris. That isn't much time." Sloan frowned at her.

"I know. But I only had four days off."

"Maybe you can get a few more. Why don't you call your boss and tell him you are in an important meeting with an old associate?" She batted her eyes dramatically.

Paris smiled and shook her head. She knew Sloan would be tickled if she told her she was her own boss and the reason she had to go home on Tuesday was Gloria Poole's thallium stress test, Martin Upland's appointment in the cath lab and a follow-up on Jillian Rema's pacemaker replacement.

"Maybe later in the summer I can squeeze in a few days to come back for a visit," Paris replied, surprising herself and pleasing Sloan.

"That would be great." Sloan grinned broadly at the idea. "Banyon has a county fair and rodeo in September. Maybe you could come for that."

"We'll see. It depends on my schedule."

"Schedule?"

"I mean the work schedule. We can't have too many people off at once." Paris wiped her napkin across the corner of her mouth. "Are we ready? I have a lot to do in a short amount of time."

"Let's go." Sloan followed Paris outside. "I have a chair to finish and deliver this afternoon, but I'll see you again before you leave, won't I?" Sloan touched Paris's arm as if to reinforce her question.

"Sure," Paris replied as her cell phone rang. "That's Malcolm. I hope he has an estimate for me," she added as she answered it on the second ring.

Sloan pointed to her truck and waved good-bye to Paris.

"Talk with you later," Paris mouthed then went back to her conversation with Malcolm. She was talking with him, but her eyes were on Sloan as she walked down the sidewalk.

CHAPTER 6

Sloan stood under the shower scrubbing and shampooing the shop dirt from her body. She was so consumed with Paris's return to Banyon she absentmindedly squirted shampoo on her hair for a third time. She rinsed it out and ran the loofa sponge over her arms and legs one last time. Sloan's body was well proportioned and trim. Her breasts were a firm round B cup with small dark nipples. She was nearly five-feet-ten, and a great deal of that was taken up by her long muscular legs. Her hair was short and a mix of reddish highlights at the temples fading to darker auburn on top and back. She had been a redhead as a child, but by college it had darkened. Her complexion was even and tanned. The last fading glimpses of her freckles were barely visible. The only makeup in her drawer was an old frosted pink lipstick and a dried-up bottle of liquid foundation she had used to cover a rash of mosquito bites on her face. Her eyes were emerald green and set off by long thick eyelashes, thick enough that she had been accused of wearing mascara twenty-four hours a day.

Sloan turned off the shower and pressed her hands through her hair. Before she could open the shower door the sound of the bathroom door opening startled her. She stood silently listening, straining to make out a figure through the frosted glass door.

"Hello?" she asked pulling the towel down and wiping her face. "Somebody there?"

"Just me," a sultry voice said as the shower door flew open.

"Shit, Allison. You scared the crap out of me," she gasped.

The woman laughed devilishly and looked Sloan up and down. "Did you think of the shower scene in *Psycho*?"

"Yes. And it wasn't pleasant."

Sloan dried herself off as Allison watched, her eyes taking in every detail of Sloan's body.

"Where is my underwear?" Sloan asked searching the counter.

Allison produced the pair of panties from behind her back and twirled them around her finger.

"You mean these?" She held them out of Sloan's reach and gave a saucy snicker. "Are you sure you need them?" She reached over and stroked Sloan's breast.

"Give me those," Sloan demanded.

"Come get them." Allison stuffed them down the front of her jeans and patted the bulge.

Sloan smirked at her and reached inside to retrieve them. Allison moved closer and slipped her hands around Sloan's bottom, firmly holding each cheek.

"Dig for them, baby," she gasped, then stuck her tongue into Sloan's ear.

"Stop that." Sloan quickly pulled the panties free and stepped back, bumping into the bathroom door.

Allison moved in and pressed her body against Sloan's, kissing her full on the mouth. Sloan didn't cooperate at first, but Allison's persistent tongue and groping hands soon had her complete attention. Sloan allowed her tongue to press against Allison's and her hands pulled her tightly to her. Allison pressed her thigh against

Sloan's pubic bone. It had been months since Allison and Sloan had dated, but they both seemed to remember the secret spots to touch and caress to arouse the other.

"Oh, baby. Yes," Allison gasped with breathless urgency. "God, I missed you." She pulled Sloan's hand between her legs and pressed it against her crotch. She painted wet kisses down Sloan's neck as she rubbed herself against Sloan's hand. "Please, Sloan. Tell me it's not too late for us. Tell me you still love me."

Sloan laced the fingers of her free hand through the back of Allison's hair and pulled her head back. She gave her a soft kiss then pushed her back. Sloan opened the bathroom door and went out into the bedroom without saying a word. She quickly stepped into her underwear and pulled on a pair of sweatpants and sweat-shirt. Allison stood in the bathroom doorway speechless.

"What's this? Why are you getting dressed?" she said, scowling at Sloan's indifference to her advances.

"Because I have things to do, that's why." Sloan pushed up the sleeves of her sweatshirt and returned Allison's stare.

"But baby," Allison cooed and sashayed over to her with a deliberate and provocative wiggle. She began to slowly unbutton her blouse in a tantalizing striptease, revealing her full braless bosom. She held her blouse open and leaned into Sloan. "I have things for you to do, too." She slid her hands up under Sloan's sweatshirt.

"Allison," Sloan interrupted and pulled Allison's hands out from their exploration under her sweatshirt. "Let me guess. Patty is either out of town or the two of you are having another argument."

Allison looked up at Sloan with big eyes and an innocent smile. "Baby, how can you say something like that to me after what we had together?"

"What we had was two weeks of sex. Then you confessed you had a girlfriend who was on a trip to California." Sloan looked down into Allison's eyes. "So what is it? A business trip?"

"Don't say that. Just remember how great we were together." Allison continued to lean on Sloan and let her hands float over her body seductively.

"Uh-huh," Sloan offered. She wrapped her arms around Allison and let her hands move down her back. When she reached her rear she cupped her hands over Allison's firm round buttocks. With the talents of a pickpocket, she plucked the ring of keys from Allison's back pocket and stepped out of her reach.

"Hey, what are you doing?" Allison grabbed for the keys, but Sloan blocked her with her body as she opened the ring and removed the one marked with a red S. She closed the ring and held it out for Allison.

"Here," she said sternly.

"What are you doing?"

"I'm reclaiming my key and my privacy."

Allison snatched her keys and scowled at Sloan.

"How do you know that is your key?"

Sloan kept it clutched tightly in her hand, suspecting Allison would love to play another game of hide and seek with it.

"Because I made it at Dad's store and gave it to you, that's how. Now"—Sloan took Allison by the hand and led her to the front door—"tell Patty hello."

Allison stepped out onto the porch and looked back at Sloan with a slow smoldering leer.

"You can go to hell." When she got to the bottom of the steps she turned back and smiled wickedly. "You weren't even that good a fuck."

Allison went to her car and roared out of the drive, slinging a cloud of dirt and gravel.

Sloan shook her head and crossed her arms.

"I'm not a good fuck?" She chuckled as the car disappeared with a noisy roar. "Damn. That sure breaks my heart, Allison."

CHAPTER 7

Paris opened the cupboard under the kitchen sink and peered in to see if the dishpan needed emptying. Not only was it full, but the mousetrap was also regrettably full and in need of emptying as well. She closed her eyes and gave a disgusted smirk at the mouse droppings across the newspaper that lined the cupboard. A mental list of rodent transmitted diseases flashed across the physician part of her brain.

Just as Paris was about to back out of the cupboard she heard the floorboards in the mudroom creaking under the sounds of footsteps.

"Hello," Paris called as she looked toward the open door. There was no answer and the footsteps stopped, leaving an eerie silence.

"Hello there," Paris repeated in a louder voice. One footstep was the only reply. Then silence again.

"Who's there? Is that you Malcolm?" Paris called warily. "Sloan? Is that you?" One footstep then another slowly moved across the mudroom floor just out of Paris's view. She leaned back on her heels to see who was around the corner. Paris pulled herself to her feet and quietly retrieved the long bladed screwdriver from the countertop. With careful steps she edged along the counter toward the door that opened onto the mudroom, all the while cursing her carelessness for leaving the back door open. In New York City she wouldn't have even considered it. But here in Banyon an open door was no big deal, at least that is what she remembered from her youth. Her grandmother would leave the house open and unlocked all day while they went off shopping or napped on the screened-in porch. But that was twenty-five years ago. This was a new millennium with new dangers and new footsteps across her mudroom floor.

"Is there somebody out there?" she asked again, summoning a courageous voice over her growing concern.

Again the footsteps stopped at the sound of her voice but no one replied. Paris moved closer to the doorway, stiffening her posture and tightening her grip on the screwdriver. She could hear the sounds of heavy breathing. Whoever it was stood a mere handful of feet away, just out of sight. Paris wedged herself into the corner and slowly raised the screwdriver over her head, ready to defend herself against the trespasser. She stood glued to the wall, waiting for the next sound, hoping the intruder would withdraw and exit through the back door as quickly as he entered. But there were no more footsteps, just measured heavy breathing. She was going to have to make a move. She knew she couldn't stand there forever. The blood was draining from her raised arm and her fingers were growing numb. With the screwdriver poised, her eyes wide and her knees quivering, she made a lunge into the open doorway to face the prowler, whoever it might be.

"Aha," she called as she turned and faced the stranger in her house. With a blood-curdling scream she dropped the screwdriver which stabbed itself into the floor. With her hand at her throat she fell against the door, trembling uncontrollably.

"Oh my God!" she gasped at the Shetland pony standing in the mudroom swirling his tail contentedly. He raised his head to sniff her hands. She backed up flat against the wall, motionless, her heart still pounding in her throat.

"Shoo, get away," she said as he snorted and sniffed her. "Get back." The little horse followed as Paris slid along the wall and around the doorjamb back into the kitchen. She backed across the room to the hall, the pony eagerly following and bobbing his head.

"How did you get in here? I don't like wild animals in my house. Get back," she muttered, waving her hands at him.

The pony continued to pursue her down the hall, her waving hand only encouraging him. As he bobbed his head and gave little snorts, a medallion attached to his leather headstall jingled merrily. He seemed to enjoy hearing it and bobbed his head all the more. Paris noticed something engraved on the medallion that resembled a name and address. But how was she going to read it without touching this persistent creature?

"I don't suppose you would go home if I opened the door and let you out?" she inquired, snatching the front door open and standing behind it.

"No, huh?" She peeked around the door as he looked inquisitively for her. He gave a high-pitched whinny and moved closer.

"No, please," she backed into the corner behind the front door as he moved in for a sniff. He gave the front of her blouse a nibble, leaving a slobber mark.

"Oh, yuck," she groaned. "Nice horsey."

Paris rolled her lips as he sniffed her hand with a quivering wet lip. While he snorted and nuzzled one hand, Paris read the information on the medallion.

"My name is Barney. In case I am lost, my telephone number is two-nine-two-four-eight-two-three, and I live with Sloan McKinley." Paris raised her eyebrows.

"Sloan, I think I have something that belongs to you," she muttered digging in her pocket with her free hand for her cell phone while Barney continued to investigate the other hand. She punched in Sloan's number.

"Hello. You've reached Sloan. I'm not available but leave your name and number, and I'll call you back."

Paris's face melted in disappointment at the sound of Sloan's answering machine.

"Sloan, this is Paris. There's a horse in my house with your name on it," she announced. "He's in my front hall eating my shirt. What do I do to get rid of him? HELP!" she added with desperation, then pushed the end button. Barney flexed his upper lip and snorted blasts of horsey breath through his flared nostrils.

"Wouldn't you be happier outside eating grass?" she asked, sliding along the wall then hurrying down the hall toward the kitchen, Barney hot on her trail. She quickly dug in her jacket pocket and pulled out a granola bar. She unwrapped it and held it up for Barney to see. As he spied the goodie and moved in for a taste, she backed toward the mudroom and the back door.

"Come on, Barney. I've got a nice healthy granola bar for you."

Barney stopped at the doorway, keeping his feet in the kitchen and stretching out his neck as far as he could reach, his lips twitching frantically toward the treat.

"Here you go," she coaxed, backing out the back door onto the stoop.

Barney held his ground, refusing to leave the kitchen. He bobbed his head and nickered at her.

"Come on outside, and you can have it." She broke off a corner and tossed it on the floor between his front legs. He sniffed it and lapped it up with a long tongue retrieval. "Come on, Barney. I have more." She continued to wave the bar, hoping he would give in.

"Now look here, Barney. This is my house, and I don't allow horses as tenants. I have some things to look over, and I need you outside. So come on out here and eat this granola bar before I do." She took a small bite herself. "Hey, not bad," she mumbled as she chewed. Barney rolled his upper lip at her and bobbed his head, as if demanding another taste. She tossed him another piece that he lapped up on the bounce. "Not bad, huh?" She took another bite. Barney nickered then whinnied loudly.

"Okay, okay. Here," she said, breaking the last of it in half and tossing a piece toward him. Her aim was off and it rolled through his legs and on into the kitchen.

"Sorry," she said with a laugh. "It's back there. No, back there," she pointed as he sniffed the floor in search of it. "Back up, silly." She came cautiously closer and squatted in front of him. She pointed between his front legs, careful not to touch him.

"It's back there. I can't get it because there's a horse in the doorway." She looked up at him and frowned. "You wouldn't know anything about that, would you?"

Barney spied the last bit of bar in her hand and gave it a lick before she realized it was coming.

"I guess you get this piece, too," she said, opening her hand. "I certainly don't want it now." Barney sucked it up and gave her hand a cleansing. Paris examined the slobber mark and curled her lip. "Thank you for that gift," she muttered. She stood up, still holding the wet hand out like it was contaminated. "Where are all the pre-op scrubbers when you need one?" She looked around for something to wipe it on, but there was nothing in the mudroom but a can of mothballs and a broken broomstick. She eyed Barney's smooth coat. "Would you mind if I pet your neck?" she asked cautiously. She reached over and rubbed her hand down his neck to dry it off. "Oh now that's much better," she declared sarcastically as she examined her hand now covered with horsehair. "Is your saliva part glue?" While she examined her hair-covered hand, Barney gave her other hand a curious lick as well. "Thank you so much."

She had moved beyond sarcasm. Now it was becoming funny. With both hands now christened, she heaved a deep sigh and held them out for Barney to inspect.

"See what you have done." He gave them both additional licks. "Go ahead have at it. By the way, that's hand lotion you're enjoying." Paris stood quietly while Barney licked to contentment. "At least they don't have pony hair on them now," she mumbled. "Okay, that's enough. Back up and let me in. I need to wash my hands." She gently pushed him back with two fingers and slid by. While she washed in the kitchen sink Barney watched intently.

"You want to wash your tongue? It must be covered in hair." She reached under the sink and pulled out the dishpan. She began to fill it so she could offer him a drink.

"Wait a minute," she gasped, then dumped the water down the drain and replaced the dishpan under the leaky drain. "I may be dumb, but I'm not stupid. If I put water in one end it will undoubtedly come out the other end. So no drink for you, Barney. Not inside my house."

"Smart woman," Sloan said sticking her head in the kitchen from the mudroom.

"Hello, there. That much about farm animals I do remember," Paris offered.

"Barney, you have to stop walking in people's houses without an invitation. You're going to get in trouble one of these days," Sloan admonished and smacked Barney on the rump. "Did you hear Paris? She thinks you are a farm animal," she said then tugged at the long blond forelock that flowed down his face. "A farm animal, can you believe it?"

"Well, isn't he?"

"Are you Barney?"

Barney whinnied loudly.

"He thinks he is a family pet with all the rights and privileges that includes," Sloan reported.

"Don't tell me you let him roam around inside your house," Paris asked skeptically.

Sloan scowled at Barney. "No, I do not. At least I try not to. Come on Mr. Barney. It's outside for you." She led him by the headstall out the kitchen door and down the steps. "You go on home," she said and gave him a swat. "Go on."

He stood motionless looking up at Paris standing in the doorway. She held out her hands so he could see they were empty.

"Sorry Barney. No more granola bar. It's all gone."

"If you fed him, he's your friend for life."

"I don't mind if he comes to visit so long as he stays outside." Paris playfully wagged her finger at him. "Do you hear me?" Paris tried to sound angry, but there was a softness in her voice.

"Sorry he came in on you like that," Sloan offered apologetically. "He's been in the family so long he thinks he can go wherever he wants. He loves an open corral gate or an open door. There's an opening in the fence just over that hill." She pointed across the pasture. "It's hidden in the trees along the property line. I hope you don't mind that I keep it open. It makes it easier to get to the pond."

"So that's how he got over here. I don't mind." Paris smiled at Barney as if it really wasn't all that terrible. "By the way, how are you with mousetraps?" she asked Sloan.

"Why? Do you have one with a problem?"

"Yes, a full one."

"Where is it?"

"Under the sink. That's what I was doing when Barney came for tea."

Sloan squatted down and peered into the cabinet.

"Houston, we have a problem," she announced. Paris looked over Sloan's shoulder cautiously, mentally chastising herself for not being strong enough to handle one small dead mouse. After all, she was a doctor and had held her fair share of human body parts in her hands. But this tiny lifeless animal with the smashed cranium was way more than she wanted to touch.

"Henry!" Sloan declared suddenly. She carefully picked up the trap, the mouse dangling by its squashed head. "Oh, Henry," she repeated tenderly.

"Henry?" Paris gasped.

"Yes. He's been a family pet for years. See the white spot on his back." Sloan petted the tiny gray body with a fingertip. "He belongs to mom."

Paris drew her hands to her face. "I'm so sorry, Sloan. I didn't mean to kill your mother's mouse. It was an accident. Really. I didn't know you had a mouse for a pet. How did he get all the way over here from your mother's house?" She looked at Henry with a pained expression.

"How am I going to tell her?" she gave a long slow sigh. "This is going to break her heart." She cradled the trap with the dead mouse in her two hands, her face pinched with anguish.

"Maybe I could get her another one," Paris offered hopefully.

"No. Henry was special. He was practically a member of the family." Sloan looked over at Paris who had deep guilt lines across her forehead. "Mom had trained Henry to fetch. Every morning, rain or shine, he would go out and bring in the newspaper for her. Even in the winter, no matter how deep the snow he would drag it in. He never let her down. She was working on training him to start the coffee maker in the morning. He almost had it, too. Another month and he would have been able to do it, I'm sure. After all, he was up early, what with his jogging and all."

Paris's guilt was beginning to lift. Her eyes narrowed as she studied Sloan's face. The more she wove her tale, the more Paris frowned at her. She finally put her hands on her hips and cast a disapproving leer.

"All right, all right. That's enough," she declared.

"What? Don't you want to hear about Henry's little sweatband mom knitted for him to wear when he went jogging?"

"No, I do not."

Sloan burst into laughter. "I about had you, didn't I?" she teased. "You almost believed it."

"You should be ashamed of yourself, Sloan McKinley. Making me feel guilty like that. Shame on you." Paris scowled at her.

Sloan kept laughing as she took the trap out the back door and emptied it.

"Admit it. You believed it."

"Oh, hush. You're terrible."

Sloan reset the trap then washed her hands and searched the counter for a towel.

"Where did you put Henry?" Paris asked peeling off some paper towels and handing them to her.

"In the yard," she replied.

"Yuck! That icky thing is going to lay out there rotting and stinking up the place."

"I put it in the yard so that old cat you've got hanging around out there will find it."

"I'll buy some cat food for the cat."

"If that lazy old cat would learn to catch mice, you wouldn't have to buy cat food, and you wouldn't need mousetraps either."

"Oh," Paris said, accepting the reasoning. "Good idea."

"City girl," Sloan declared, patting her on the head.

"I should tell your mother on you," Paris warned, wagging her finger. "Teasing me like that. A family pet. Really." She was doing her best to act angry.

"Damn, Paris. Don't do that. The last time you told my mother on me she blistered my ass with her hair brush. I had bristle rash for a week."

"When was that?"

"I think it was your third summer at your grandmother's. Remember we were playing cowboys and Indians. You were a sheriff and I was an Indian chief."

"I remember that. I was supposed to bring you in for horse rustling or some such crime against humanity." Paris smiled and leaned against the counter.

"And I snuck up on you and scalped you."

"Yes. You cut off my bangs and waved them around, doing a war dance. It was just a couple days before I was to go home and start school."

"Your grandmother about had a hissy-fit about your bald fore-head."

"My school picture was very strange that year," Paris added with a chuckle.

"You were supposed to say you got your hair caught in the gate."

"Like anyone was going to believe that story."

"I could hardly look at a pair of scissors without my butt hurt-

65

ing until I was in third grade." Sloan rubbed her bottom as she remembered the licking she took.

Paris cooed sympathetically and patted Sloan's tush. A surprising tingle raced across her own butt at the thought of Sloan's punishment and the sharp whacks that must have reddened her tender skin. "I'm so sorry," she replied, full of regret. "Consider us even then for the Henry joke."

"I don't know," Sloan said doubtfully. "My butt hurt a lot more than that."

"But it took six months for my bangs to grow out."

They laughed.

"So, have you decided to give up your city-girl ways and move to Banyon?" Sloan asked jokingly as she sat on the counter.

"I have my career in New York, Sloan," she explained.

"You can have a career in Banyon," Sloan replied cheerfully. "Besides, Banyon has something New York doesn't have," Sloan inserted.

"What's that?" Paris asked, crossing her arms. She expected her to say either horses in the kitchen or something to do with wide open spaces.

Sloan smiled coyly, a twinkle in her eye.

"Someone who wishes you'd stay," she said softly.

"Thank you, Sloan," she replied touching her arm. "I appreciate that." Paris tried to make light of Sloan's remark and avoid her stare. She didn't want to admit to herself how captivating she found Sloan's eyes.

Sloan hopped down from the counter and headed for the back door.

"Since this is your last night will you have dinner with me?" she asked, turning back to Paris.

"Sloan, I'm sorry. I have a meeting with Malcolm tonight. We are going over the repairs." She decided not to add that she also intended on talking with him about selling Maybelline. "I'm meeting him at a restaurant in Aurora."

"Oh," Sloan replied, her face melting at the news.

"I'm sorry." Paris offered a warm smile. "But I have to take care of this before I leave in the morning."

"I understand," she justified, trying to sound nonchalant.

"I'm sorry," Paris repeated, reading the disappointment on Sloan's face.

"I better go. I've got a customer bringing a sketch over for a light fixture he wants me to make out of deer antlers."

Paris followed Sloan out the back door and walked her to her truck.

"It was great to see you, Sloan," she said, giving her a hug. "I will keep in touch. I promise."

Sloan held the hug a long moment before releasing Paris and smiling warmly at her.

"You better," she warned then hugged her again. Sloan climbed in her truck and waved as she slowly pulled away.

Paris could see Sloan's eyes staring back at her in the rearview mirror. A surprising knot formed in her stomach as the sound of Sloan's truck faded down the road.

Paris met Malcolm for dinner at six. They discussed each of the major repairs and how they were to be completed. Malcolm reminded her that his brother, Raymond, was a contractor and carpenter; and that he could do most of the repairs at a considerable savings on the labor. Paris also questioned Malcolm about real estate prices in the Banyon area and commissions for the sale if she decided to liquidate the property.

"Have you decided to sell?" he asked, leaning over and fixing her with a shrewd gaze.

"I haven't yet," she replied, uncomfortable with his demeanor. She didn't want to be rushed. The farm belonged to her, and she could take all the time she needed, in spite of Malcolm's beady little eyes staring insistently at her. "I'll let you know when I decide."

"By the way, did you bring the key back?" he asked.

Paris took it from her pocket and placed it on the table. She decided not to mention she had a copy made. It wasn't any of his business anyway.

"I'll be in touch with you to see how things are going. Please remember," she added, giving him a deliberate gaze of her own. "No smokers."

"Absolutely," he quickly agreed, as if it was his idea all along.

Paris was slightly surprised when Malcolm bought her dinner since he didn't strike her as being particularly generous. But at least the business part was settled, for now. She headed for Purdy and a hot bath before packing for her flight home. The decision on what to do with the house still swirled around in her mind. She finished packing and dropped the envelope with the papers about the house back into her carry-on.

"I don't know what to do, Grandmother," she said, letting her fingers linger over the envelope that contained her grandmother's letter. "I just don't know."

CHAPTER 8

Paris had been back in Manhattan less than a week when she left Bill Hays a message to meet her for lunch. She waved at him to join her as he entered the hospital dining room with his tray. She was sitting in the far corner of the room away from the noisy crowded tables of hospital employees. She preferred peace and quiet, if even for a few minutes before returning upstairs.

Bill set his tray on the table across from Paris. He had his usual Thursday lunch. Meatloaf, sliced tomatoes, cottage cheese, a slice of rye bread and a glass of iced tea. Meatloaf was the cafeteria's special of the day. Bill was predictable with his lunch and with his work. He started his hospital rounds at six forty five and was in the office by eight thirty. He wore highly polished black oxfords even with brown slacks. He could interpret an EKG faster than anyone Paris had ever met, but he could not set the timer on a thermostat. His glasses were usually on the end of his nose perilously close to falling into his soup or onto a patient's lap. While on a flight from

Chicago to New York, he saved a man who was having a heart attack, but he has yet to remember his wife's birthday or their anniversary. Bill graduated in the top ten percent of his class at Dalhousie Medical School in Halifax, Nova Scotia, but he flunked high school typing and choir. He hitched his chair in tight to the table and tucked the end of his tie in his shirt to protect it from flying meatloaf.

"So, Paris," he said, peppering everything on his plate with an even black dust. "What's up?"

Paris placed her fork on her plate and folded her hands in her lap. Her mind was wrestling with the decision on whether to return to Banyon and oversee Maybelline's repairs or leave the job to Malcolm. She thought the matter was closed. She thought she was comfortable with it. But something just didn't feel right. The third option of selling the place as-is still lurked in the shadows as well. Paris was a dedicated and compassionate doctor, but for the first time since Gabby's death, she felt something other than her practice gnawing at her.

"How was Missouri?" he asked noticing Paris's distant expression.

"Fine. Warm," she replied, dabbing her napkin across her mouth.

Bill measured three teaspoons of sugar into his iced tea but didn't stir it. A quarter inch of sugar settled to the bottom of the glass like silt.

"How's your mother?" he added.

"She's fine. Giving orders to the bridge club in Florida and changing the color of her hair every other month." Paris gave a half smile.

Bill chuckled and let Paris decide when it was the right moment to tell him what she wanted to talk about.

"It's the house, Bill. The one I own in Banyon," she started.

Bill nodded, testing his meatloaf.

"It needs some repairs before it can be rented out again."

"Major stuff?"

"Not terribly. It's just an old house with old house ailments," she reported.

"Didn't you have the same problem a few years ago?"

"It seems like I have repairs between every renter."

"Renters are tough on a place. I own a couple of little houses over in Jersey. Every time I go out there it's one problem or another, clogged toilet, hole in the wall, broken window." Bill frowned and continued eating. "Isn't your property management company overseeing the house?" he asked skeptically.

"I thought so."

"But?" he queried.

"I told Malcolm to go ahead and make the repairs. He's going to call me when it's finished. I had given some thought to selling the place. I live so far away and don't have the time to go out there very often. I thought the best thing was to just sell it and forget it," Paris tried to sound detached and emotionless.

"My guess is you don't want to sell your grandmother's home, Paris. If you did, you would have done it a long time ago. And—" he started then took another bite of meatloaf.

Paris waited and watched as he swallowed and washed it down with a gulp of tea. "And what?"

"And if you really wanted to divest yourself of the property in Banyon you wouldn't use the past tense when you mention your thoughts of selling it. I think you want to keep it. I think you want to hang on to it as a memento of your childhood. You have told me on several occasions how much fun you had spending your summers in Missouri. That old house holds your sense of family, your sense of stability. You live in New York, but your roots are in Banyon, Missouri."

"I was raised in upstate New York, Bill. Not Banyon," Paris reminded him.

Bill leaned back in his chair and wiped his mouth with his napkin.

"If you say so."

"But I have been giving some thought to my decision to let Malcolm handle the repairs," Paris offered.

"Don't you trust him?" Bill asked.

Paris thought a minute.

"I'm not sure if that's the problem. But it sure has been on my mind since I got back from Banyon."

"Why didn't you stay and oversee the repairs?"

Paris laughed sarcastically. "And my patients? What do I do with them? Take them with me?"

Bill stared at her with narrowed eyes and a set jaw. He didn't say anything.

"What?" she asked.

"It has been five years since you took any time off other than a day or two for a medical conference. You act like we can't survive without the almighty Doctor Paris DeMont."

Paris looked at him with pained and unsuspecting eyes.

"Paris, you're human," he continued. "You need to take a vacation now and then just like the rest of us. You need to get away and have some R & R. I know you have your reasons. I know you are dedicated to your practice and your patients, but you have to get away." He leaned forward and spoke deliberately. "You need to be Paris DeMont for awhile. Not just Doctor DeMont. What would Gabby say?"

Mentioning Gabby's name seemed to slap Paris across the face. She sat up defensively. Before she could reply Bill had placed his hand on the table and slid it toward her as if to pacify his harsh words.

"I'm not sorry for saying that," Bill added quietly. "I'm just sorry I had to say it."

Paris lowered her eyes.

"Gabby would say Paris is doing just fine," she said quietly.

"Then what is this lunch meeting all about?"

Paris realized the decision she was about to announce was going to bring a smile to Bill's face.

"What would you say if I told you I was taking a couple weeks off to go back to Banyon?" Paris propped her elbows on the table and folded her hands under her chin.

Bill stopped his fork in mid-bite. His eyes rolled up to meet hers. A grin instantly brightened his face.

"I'd say that's great. I'd also say take a few months, not a few weeks."

Paris shook her head.

"Two months. Make it two months," he insisted.

"Two weeks," she argued. "Maybe three."

"When are you going?"

"I don't know. I hadn't decided I would go until today."

"Tell you what. Today's Thursday. You're on call this weekend. How about you leave Monday? The girls in the office can juggle the patient's appointments. Joe and I can pick up the load next week."

"I thought you were taking a couple of weeks off to go to Florida," Paris declared curiously.

"Nope. I was just waiting for a reason to get out of a trip to Disneyland with the grandkids."

"Bill, your wife is going to kill you."

"No, she won't. Not when I tell her why."

"Thank you, Bill," Paris replied sincerely.

"Three months is a good round number," he offered.

"Weeks, not months," she insisted.

Bill fixed her with a concerned stare. "If you need more time, you call me. Okay?"

"I will. And if you need me, you'll call me, right?"

He nodded.

A confused mixture of excitement over returning to Banyon and guilt for taking the time off buzzed around Paris all afternoon. As much as she tried to keep her emotions balanced, the excitement was far stronger than the guilt. It was a strange but invigorating feeling Paris hadn't expected when she made the decision.

CHAPTER 9

Paris finished a long Friday in the office and spent a tiring weekend on call for the patients she, Bill and Joe had in the hospital. When she left the hospital Sunday evening she stopped by her office and left her stethoscope and pager in her desk instead of bringing them home with her, a subconscious tribute to her decision to take time off from work. She opened her suitcases and began sorting through her closet. A giddy excitement over going back to Banyon was enough to start Paris whistling while she packed. While she collected her cosmetics from the bathroom, she called her mother to let her know where she would be. Paris was formulating her explanation on why she was returning to Banyon when Liz's answering machine picked up.

"Hello Mother. I'm taking your advice and going on vacation for three weeks. I'll be in Banyon, but you can call me on my cell phone if you need me. Hope you are well. Tell the gals in the bridge club hi for me. I love you. Bye."

Paris arose early Monday morning, anxious to get out of town before seven and the rush hour traffic. She knew her BMW Z3 wasn't going to be the most comfortable car to drive halfway across the country, but having her own vehicle instead of a rental seemed like a smart idea. The two-passenger roadster limited the amount of luggage she could take, but she didn't need all that much for just three weeks.

She was out of Manhattan and headed for U.S. 95 before the rush hour traffic came to gridlock. She eased back in the driver's seat, slipped in a CD and cruised westward. There was something about the trip and returning to Banyon that captivated her. It was more than just getting away, more than just overseeing Maybelline's repairs. Whether it was reliving the happy times of her youth or something to do with Sloan, she felt a rush that pinked her cheeks and stirred her soul.

She crossed the Mississippi River at St. Louis Tuesday afternoon. A gentle summer shower followed her across the state and didn't end until she was almost to Banyon. She had taken the same route just over a week ago from Springfield to Banyon but somehow there was a deeper thrill this time as she entered the rolling hills and rich farmland.

She pulled into the drive and circled around to the back of her big farmhouse. The sun was beginning to melt into the horizon and cast long shadows across the meadow. The gentle scent of wild heather floated over her as she climbed out of the car. The clicking of crickets were the only sounds in the evening air. Manhattan's congestion and confusion seemed a million miles away. She went to the fence and gazed out over the meadow where the pond shimmered like fine crystal. A satisfaction settled over her as if she had returned to an old friend. It was a warm feeling. She hated it. She didn't want to feel warm and fuzzy about Maybelline. She didn't want the grip of contentment to influence her decision about what to do with the house. She wanted to remain objective.

She opened the gate and strolled down the hill toward the

pond. As she crossed the footbridge to the island she saw a blue plastic tarp draped over a stack of boxes. Several folding tables were leaned against the pile. She pulled back the tarp to find the same boxes of wedding decorations she had seen in the barn. The corrugated paper bells had been used and mashed. The napkins had been opened and the pillar candles had been burned down several inches. An empty champagne bottle and two long-stemmed champagne flutes were tucked in the corner of a box, protected by one of the paper tablecloths.

"So, Kathy and Ryan. You must have tied the knot after all." Paris muttered, poking through the remains of the celebration. There was a battery-operated boombox under the tarp. It had huge speakers that looked like the exhaust ports on a spaceship. She pressed the play button and was instantly blasted back on her heels by a loud twanging guitar accompanied by drums and bass. She quickly pushed stop, the sounds echoing across the pond and back again. The loud noise had disturbed a flock of birds that were roosting in the trees. "Nothing like a little peaceful music for a wedding," she chided under her breath.

It dawned on Paris that not only had this Kathy and Ryan gotten married on the island, but they had done it without her knowledge or consent. She knew the house had been empty for nearly two months. If they had moved out of the house they no longer had a legal or ethical right to use her island for their nuptials without contacting her. Malcolm hadn't mentioned it. The legal and insurance responsibilities for any accident that might have happened raced through her mind like stinging rain. The thought of someone falling off the bridge and breaking a leg or, heaven forbid, a drowning stopped her blood cold. But the ceremony was over. The damage was done.

The sun was long gone, and the last glimmers of light were blending images together in muted shades of gray and green. The faint sound of an engine came from over the hill and grew louder. Soon the beams of a pair of headlights came bouncing over the crest of the hill and headed toward the pond. The roar of the ATV stopped at the far side of the bridge.

"Who's there," an angry voice demanded from behind a flashlight.

Paris shielded her eyes as the flashlight captured her face.

"It's me. It's Paris. Is that you, Sloan?" Paris strained to see beyond the flashlight.

"Yes. Damn, woman. I thought someone was down here robbing the place." Sloan crossed the bridge, sweeping the flashlight along in front of her. "You're back," she said, her eyes wide with pleasant surprise. "Is something wrong?"

"No. I just decided to take a few weeks off to see about getting the house in order." Paris wrestled with the idea of asking Sloan if she knew anything about the wedding supplies but decided it was something she could handle herself.

"To sell or to rent out again?" Sloan asked.

"To tell the truth, I don't know. One minute I'm just going to sell it and be done with it. Then I remember all the summers I spent here, all the wonderful memories and fun I had with Grandmother and with you. I need to decide once and for all. Maybe that's why I'm here."

"Where are you staying tonight? You are welcome to stay with me," she offered brightly.

"I called the hotel in Purdy where I stayed last week. They are holding a room for me, but thanks. I had to come by the house first. Just for a minute." Paris looked out over the pasture as the last faint light of the day surrendered to the night. "It is so peaceful," she said quietly so as not to disturb the serenity.

Sloan watched Paris enjoying the moment.

Paris took a last quenching breath. "I guess I better go. Will I see you tomorrow?" Paris asked as she led the way across the bridge.

"You can count on it," Sloan replied, carving a path with her flashlight. "I'm glad you're back," she added as they walked up the hill. There was an excitement in Sloan's voice she was trying to restrain.

Paris climbed in her car and waved at Sloan then pulled away. Sloan stood watching and listening as the sounds of the car faded into the darkness. Paris was back, and Sloan's grin couldn't be any wider.

Paris was up early the next morning, anxious to return to the house. She pulled into the drive, unlocked the back door and went inside. She couldn't tell if anyone had been working on the house or not. She called Malcolm's office and left a message for him to call her.

Paris opened the basement door and peered down the stairs into the darkness. She flipped on the basement light and started down the narrow stairs. A damp musty smell filled her nose as she descended the wooden steps. Like all hundred-year-old houses, the basement was dirty and dank. The windows were small and offered little light. The two bare light bulbs suspended from the rafters dimly lit the vast expanse. There was a box of aerosol cans at the bottom of the stairs, one of which looked like it had been used. She took one of the cans from the box and read the label of the bug spray. There were five more cans in the box, all new and full. She wondered why Malcolm was spraying Raid since she remembered paying for a professional exterminator to spray twice a year. Surely his formula would handle any extra little critters lurking around in the basement. She looked up in the ceiling joists but couldn't see anything crawling. As she started back up the steps she saw four sections of lumber stacked behind the stairs. They looked like well-aged timbers just like the ones in her joists. They had been neatly sawn into four foot sections. The cut marks looked fresh. She assumed they were to be used to reinforce the floor in the mudroom. At least they are getting things going, she thought. She walked to the back corner of the basement which would be directly under the mudroom. There was no light bulb in the socket. She squinted up at the joists but it was too dark to see. She dismissed the uneasiness she felt as just travel fatigue. She went upstairs to wash her hands. When her cell phone rang she wasn't surprised to see Malcolm's number on the screen.

"Hello Malcolm," she said cheerfully.

"Miss DeMont, I heard you're back in Banyon." There was nervousness in his voice.

"Yes, I decided to take a few weeks off. And what better place to take a vacation than at my own house." She spoke happily, intentionally testing his opinion.

"Well, well. This is a nice surprise. We've got a lot of repairs going on at your house so it's going to be a real mess for a while. We'll be spraying some insecticide and doing some noisy construction. I wouldn't want anyone to get hurt. I'm always real careful about safety, you know."

"I'm glad to hear that, Malcolm. And I won't be in the way. I would like to keep track of the work, though. The house seems to be deteriorating faster than I thought it would."

"Yes. It sure is a shame how these old places go south once they get a little age under the shingles." He tried to sound deeply concerned.

"What kind of repairs are you planning for this week?" she asked.

"We had to order some parts. It'll be a few days before they'll be in. Repairs are always held up when you have to special order parts. I was going to check this afternoon and see if they were in yet."

"Like what?"

"Electrical parts. Electrical cable, junction boxes, ground fault interrupter switches. You got to have GFI plugs in the bathrooms, Miss DeMont. Yes siree. Gotta have those. If you didn't put those in and touched the switch with wet hands you'd get zapped for sure. It could kill you, you know."

"Can't you get those things at McKinley's hardware store?" she asked.

"You'll need a GFI plug in the laundry room, too. And one in the kitchen, two would be better." He rambled on, ignoring Paris's question. "One by the sink and one by the stove. That's a two-twenty line."

Paris didn't know what a GFI plug was, but it sounded like a safety feature she couldn't afford to do without.

"You staying at the motel over in Purdy again?" he asked, changing the subject.

"Yes," Paris replied.

"The crew will be out in the morning, but you don't need to worry about being there. There'll be a lot of hammering and pounding so you might want to give us a few days before you venture out to the house again. I hear there's a real nice strip mall in Aurora. You might like to check that out. My wife says she likes to shop over there. Hell, she likes to shop anywhere." He laughed robustly. "I do have something you could do. Maybe you could select the new ceiling fixtures, one for the hall, one for the downstairs bathroom and one for the master bedroom. All of them are damaged. There's a place in Springfield that has hundreds to choose from. Reasonably priced place, too. They are nice folks over there. They'll let you wander around for hours while you decide." He chuckled as if he doubted Paris's ability to make an expeditious decision on a light fixture.

"Could we just get them here in Banyon at McKinley's hardware store?" she asked, again trying to pin him down.

"Well, you might be able to," he replied with hesitation. "But the prices will probably be a lot higher, and you won't have near as many choices. You might want to look over some paint samples while you are in Springfield. We'll have to repaint after the bathroom tile gets replaced. I'm sure you can select a better color than I can. I'll call them and let them know you are coming over today. They'll give you a good price on the fixtures. Tell them I sent you." His tone grated on Paris's nerves.

"I'm going to check McKinley's first," Paris said frankly.

"Suit yourself, miss," he said finally. "I'll talk with you later."

Paris hung up, a smirk still on her face from Malcolm's condescending attitude. She made a list of some basic needs for the house and headed for the store. She spent the morning in town shopping and browsing. The summer day was beautiful and the square was busy with pedestrians and other shoppers. She ate lunch at Rita's Cafe and treated herself to a piece of homemade coconut cream pie for dessert. She returned to the house and carried in a package of toilet paper, paper towels, plastic cups, a mop, a broom, detergent, hand soap, a small wastebasket and a toilet brush. If she was going to spend any time at all in the house she at least wanted it clean.

Paris opened the cupboard under the sink and dumped the dishpan. She was relieved there weren't any of Henry's relatives in the mousetrap. As she was about to close the cupboard door something else caught her eye. An ad in the newspaper that was lining the shelf, partially obstructed by the trap, said something about renting a local island for weddings. She used her car key to carefully move the trap so she could read the ad. She got down on her hands and knees, turned her head sideways and read the ad out loud.

"Picturesque Island in Romantic Setting—Banyon Area. Available to rent for weddings, receptions, reunions or other special occasions. Contact Malcolm Vetch at Ozark Properties." A small icon of a weeping willow tree was just above the telephone number. The newspaper was dated months ago. "It couldn't be mine. Surely he would have asked me first," she muttered.

"Knock, knock," Sloan called from the mudroom.

"Hi. Come on in," Paris replied as she closed the cupboard and stood up.

"You left the back door open again," Sloan admonished.

"Oh, gosh. Don't tell Barney."

"My lips are sealed," Sloan joked. "So, what's up in the world of home repairs?"

"Good question. Speaking of questions, I have one for you. Do you know what GFI plugs are and do I need them?"

"GFI means ground fault interrupter plug. They trip the circuit to protect you from electrocution if you touch an electrical source with wet hands. They are usually in bathrooms and kitchens. Laundry rooms, too. They also have master GFIs that go in the breaker box. One can do the whole house. Or you can have one for each circuit where there might be a water source. It depends if those rooms are on the same circuit. And yes you need GFIs, but I would assume you already have them. Let's check." Sloan first checked the breaker box on the wall in the mudroom then went into the bathroom next to the kitchen.

"Yes, you have one. See this red button on the outlet? You press it to test the system." She turned on the bathroom light then pressed the test button. The light immediately went out. "This one works fine." She went to the breaker box and reset the circuit. The light came back on. She then checked the upstairs bathroom and it, too, had a working GFI plug in the outlet by the mirror. "You have one in the kitchen and one in the laundry room, but they are on the same circuit as the bathroom so they are redundant," she explained after examination.

"Why would Malcolm say he is going to install some? He said I needed them."

"Looks like he didn't check to see if you already had them."

"One more thing," Paris stated. "I may be just overly suspicious, but would you take a look at some beams in the basement with me?"

"Sure," Sloan agreed and started down the basement stairs.

Paris showed her the sections of cut timbers behind the steps and explained the sagging floor in the mudroom. Sloan moved one of the light bulbs to the empty socket so they could see the area under the mudroom.

"Look," Sloan said pointing to the cross beams. "There are sections missing."

Paris scowled up at the four gaps in the overhead beams. Sloan carried one of the cut timbers over and held it up.

"This one came from right here. See how the swirls in the grain match." She held up the other cut sections and was able to find a matching spot for each of them. "I'd say these were cut from here. Did you tell Malcolm to do this down here?" Sloan asked.

Paris shook her head adamantly. "No, I didn't." Paris narrowed her eyes and rippled her jaw as she studied the ceiling. Finally she turned out the light and headed for the stairs.

"Have him test the GFI plugs, but I think he'll see you don't need them replaced and you certainly don't need any more," Sloan said, following her up the stairs. "They don't wear out very often. It's like installing a light switch. They usually last a long time. And yours look fairly new."

"Are GFI plugs and electrical cable special order items?" Paris asked.

"No," Sloan replied, staring at Paris curiously. "Who told you that? Dad carries all that stuff. That's basic electrical supplies. The cable you're talking about is that heavy white wire they use to string the electrical circuits in a new house. It's usually hidden in the walls. You'd only need that if you were adding on a room or doing major remodeling."

"I'm sure there is a perfectly legitimate explanation for all this," Paris offered. "But I definitely want to ask some questions." She looked around the kitchen then stared out the window.

"What's wrong?" Sloan asked, reading the worry on Paris's face. "Anything else I can help you with?"

"No. Thank you for your help, though." Paris gave a smile and squeezed Sloan's arm. "I just keep thinking about what to do with the house. I don't know why this decision is so hard for me."

"You mean whether or not to sell?" Sloan asked cautiously.

Paris nodded.

"I'll tell you what. I have something to take your mind off the house and off the decision." Sloan smiled broadly. "An invitation."

"Invitation for what?"

"You are invited to the McKinley barbecue on Saturday. Mom and Dad insisted you come. The whole family, and it is getting big, is going to have the annual family hog slop." Sloan laughed a cock-eyed laugh.

"Hog slop?" Paris frowned then chuckled.

"Dad roasts a pig. Everybody brings a couple of covered dishes. Last year we had almost a hundred people."

"A hundred? I didn't know your family was that big."

"We add in the aunts, uncles, cousins, a stray boyfriend or girl-friend or two and before you can stomp a cow pile you've got a loud and hungry crowd." Sloan beamed.

"Hog slop, eh?" Paris pondered, tugging at her ear.

"When you say it, it does sound a little gross," Sloan replied with a wrinkled nose.

"It might be the perfect name for a big family gathering."

They both laughed.

"So, you'll come?"

"Sure. I'd love to," Paris nodded. "What can I bring?"

"Nothing."

"Oh, no. If I can't contribute to the food, I'm not coming." Paris looked stern and defiant.

"How about bringing some pop or something, whatever you like to drink."

"That I can do. But isn't there any place where I can get a tray of something, cheese or hors d'oeuvres?"

Sloan snickered. "If you showed up with a deli tray of fancy tid-bits you'd be laughed into the next county. My family eats starch, carbs, he-man food." Sloan flexed her biceps in a mocking pose. "No celery sticks or rice cakes for them."

"How high are their cholesterol levels?"

Sloan rolled her eyes skyward. "It isn't quite that bad. But they eat potatoes and white bread. I've gotten most of them to use no-fat or at least low-fat foods as much as possible. Mom's been feed-ing dad low-fat stuff for years, but he doesn't know it. He thinks he's still eating chicken fried in lard."

"Good for her."

"Mom remembers you. She said you were that cute little girl with long legs and a soft smile."

Paris blushed.

"She was right," Sloan added watching Paris smile sheepishly.

"What time, and where is this hog slop?" Paris needed to change the subject. Sloan's watchful eyes were making her feel self-conscious.

"It's at the folks. We start gathering about three."

"I'll need directions. I'm afraid I don't remember how to get there."

"I thought I'd pick you up. There are usually so many vehicles in the yard, one less car would be good. In case you're wondering, this barbecue is a jeans affair. You can leave the slacks with the tidbit tray." Sloan pointed to Paris's linen slacks.

"Jeans, huh?" Paris tried to remember if she brought any.

"What's wrong with jeans? Don't they wear jeans in New York City?" Sloan asked defensively.

"Yes," Paris replied. "It's just that I'm not sure I packed any."

"How can you travel and not take jeans? My God, woman," Sloan teased.

"I don't wear them very often. I work long hours, and I don't wear jeans at work."

"Weekends?" Sloan prodded.

"I work a lot of weekends, too. But maybe I dropped a pair in my suitcase."

"What size do you wear? We look about the same size around. You could borrow a pair of mine. They'd be too long for you, but with shoes on it wouldn't matter."

"Thanks but if I didn't bring any, I can buy a pair," Paris said, not wanting to be a bother.

"Sevens? Nines?" Sloan persisted.

"Well—"

"Nines, right?"

"Yes, something like that. But really, I can get some."

"I'll bring you a clean pair. I'll even iron them for you. I must have a dozen pair. Do you like the trim fit or the relaxed fit?"

Paris's eyes widened as if she had no idea.

"Trim fit," Sloan declared with a saucy smile.

CHAPTER 10

Paris wasn't surprised when no one came by the house the next morning as Malcolm promised. Nor was she surprised when he suddenly had to go out of town for a family emergency. Against her better judgment she decided to give them the benefit of the doubt and wait a few more days for the repairs to begin.

According to the newspaper, Friday was to be a warm sunny day, and Paris planned to use it to air out the house. She opened as many windows as she could, propping some with sticks to keep them open. She then cleaned what looked like years worth of dirt from the window sills. She mopped the bathroom floors, scrubbing away the sticky hairspray residue left by the previous tenant. While she was in the mood she also swept and mopped the kitchen and mudroom floors. By noon she was dripping with sweat, but she had found her groove. She cleaned the refrigerator and stove, removed the cobwebs from the light fixtures and corners, dusted the woodwork and swept off the huge front porch. What started out as a day to air out the house turned into a full, long day of cleaning. By dinnertime she was tired and sweaty. The small fan she had found in the pantry stirred the hot air around the kitchen but did little to cool her. She had a fresh change of clothes in the car and promised herself a long, relaxing bath, but first she wanted a stroll across the meadow and around the pond.

As she descended the slope a meadowlark called his evening lament. The pasture was alive with the scent of growing things. She crossed the bridge onto her island and meandered through the waving branches of the willow. It was cool and peaceful in the shade of the big tree, a tree she had always found comforting and reassuring. She sat down in the grass and leaned against the trunk of the tree. The waning evening light was reflected in the water, bathing the meadow in a warm, golden glow. Paris closed her eyes and took a deep breath, drinking in the smells of country summers. It was a pure yet heady smell of grass and trees, of heavy humid air, the smells of her childhood summers. She watched the ripples as they drifted around the island in a hypnotic and tranquil flow. The little girl in her wanted to slip off her shoes and wade in, or better yet, jump in. But cardiologists from Manhattan didn't jump into farm ponds, even though it did look cool and inviting. She remembered hot summer days and the way the muddy pond bottom squished between her toes. She also remembered her grandmother sitting on the bank dangling her feet in the cool water as Paris splashed and frolicked on an old inner tube. They were more than memories. They were life-altering experiences. That's what Grandmother West would tell her. Don't be afraid to try things, she would say. How will you know what you like if you don't try it?

The sunset had exploded over the pond like a brilliant, wild fire and was fading to a pale glow. A haze covered the meadow with a silvery fog. Paris kicked off her shoes and walked to the edge of the water. She brushed a toe across the surface. It was cool and refreshing.

"What the heck," she muttered, checking to see if she was alone. She then peeled off her shirt, shorts, bra and panties. She waded in up to her knees then dove across the surface of the water. She gasped at the shocking temperature. A toe's worth was cool, but a naked body fully submerged was more. It was cold. But she was determined to experience it. She swam a complete circle around the pond, under the arched bridge, and back to the bank where she had left her clothes. She had gotten used to the crisp water temperature and lazily floated along enjoying the last light of day. Paris scolded herself for not experiencing this sooner. She floated on her back, watching the first twinkling star dot the twilight. Her nipples bobbed along on the surface, erect and hard from the chilly water. A dragonfly zipped across the water, touching down here and there. She wondered if he was getting a drink or just cooling off like she was.

Paris lazily pulled a backstroke then another, aiming herself toward the bridge. The bulging croak of the bullfrog echoed over the pond. There was nothing in New York City like this. Nothing even close. If she jumped in the pond in Central Park in the nude and took a lazy swim she'd either be raped, shot or arrested. Maybe all three. The thrill of ownership suddenly swept over her. Not only was she skinny-dipping at twilight, she was doing it in her very own farm pond. Her smile grew wider as she listened to the sounds of summer's innocence.

She drifted backward, waiting to float under the bridge, knowing it was close. As she floated under the arch she looked up and was greeted by a pair of bare feet dangling from the bridge. Someone was sitting on the bridge watching her. She gasped and pulled her body down into the water. Paris stayed under the bridge, waiting to hear who was up there. The dangling feet suddenly disappeared and were replaced by Sloan's smiling face.

"Hi," she said, looking under the bridge at Paris.

"Oh my God, Sloan. You scared the crap out of me," Paris replied angrily. She remained under the bridge, treading water.

"Sorry." Sloan continued to watch Paris, her head hanging upside down through the railings.

"How long have you been up there?" Paris blushed at the realization she had been floating fully exposed.

"Not too long." Sloan seemed to know Paris was embarrassed. "I told you I'd be back to bring you some jeans for the barbecue," she declared, trying to justify her late evening visit.

"I know. But I thought you meant tomorrow."

"Oh." Sloan was having trouble making conversation while hanging upside down and staring at Paris's glistening skin. The greenish pond water masked Paris's breasts like a daringly low cut gown, high enough to hide her nipples but low enough so she wished it didn't. "Are you coming out from under the bridge or are you spending the night under there?"

"Sloan, you know good and well I'm naked. I'm not coming out until it is completely dark." Paris slapped a splash of water in Sloan's direction. "So go away." Paris was normally shy and modest about her body, anything but an exhibitionist. But somehow the idea of Sloan seeing her naked was far less than a tragedy.

"I've got news for you. There's going to be a full moon tonight. See?" Sloan pointed toward the huge yellow ball rising out of the horizon. "It isn't going to be dark tonight, at least not enough to hide your lily white skin."

"Very funny." Paris tried to cross her arms to cover her breasts, but she couldn't tread water without them for balance.

"Either you come out of there or—" Sloan's face disappeared, and Paris could hear her footsteps cross the bridge to the island.

"Or what?" She listened intently for the footsteps to return, but they didn't.

"Or I'm coming in, too," Sloan called from the island.

"You wouldn't dare," Paris scoffed. As soon as she said it she knew she had dared the wrong person. The sound of a splash and the rush of ripples toward her told Paris that Sloan had taken the dare.

"Damn! This is cold," Sloan yelled as she swam under the bridge. "Hello." Sloan gave a broad grin. "You were saying."

"You're naked," Paris said with a frown.

"So are you," Sloan justified. "Besides we used to see each other naked all the time. It didn't bother you back then."

"We were six years old. By the time we were twelve you wouldn't even show me your new underwear when it was still in the package let alone on your butt." Paris began to ease her way out from under the bridge. Sloan followed at a respectable distance.

"It isn't very deep over here," Paris said, feeling the soft mud oozing up between her toes. "In fact, I don't remember it being very deep when we used to play down here. I thought we could touch almost everywhere."

"Malcolm had this part dredged up a few years back. He had a backhoe down here making the area under the bridge deeper." Sloan picked a rock off the bottom with her toes then skated it across the surface.

"I remember him telling me something about the pasture flooding. He must have done it to fix that."

"Are you kidding?" Sloan gave a mocking laugh. "Malcolm heard that Melinda Mathews was visiting her brother who was renting the house, and she dropped her engagement ring in the pond as they were crossing the bridge. From what I heard it was a huge rock. Worth a couple grand. They searched for it for hours and hours but finally gave up on it. Figured it was lost in the mud. So Malcolm and his brother rented a backhoe and dug for two days trying to find it."

"Did he find it for her?"

"No one knows. He closed off the meadow and wouldn't let anyone down here. I heard Melinda never saw it again."

"If he had found it surely he would have given it back to her, wouldn't he?" Paris speculated.

Sloan raised her eyebrows in doubt.

"Look at that moon, Sloan," Paris said in awe as she caught a glimpse of the huge golden globe. "Have you ever seen so beautiful a summer night?" The moon had risen off the horizon and cast a brilliant light over the swimmers, glistening on the surface of the water like tiny twinkling lights. Paris had been drifting and walking further away from the bridge where the water was shallower. She was so engrossed with the moon's spectacle she didn't realize her breasts were now fully above the water's surface.

"Yes, very beautiful," Sloan replied quietly, noticing Paris's breasts and erect nipples glistening in the moonlight. She tried to will her attention away from Paris's supple whiteness, but it was not to be. She had never seen a woman with such extraordinary beauty before. She told herself it was the romantic setting, the moonlight, the water droplets on Paris's perfect skin, the warm summer night all conspiring against her. But she couldn't help it. Paris was beautiful. Sloan had always thought Paris was beautiful, even as a skinny, gap-toothed six-year-old. She had perfect posture, a bright smile, soft radiant skin and satiny smooth hair. One of those girls it would have been easy to hate out of jealousy. But Paris was also kind and funny and caring. Sloan had never hated her for her looks. She had admired it, praised it, even coveted the moments she could sit and stare at Paris's exquisite beauty. Sloan's brain had begun taking snapshots of Paris's full round breasts.

"Look over there," Paris pointed at the island. "Look at the fireflies under the willow." Paris had turned around, her shimmering shoulders toward Sloan.

"Uh-huh." Sloan blinked and looked in the direction of the willow as if coming out of a trance. "Be right back," she added, splashing toward the island. She hurried up the bank, grass and dirt sticking to her wet feet and ankles. Sloan's body wasn't thin and pale like Paris's. She was tan except for her bottom and tank top area that were nearly white. Her thighs were well defined and muscular. Her hips were trim like an athlete's.

Paris could see the white outline of Sloan's rear darting back and forth in the darkness under the willow branches. Suddenly she ran back down the bank, her small firm breasts dancing in the moonlight. She splashed her way toward Paris, holding her left fist high over her head.

"What are you doing?" Paris said turning her face as Sloan thrashed closer.

"Give me your hand," Sloan ordered.

"Why? What do you have?" Paris asked, holding out her hand.

Sloan opened her fist and carefully took out the lightning bug.

"What are you going to do with that bug?" Paris asked pulling her hand back.

Sloan took her hand and waited for the lightning bug to light up again. When it did she pulled off its lit abdomen. Paris wrinkled her nose but didn't say anything. Sloan placed the iridescent bug's body on Paris's ring finger, the bug's body fluid acting like glue.

"There. Looks just like a diamond ring. At least it will for a few minutes." Sloan smiled. "Don't you remember when we used to do that?"

Paris held out her hand and admired it in the moonlight, as the happy memory presented itself.

"Thank you, Sloan. My very own bug ring." She smiled back and playfully kissed Sloan on the cheek. The feel of Paris's lips against her cheek and the brief touch of her breasts against her own gave Sloan an explosive rush of emotion she hadn't expected. Sloan swallowed hard and diverted her eyes for a moment. When she looked back at Paris's soft eyes she couldn't stop herself. She leaned over and kissed Paris fully on the mouth in a firm yet tender kiss. The simple act took them both by surprise. Paris's eyes widened as Sloan pulled away, a blush visible on her face even in the pale moonlight. Neither one said anything as they stood armpit-deep in the water, staring into the each other's eyes. Sloan watched Paris's expression for a sign of how the kiss was received. She hadn't meant to throw a wet blanket on the evening's fun. It just happened. Sloan also regretted that she couldn't find the courage to do it again.

Paris offered a nervous smile and diverted her eyes.

"I'm sorry," Sloan began, but Paris cut her off and moved away.

"Time to get out. I'm all pruny, and it's getting chilly." Paris quickly climbed out and grabbed her clothes. She disappeared beneath the willow branches and dressed.

Sloan took her time climbing out, allowing Paris a moment of privacy. She stepped into her shorts and pulled the T-shirt over her head. She stuffed her bra and panties in the pockets then waited on the bridge for Paris to finish dressing. Guilt was ripping at her gut over being so forward. But something else deep inside was tingling wildly at the thought of Paris's lips against hers. She leaned against the railing, looking down into the dark water.

CHAPTER 11

Sloan picked up Paris at two-thirty Saturday afternoon. She turned off the country road, crossed the metal cattle guard and pulled into her folks' yard where more than a dozen vehicles made the McKinley farm look like the McKinley used truck lot. A few cars were tucked in between the big pickups like weeds in a rose garden. Sloan pulled in next to a mud-covered pickup with a hay spike on the back. She unloaded the cooler containing her casseroles and carried it around to the backyard.

"I'll be back to get those cases of pop in a minute," she said over her shoulder.

"I can get them," Paris replied dragging one to the open tail-gate.

"Let me give you a hand there, Paris," Charlie yelled, hurrying to help. "How's my favorite customer?"

"I'm fine Charlie. How are you?" She gave him a hug. "Thank you for letting me gate-crash your family barbecue."

"Hell, you ain't gate-crashing. You're invited and welcome as you can be. Make yourself at home. Come on in the backyard and meet the family." He leaned toward her to whisper. "I don't know half of their names. Too many cousins and kids. I just call them bud or sis."

"Uncle Charlie, where's the horseshoes?" asked a group of teenage boys.

"On a peg in the tack room, Bud." He smiled at Paris and nodded. She returned the nod understandingly.

"My land o' love. Paris DeMont." A broad and smiling woman came hurrying toward Paris with her arms wide. She gave her a bear hug that locked Paris's arms to her side. "Let me look at you." She held Paris's shoulders and pushed her back, turning her one way then the other. "Look how you have grown. You're not a little girl anymore." She hugged her again. "How many years has it been, dear? Twenty? Twenty-five?"

"Mom, you're going to smash her," Sloan said, noticing Paris's bewildered look.

"Hello, Mrs. McKinley," Paris said, grateful to Sloan for revealing the woman's identity. "It's nice to see you again."

"Mrs. McKinley?" she laughed and waved her off. "Call me Shirley. The first year you came to visit your Grandmother Pauline you called me Mrs. *McKinwee*. It was so cute. I think you were about five or six."

"Shirley!" called a woman from the kitchen door. "The meringue won't stiffen. How am I going to finish these pies if the meringue won't stiffen?"

"You make yourself at home, honey. I best go add the cream of tartar before my sister has a conniption fit." She hurried away, pushing her hair back from her face.

"Hi, Paris," a woman called. She was carrying a pan of barbecue sauce toward the cookers. "Sloan, don't forget you promised to babysit the twins on Monday," she added.

"That's Stacy," Sloan said. "Remember, she was the pain in the ass every time we wanted to go ride bikes. Mom made us take her

94

along. She had that little bike with one training wheel bent out to the side."

"Oh, yes. I remember. She said it was her landing gear." They laughed, and Paris waved at Stacy.

"Stacy's husband is over there." Sloan pointed at the group of men drinking beer and tending the row of cookers. Sloan leaned over and whispered to Paris. "He's got the cutest butt. It looks great in a pair of jeans. He's a real sweetheart. The twins have his gorgeous eyes. We McKinleys don't have gorgeous eyes. We have to marry them into the family."

"You do too have gorgeous eyes," Paris insisted, giving Sloan's green eyes a long look.

"Sloan, don't tell me. Is this our Paris—the little girl with the skinny legs?" A man said as he hurried over to them. His eyes were bright and sparkling, just like Sloan's. He had a dimple in his right cheek when he smiled.

"Paris, you remember Devon. He's the brother who always had his nose in a book."

"I did not," Devon argued. "Just sometimes." He grabbed Paris and gave her a hug, swaying back and forth. "It's so good to see you again after all these years."

"Hi, Devon. The only thing I remember about you is the big glasses you used to wear. And that one time you got in trouble for spilling your mother's fingernail polish all over the back seat of the car."

"Oh my goodness, yes. I had forgotten that. It was frosted pink. I loved that color. It was an obsession of mine." Devon fluttered his hand as if he was air-drying his nails.

Paris looked over at Sloan. She didn't want to make assumptions, but she wanted to know if her instincts were correct, the ones that told her Devon was gay.

"Yes, Paris," Sloan whispered loudly enough so Devon could hear. "Dev is the pink sheep of the family."

"And you're not?" Devon said with narrowed eyes.

"Heck no," Sloan replied, giving him a playful shove. "I'm the lavender sheep of the family." Sloan and Devon smiled at each other with sibling understanding.

"James," Devon called as a man stepped out the back door. He motioned for the handsome middle-aged man to join them. There was a proud and fond look on Devon's face as he watched the man cross the yard to them. "James, this is Paris DeMont. The one I was telling you about."

"Hi Paris," James said immediately, giving her a kiss on the cheek and a small handshake. "I'm James Fenadey. Glad to finally meet you. Sloan hasn't stopped talking about you since you got to town." Sloan gave him a shove and a leer. "Well, you haven't, sweetheart," he replied, leering back at her. He gave Devon a kiss and rubbed his back tenderly.

"James is the other half of Tweedle Dum and Tweedle Dee," Sloan said then winked at James.

"It's so nice you could join us, Paris. Your presence adds a degree of respectability to the festivities," James said.

James and Devon had been partners for nearly ten years. Shirley and Charles had welcomed him into the clan with open arms. They had come to grips with Devon's homosexuality when he was in high school. His coming out had paved the way for Sloan to admit her own lesbianism. Devon and Sloan had taken long walks as teenagers, discussing their feelings of confusion and their fears of telling their parents and friends the truth about their sexuality. It had become a secret each protected about the other.

When Devon came out to his parents, Sloan was there to offer her approval and support, just as he was there for her. If there was one thing Shirley and Charles were proud of it was their family's warm acceptance for all its members. They told James he was part of the family, for better or worse. It had become frustrating for them as Sloan bounced from woman to woman with relationships never lasting more than a few weeks. Shirley wanted to show Sloan they welcomed her partner into the family web, but there never seemed to be anyone who challenged or satisfied Sloan's needs.

"And you? What do you do, Devon?" Paris asked.

"KKAT, Ninety-five point two on your FM dial. Classic country, classic rock, classic music from the heartland," he reported as if reciting a commercial. "DJ, program director, advertising manager, janitor, you name, I've done it."

"Wow," Paris replied. "You sound busy."

"Overworked and underpaid," he added jovially.

"How about you, James? What keeps you overworked and underpaid?"

"I work for a travel agency," he said shyly. "You know, tours, charter flights, cruises."

"Now that sounds like fun."

"What is this *work for* stuff?" Sloan asked with a glower. "He owns the travel agency, Paris."

"Only half of it," James corrected. "My brother owns the other half."

"He has a twin brother with the most gorgeous, long eyelashes." Devon gave a heavy sigh and a dreamy moan.

"Devon!" James declared, perching his hands on his hips.

"Well, he does."

"We are identical twins you know."

"I know," Devon flashed a seductive look into James's eyes. "And you are handsome, too."

James's stern expression melted into a soft smile as Devon touched his arm tenderly.

"How about a pop or something, Paris?" Sloan asked as Devon and James went to help with the food table.

"Love one," Paris replied, following Sloan to the ice tubs. "Tell me again your brothers' and sister's names. I don't remember them all."

"Mitchell is oldest and the biggest. He's the one wearing shorts and cowboy boots. That always gives Dev a heart attack. Mitch's wife is Erika, and they have three kids. Then Dev, me and Stacy. Her husband is Brad. Then there's Bobby, the baby of the family. He looks like a miniature Mitchell, except for the shorts and boots. His fiance is Sara. How big is your family?" she asked.

"Two."

"Two? No, I mean the whole shooting match. Cousins, aunts, uncles," Sloan corrected.

"Two." Paris repeated, then gave an apologetic smile. "Mother and I. My father died several years ago. They were both an only-child, and so was I. I think there was a cousin somewhere in Canada, third or fourth cousin, but I'm not sure he's still living."

"You're lucky. You don't have half a dozen people questioning your every decision."

"Oh, I don't know about that. Mother has an opinion for everything I do." Paris smiled at the thought. "But she means well. And I have friends and business associates who love to stick in their two cents worth. But they all love me. I think you're the lucky one," Paris said sincerely.

"Once in awhile maybe we can trade." Sloan fished around the galvanized tub of ice and pulled out a can of pop. She wiped off the drips then offered it to Paris. "Isn't this what you drink?"

"Yes, thank you. How did you know I like Diet Coke?"

" 'Cause I saw a can of it on your kitchen counter."

Paris was impressed that Sloan had noticed that and remembered it.

"Sloan," called a pair of eight-year-old girls as they ran through the crowd. "Sloan, will you put the bridle on Barney? We want to ride him." They were barefoot and wearing matching jeans and T-shirts that read *Grandma likes me best*.

"Lucy and Lori, this is Paris," Sloan said as the girls each took one of her hands and began pulling her up from her chair.

"Hi, Paris," they quickly announced in unison then returned to the task of raising Sloan into action.

"They belong to Stacy," Sloan added.

"Hi Lucy and Lori." Paris smiled at the two and thought how much they looked like her memory of Sloan at that age.

"Okay, okay. But one at a time, girls. And no galloping. Barney's too old for that."

"Oh, boy," they squealed and ran off toward the barn.

"Want to come help?" Sloan signaled toward the barn with a nod.

Paris followed as Sloan headed through the crowd to the barn. Inside the tack room she found a leather headstall and reins hanging on a burnished peg. She also collected a small horse blanket that had been customized with a pair of canvas straps to keep it snug around Barney's fat tummy.

Sloan went to the corral and whistled him up. The pony lifted his head from the strand of hay he was enjoying and twitched his ears at her.

"Come on, you old glue pot." Sloan opened the corral gate and walked toward him, holding up the headstall. "Come on fatty. The twins want to ride. And you need the exercise." Barney stared at her for a brief moment then lowered his head and slowly walked toward her, stopping a few feet away. Sloan patted him on the neck and scratched his chin. "You be nice to these girls or no oats for you," she said as she slipped the harness into place and snapped the blanket over his broad middle.

"How old is he?" Paris asked watching Sloan lead him out of the corral into the pasture.

"We aren't sure, around eighteen. He's carried many a McKinley, that's for sure. No one pays much attention to him anymore. The kids would rather play video games or play on the computer than be outside in the fresh air. That's why I keep him at my place. He likes to have people around. He's more like a family pet. I brought him over this morning for the little kids. They like pony rides."

The twins waited on a tree stump just inside the pasture. "I'm first," Lucy said jumping up and down.

Lori watched expressionless as Lucy took the reins and swung her leg over his back. Sloan saw Lori's disappointment and patted her head.

"Come on, Lori," Sloan said taking her by the waist and placing her behind her sister. Her face instantly lit up as she wrapped her arms around Lucy's waist.

"Hang on tight," Sloan said. "No running, okay?"

"Okay, we won't," they said with matching smiles. Lucy pulled the right rein and urged Barney out into the pasture. He obeyed, plodding along deliberately.

Paris watched from outside the fence as the happy little girls steered Barney around every tree, bush, rock and cow pile along their adventure.

"Looks like fun," she said, resting her arms over the top board of the fence.

Sloan leaned back against the fence near her to watch.

"Yep. The twins are about the only ones who ever ride him anymore."

"They remind me of us way back then." Paris smiled reflectively.

"Do you remember the raft?" Sloan asked, also lapsing into memories.

"Oh, yes. When you look back on it, I guess you started building rustic things pretty young."

"You're right. Although my technique wasn't that great at age eleven."

"How many splinters did we get making that thing?"

"Zillions, as I remember," Sloan replied as the memory came into focus.

Sloan got out of the car and waved good-bye to her mother. Paris was waiting for her on the back steps and came running over.

"Dad let me have some nails and a hammer," Sloan said opening her knapsack and showing Paris her haul.

"Grandma said we can use the stack of boards behind the barn. Some of them are split, but we can tie them together or something."

"You don't tie them together, silly. You nail 'em." Sloan pulled out the old paint-splattered hammer and waved it in the air. "I can do it. I can hammer anything."

"Watch where you're swinging that thing," Paris warned, pushing her away. "Let's get the boards. We can put them on the wagon and pull them down to the pond."

They wrestled the old barn boards onto the wagon and pulled them down to the bank of the pond. After hours of planning, stacking and nailing, they finished the USS Banyon, a mighty fighting ship, strong enough to sail them off into any fantasyland. After a lunch of cheese sandwiches and apples, they had permission to launch it. With great ceremony and Grandmother's help, they pushed it down the grass into the pond. It immediately sank under the greenish pond water, leaving Sloan and Paris white-faced with disappointment. After several agonizing seconds, it majestically rose to the surface. The girls cheered wildly and waded in to grab the rope they had tied to the front.

"Now you two are to be careful, you hear me Paris Elizabeth?" Grandmother warned with a wagging finger. "You, too, Sloan. No nonsense. You sit down and hold on. If I didn't know you could swim, there'd be no raft at all."

"Yes, Grandma."

"Yes, ma'am," Sloan agreed.

"I'll be watching from the kitchen window, so if I see any foolishness, I'll be down here in a flash."

"We'll be careful."

With a worn down bristle broom and a plastic rake for oars, Paris and Sloan climbed aboard and steered away from the bank to begin their odyssey around the island.

"You watch out for pirates, you hear?" Grandmother called out as she turned and headed up to the house.

"Yeah, pirates," Sloan gasped with excitement. "We can be looking for buried treasure. Then we can be attacked by pirates with peg legs and eye patches."

"And we can rescue the stolen amulet."

"What's an amulet?"

"A necklace worth a bazillion dollars," Paris answered as if passing along secret information.

"Okay. And I will fight the pirates and whack 'em with my sword." Sloan carved her trusty rake through the air. "It might be dangerous," she warned, peering out over the sea before them. "Those pirates are really, really mean."

"If you get wounded, I'll bandage you," Paris offered courageously.

"Thanks, but I can take 'em. I've got the best sword in the whole wide world."

Paris reached down and grabbed a stick that was floating by. She broke it in two equal pieces, each about a foot long, and handed one to Sloan.

"Here's our knives. I think pirates had knives, too."

"Thanks." Sloan took hers, gave it a testing thrust into the air then stuck it in her belt loop. "We'll rescue that—that . . . What is it again?"

"Amulet," Paris offered.

"Yeah, amulet."

Paris fashioned a necklace out of the long grass and tied on a yellow dandelion flower for the priceless gem. It took two circles around the island to find the pirates and claim the amulet as their own.

Sloan stood on the raft, well out of Grandmother's view, wielding her trusty sword, jumping out of the way as the peg-legged pirate tried to run her through. Just as the last heathen leaped on board, and she was faced with certain doom, she gave a mighty lunge, and he fell overboard into the waiting crocodile's mouth.

Paris ran ashore, plucked the necklace from the branch of the big willow, where the pirates had hidden it and ran back to the USS Banyon only to find Sloan sprawled across the deck, her sword in her hand, her body lifeless from the injuries of battle.

"Are you okay," Paris asked from the shore.

Sloan raised her weary head and gave a dramatic gasp. "I think they got me." She lay back motionless.

"Where," Paris asked and climbed on board, ready to tend Sloan's wounds.

"They got me in the spleen," she muttered without moving.

"Where's your spleen?" Paris asked ready to do her duty as a high seas Florence Nightingale.

"I don't know. By my heart I think. Yeah, it's by my heart." Sloan clutched her chest and gave a faint cough.

"I'll save you. I can fix it." Paris went to work, maneuvering her *hands over Sloan's wounded spleen, waving them as if she were kneading dough, then spreading butter. "Hold still. This is the tricky part."*

Sloan obeyed. "I can take it. The pain doesn't bother me."

"Shhh. I'm operating." Paris wrinkled her brow, taking her duty seriously. "There. I saved you. I fixed your spleen. It was broken in two places."

"Yeah. They got me good. But I made 'em all walk the plank. They're crocodile food now." Sloan sat up, her recovery complete. "Did you get the amulet?"

"Yes." Paris held it up proudly. "Want to wear it?"

"Naw. You wear it. You found it."

"Okay." Paris slipped it over her head. "You want some milk and cookies?"

"Yeah. I'm starving."

They beached the raft and ran up the hill, the prized amulet still around Paris's neck.

"How's your spleen?" Paris teased, watching the twins return to the stump and trade places.

Sloan laughed and grabbed her chest dramatically. "Still broken, I'm afraid. Right here under my heart."

"Darn ol' pirates," Paris teased.

"Guess you'll have to fix it again," Sloan said softly and winked at her.

Sloan's remark caught Paris off-guard, penetrating her right down to the protective layer she had locked around her emotions. Paris gave a shy smile. Suddenly the air had stopped moving and a dry heat floated over Paris. A deep shiver started in her toes and moved up her body, not stopping until it had parted her lips and flushed her face. They stood across the fence from one another, a breeze stirring their hair, silence heavy between them. Sloan's eyes had completely captured Paris, and she was powerless to look away.

"Sloan," Shirley called from the kitchen door. "You and Paris come on up. We're ready to eat."

"Okay. We're coming, Mom," Sloan called back, releasing Paris from the stare.

The twins dismounted and ran ahead. Sloan tended to Barney then took Paris by the hand and led her through the maze of tables and lawn chairs to the grassy area by the back door. Shirley was wiping her hands on her apron as the crowd gathered in anticipation. When everyone was present and their attention was fixed on Shirley, she laughed with embarrassment and loudly cleared her throat.

"What's the official count, Mitchell?" she asked loudly.

"One hundred and eight, not counting Uncle Al's dog," he yelled, bringing on a cheer from the family. "And a big welcome back to Paris," he added proudly. The crowd cheered even louder and waved in her direction.

"Then I guess we're all here," Shirley said, looking over her extended family with a proud grin. "Charlie said the barbecue is ready so here we go." There was a noticeable hush over the gathering.

She took a deep breath, cupped her hands to her mouth and began an ear-splitting squeal.

"Soooooooeeey!" she screamed with all her might. "Sooey sooey sooey. Come and get it," she yelled, her eyes closed tight as she bellowed across the yard.

The crowd erupted with applause, hooting and snorting as she finished. Paris laughed and applauded. Sloan whistled and cheered. Shirley blushed again at the applause and waved off the attention.

"Grab you a plate now before it gets cold," she continued, shooing people toward the food line.

Sloan pulled Paris along as the crowd meandered toward the long table made from two four-by-eight sheets of plywood covered with checkered tablecloths.

"Hope you came hungry," she advised, handing Paris a paper plate and taking one for herself.

"Yes, I'm famished." She looked down the long table of food with a stunned expression. "There's enough food to feed the entire state."

"Almost. Mom will be nagging if you don't go back for seconds and thirds. And be sure and save room for hand-cranked ice cream and Aunt Bess's apple cobbler." She licked her lips dramatically. "It's good stuff."

They moved down the line making selections and speculating about various casseroles, salads, vegetables, corn on the cob, fresh sliced tomatoes, homemade apple sauce, deviled eggs, bread and butter pickles, seasoned baked beans, skillets of fried potatoes and onions, homemade rolls and finally three kinds of pork—plain smoked, mild barbecued and oh-my-God-this-is-spicy.

"See the three big pans of pork. The white pan is just smoked pork without any sauce. The silver pan has mild barbecue sauce and is really good."

"And the red pan?" Paris asked tentatively.

Sloan smiled wickedly.

"It'll melt the fillings in your teeth."

"Wow. That hot?"

"Yes ma'am."

Paris eyed the three pans trying to decide.

"The best way to do it," Sloan inserted, taking a serving spoon full of the smoked meat. "Is to take a little of the mild and mix it with the plain smoked stuff. You get the barbecue taste without hiding the smoke flavor." She took some of the mild-sauced pork and plopped it on top of the plain.

"That looks so good and it smells terrific." Paris took a deep pleasing whiff. "There's a bistro in Manhattan that specializes in barbecue. A little scoop of it served with cole slaw and a hush puppy is eighteen dollars."

"Bet it isn't as good as Dad's."

"I'm sure it isn't either. There's no buffet like this in New York."

"This isn't a buffet," Sloan said with an elegant wave of her hand. "It's a trough," she added, then laughed.

"I refuse to call this scrumptious looking feast a trough or a hog slop," Paris replied, fixing Sloan with a serious look.

"Hey, Paris. If you don't call it by its rightful name you'll have to wash all the dishes by hand," Mitchell called from across the table. He was heaping scoops of the filling-melting barbecue onto his plate.

"That's right, Paris," Stacy added, as she helped the twins fill their plates.

"I'll help you do the dishes, Paris," Lucy said with helpful enthusiasm.

"Me, too," Lori chimed in, equally excited to offer her assistance.

"Then I guess I'll be doing the dishes," she said resolutely. "You girls count all the serving bowls so I'll know how many I have to do." She smiled over at their eager little faces.

"Okay," they agreed.

"Nope," Mitchell corrected. "They can't help. You have to do it all by yourself. Every platter, dish and pan. Everything." He stuck his finger in the barbecue sauce then licked it.

Paris looked around at all the attention she had attracted.

"In that case, Shirley," she called. "Great hog slop."

Everyone laughed and cheered wildly at her revelation.

"But I do want to help with the dishes," she quickly added.

"Fine with us," Mitchell said with a big grin.

"No, she isn't," Sloan declared in his direction. "You know the rules, Mitch."

"What rules?" Paris asked.

"The guys have to do the dishes. The women prepare the food and the men have to clean up afterward. Mom has a fruit jar in the kitchen and it costs them ten bucks every time they break something." Sloan leaned over and whispered in Paris's ear. "It cost Mitch forty bucks last year."

Sloan led the way to a picnic table and waited for Paris to climb in before swinging her leg over the bench and settling in. For over an hour they ate, joked, visited and returned for seconds. Mitchell teased Sloan and Paris about the summer they got poison ivy from using the wrong leaves for toilet paper on a trek through the woods. Stacy remembered admiring Paris's long blond braids.

"How come I never got to play on that island with you two?" Stacy asked.

"Cause you were a brat, that's why," Sloan replied, then flipped an olive at her.

"Hell, she's still a brat," Mitchell yelled from the next table.

Finally a satisfied lull fell over the crowd as the eating wound down. Plates were stacked into trash barrels, dishes collected, leftovers packaged and a general policing of the area was started.

"You make yourself at home, Paris," Shirley advised as she carried a stack of dishes to the house.

Paris picked up two salad bowls and began to follow her toward the kitchen door.

"Oh no, Honey." Shirley frowned at her and blocked her entrance. "You are not doing that. Charlie, take these bowls from Paris."

"Give me those," he chided. "You get out of here. Go visit with Sloan. Get a ride on one of the horses. Play horseshoes."

"You're our guest, honey." Shirley smiled warmly. "Next time you can help. But this time, you go have fun. Get acquainted." Shirley motioned for Paris to mingle.

"Thank you, Shirley. The food was delicious." Paris rubbed Shirley's arm. "I appreciate your inviting me."

Shirley leaned over and kissed Paris on the cheek.

"Anytime, Paris. Anytime at all. You are always welcome here. Now go on. But not too far. There'll be desserts later." Shirley hurried inside with her load.

Paris tried to hold back the lump that was rising in her throat. Sloan's family had taken her in, lock, stock and barrel. It was as if the thirty years since she had last seen them had just melted away.

CHAPTER 12

Paris looked out over the yard. Mitchell was playing with his kids. Devon and James were cleaning tables. Stacy and her husband were exchanging kisses. Children were swinging on the corral gate. Sloan was helping move tables. Those who weren't working were visiting and laughing. Everyone had a place in the family scheme. No one was left out. No one was sitting alone. The twins skipped over to share their bubble wands with Paris. Sara waved at Paris from across the yard. Charlie pointed out the horseshoe pit. Paris had been taken in by the McKinleys. She was surrounded by this family and made to feel welcome.

Paris felt tears welling up in her eyes. The warmth of Sloan's family was stirring memories deep within the recesses of her mind. She walked across the yard and through the gate into the pasture. She meandered down the hill toward a row of trees and the sounds of a babbling stream. She slipped through the trees and sat on a large rock along the bank.

As much as she tried to block them out, memories of large gatherings with Gabby's family came flooding over her. She missed the warm acceptance and the hectic commotion. She missed the big meals and the kind words. She missed Gabby. The McKinleys had re-created those special family times with such exact precision it was impossible for Paris not to relive them. The faint sounds of laughter rolled down the pasture. The well of emotions was too much for her. Paris hid her face in her hands, tears spilling out between her fingers as the memories consumed her.

Sloan finished with the tables and rolled a full trash barrel behind the house. She scanned the crowd for Paris. She checked in the house, then the barn.

"Have you seen Paris, Dad?" she asked as he dampened down the cookers.

"She was over by the corral gate a little while ago."

"Are you looking for Paris?" Lucy asked, dipping her bubble wand in the bottle then waving it through the air.

"Yeah. Have you seen her?"

"She went that way," Lori said pointing her wand toward the pasture. "I shared my bubbles with her. She blew some really big ones."

"I shared mine, too," Lucy added quickly. "She said she used to blow bubbles when she was our age."

Sloan smiled warmly at them and brushed the hair out of Lori's eyes. "That's great, girls."

"She looked like she was going to cry," Lucy added sadly.

Sloan wrinkled her forehead and scoured the pasture for any signs of her.

"Which way did she go?" she asked cupping her hands to her eyes for a better view.

"I don't know. Down there somewhere." The twins skipped off, leaving a cloud of bubbles in their wake.

Sloan stepped inside the corral, untied one of the bareback horses and led it into the pasture. She held the reins in one hand and grabbed the base of the mane with the other, then threw her leg over and pulled herself up with a groan. She headed across the pasture at an easy lope. Sloan had a good idea where Paris might be. Charlie had thinned the trees in a section along the stream where there was an outcropping of rocks. It was a quiet spot—a spot Sloan had used to find solitude and peace. It was the perfect place for Paris to sit and contemplate whatever was bothering her.

Sloan stopped at the edge of the trees and slid off the mare. She tied the reins to a branch as she searched through the woods for any sign of Paris. The muffled sound of a sniffle came from the direction of the big rock. Sloan quietly made her way through the oak trees toward the sound. Paris was wiping her eyes and collecting her emotions. Sloan watched from behind a tree, unsure what could be wrong. She finally cleared her throat as a warning she was nearing.

"Hi," Paris said with a startled look.

"Hi, yourself." Sloan moved closer. "You've found my favorite spot on this whole place. I used to come down here when I needed to get away from too much family." She offered a small smile as if to say it was all right if that's what happened.

"Your family is wonderful. Really. They are so nice to me."

"Sometimes they're okay." Sloan eased herself onto a rock next to Paris. "Sometimes they get a little carried way and say or do hurtful things." Sloan continued giving Paris a chance to admit whatever had caused her tears. She wanted to give Paris a hug. She wanted to wrap her arms around her and protect her. The thought of someone in her family saying something to upset Paris gave Sloan a gnawing pain in her stomach.

Paris looked out over the stream and watched the water bubble along its path.

"You have a nice family, Sloan."

Sloan watched Paris's face as she studied the stream.

"You fit right in, Paris. They have taken to you wholeheartedly."

Paris nodded in agreement but kept her eyes on the gently rambling water.

Sloan leaned forward and touched Paris's arm.

"What's wrong? What's upset you?"

Paris drew in a deep breath and straightened her posture.

"Nothing. Nothing is wrong." She looked over at Sloan with a determined smile, but the tracks of her tears gave away her mood.

Sloan moved closer and wrapped an arm around her waist. "Come on. Tell me what's got you sitting on a rock by a creek all by yourself when there's homemade apple pie up the hill." Sloan rubbed her back tenderly. "If someone said something to hurt your feelings I'll go punch their lights out, unless it's one of the kids. In that case, I'll stand them in the corner for a week." Sloan smiled, trying to lighten Paris's depression.

"Actually, it *was* something someone said," Paris started.

"Who?" Sloan asked with an angry frown.

"Everyone." Paris looked straight at Sloan.

Sloan stared back with a confused expression.

"Everyone said such kind things to me," Paris continued. "They were all so nice. Maybe it would have been easier if someone had been mean."

"Okay, now I'm lost," Sloan muttered. "You are crying because everyone was kind."

"It just brings back some memories that are close to my heart."

"Of your family?"

"Sort of." She pulled her feet up on the rock and wrapped her arms around her knees. "It was Gabby's family."

"Gabby?"

"Gabriella Maria Buttichi," Paris said proudly. "Gabby for short."

"She's the one who died?"

"Yes."

"Tell me about her family. Tell me all about Gabby's family." Sloan leaned back on her hands, ready to hear Paris's story.

"Are you sure you want to hear this? Do they need us up there?" Paris motioned up the hill.

"Nope. They don't need us. Tell me about your memories of Gabby's family," Sloan urged softly.

"Okay, but tell me if you get bored," Paris said, then looked over at Sloan. "Promise?"

111

"I promise."

"Let's see. Gabby's family. Where do I start. Gabby was Italian. All of her family was Italian. They still live in Yonkers, off Yonkers Avenue in a two-story frame house. It's the house where Gabby grew up with her parents and her two brothers. Her grandparents lived next door for years then moved in with Rose and Dominic after all the kids moved out. Rose and Dominic Buttichi were good, hard-working people. They still are. Grandpa Joe died about ten years ago. Grandma Maria passed away just last year. They were Rose's parents. Joe was a barber in Yonkers for nearly fifty years. Maria came over from Italy with her older brother when she was about fourteen years old. I say about fourteen because she didn't really know exactly how old she was. But something like fourteen in nineteen thirty-eight. Her older brother, Aldo, was about sixteen. They came across on a ship that landed at Ellis Island. The immigration official couldn't pronounce their last name so it was changed to Molinari.

"As Maria's parents could afford it, they planned to send the six children, two grandparents and themselves over to America. They had some friends in Yonkers who had immigrated a few years before so they were to live with them for a year or two. But right after Maria and Aldo arrived, the war broke out. They couldn't send anyone else over, and it wasn't safe for Maria and Aldo to return to Italy. So they were stuck in Yonkers living with this other Italian family. They couldn't speak English so school was impossible. Aldo worked on a garbage truck. Maria worked in a uniform factory. Her job was to collect the usable scraps and pack them in barrels. She was paid two dollars a week, which went to the family she lived with for her room and board. When Maria was sixteen she met Joseph Grecco at a church Christmas program. By Easter they were married and living in a two-room apartment over the barber shop where he was an apprentice."

"She was awfully young," Sloan inserted.

"She told me once that Joe was an older man so she thought it would be all right to marry him."

"How old was he?"

"Eighteen." Paris smiled at the thought. "Maria was a little woman, barely five feet tall. Joe wasn't much bigger. They had two children, Joseph Jr. and Rose, Gabby's mother. Rose was born on V-E day. Joe wanted to call her Victoria, but Maria wanted to name her after her mother. Rose is a very strong woman. I don't mean muscular strong, but strong willed and strong natured. She worked sixteen to eighteen hours a day to take care of her home, family and friends. If someone is sick Rose will make chicken soup. If there is a new family in the neighborhood she'll cook some pasta for them as a welcome. If someone at the church is in need Rose will donate clothes or a lamp or whatever she can spare. When Gabby was working her way through college and living in an apartment in Queens, her mother was always cooking extra and sending her home with enough food to feed an army." There was a sparkle in Paris's eyes as she retold it. "She used to make cannoli and send one home with Gabby in a little box just for me. It had extra chocolate on it." She turned to Sloan. "Have you ever eaten cannoli?"

Sloan shook her head.

"It is wonderful." Paris licked her lips. "Pastry shell with ricotta cheese mixed with powdered sugar and pistachios, then topped with more pistachios, chocolate shavings and powdered sugar. Yum!" Paris laughed devilishly. "No calories there."

"Then you need to eat some cannoli. You're too thin," Sloan advised.

"That's what Rose said." Paris lowered her eyes for an instant. "Gabby said that, too. She said I'd never be a good little Italian unless I got some meat on my bones."

"So Gabby was a good little Italian?"

"If you mean was she fat, no. She wasn't. She had a great body. Long legs, toned muscles, like an athlete in training."

"What did Gabby do for a living?" Sloan asked. "Was she into sports?"

"She was a paramedic. She said that kept her in shape. Carrying

113

those heavy medic bags and stretchers. She and her partner had to carry a two-hundred-and-fifty-pound man down a two-story spiral staircase once. The stretcher didn't fit. Neither did the backboard. So they had to carry him down trying to keep him semistraight."

"Rose and Dominic must have been very proud of her," Sloan offered.

Paris smiled broadly. "Oh, my God, yes. You would have thought Gabby had won an Olympic gold medal when she got her license. Rose introduced her as my daughter, the paramedic. Dominic had a picture of her in her uniform hanging over the cash register in his butcher shop."

"Is it still there?"

"Yes. It has a smudge mark on it where he touches it every morning when he opens the shop."

"What happened to Gabby?" Sloan asked carefully.

Paris straightened her legs and stretched. "I thought I was going to tell you about her family?"

"I'm still listening." Sloan realized the subject of Gabby was going to be limited to her family and the fun times. The subject of her death was off-limits. "I bet they didn't have barbecues like ours," Sloan boasted teasingly.

"You haven't eaten until you've been to an Italian family meal. It was usually a Sunday afternoon about four o'clock or so. Grandma Maria would meet us at the door. She would be wearing a flowered dress, green apron and orthopedic shoes that tie. Sometimes she wore white anklets with them. Sometimes it was knee high stockings. She had curly gray hair that she kept short. Gabby called her an Italian Brillo pad." Paris laughed at the thought.

"Like my Grandma McKinley," Sloan added.

"Like everyone's grandma, I think. She'd give us a hug and a kiss on each cheek. Then she'd pinch our cheeks and call us her *bella bambina*. She and Rose would have started the tomato sauce for the pasta early in the morning before they went to Mass. It would simmer all day filling the house with the most agonizingly

114

delicious aroma. Grandpa Joe would crack an egg onto the surface of the sauce and put the lid on. He'd come back five minutes later and lift out a perfectly poached egg. All through the day Maria, Rose and Joe would test the sauce with crusts of Italian bread. Maria and Rose would argue over how much garlic or oregano it needed. Grandma Maria would pinch the air with her fingers." Paris demonstrated. "And she would say 'you no have enougha garlic ina the gravy, Rose. What's amatter with you. I told you and told you. You gotta have enougha garlic or it won'ta tasta good'." Paris threw her head back and laughed. "Garlic was Grandma Maria's answer to everything from colds to bunions."

"Garlic in the gravy?" Sloan made a face.

"Gravy is what they called the pasta sauce. And they called the pasta macaroni. Gabby's dad's job was to taste the macaroni and see if it was done. That was Rose's way of getting him into the kitchen to lift the big pot over to the sink."

"How many people would be at those shindigs?"

"Maybe twenty, twenty-five. The dining room table was opened all the way out with a card table added to each end. There were no tablecloths when we were eating pasta because the sauce would stain it. There were always several baskets of Italian bread on the table. The smell of the bread is an aroma from heaven." Paris closed her eyes and took a deep breath as if a loaf had just been pulled from the oven.

"So you had spaghetti sauce with bread," Sloan said.

"That was just the beginning. We'd have roasted chicken with browned potatoes, a huge salad, green beans with olive oil and garlic cloves. Then came the desserts." She grinned broadly.

"Desserts?"

"Cannoli, sfogliatelle, tiramisu, peaches marinated in wine, spumoni ice cream, pizzelle, biscotti."

"All that?" Sloan's eyes widened.

"No, not all of it, but there was usually two or three. Enough to make the decision of which one to have sheer agony."

"Sounds incredible."

"And everyone talked at once. There were forks and spoons waving in the air all around the table. Gabby told me her family was like any good Italian family. They couldn't talk without using their hands. One time Dominic was holding his wine glass and talking with Grandpa Joe about a football game. He got so excited that when he gestured he broadcast the whole glass of wine across the table."

The retelling of Gabby's family gatherings seemed to be cleansing for Paris, leaving her relaxed and contented.

"Did that story bore you?" she asked.

"No." Sloan replied and touched Paris's arm. "I'm glad you shared it with me. Thank you. It must have been very hard for you."

Paris's eyes told Sloan how devastating Gabby's loss had been. Sloan wanted to ask more, but she felt the time wasn't right. Paris would surely tell her about Gabby, their life together and her sudden death, but Sloan knew it wouldn't happen until Paris was ready.

Paris combed her fingertips through the stray wisps of hair around her face that had escaped her braids.

"I give up," she muttered disgustedly. "I'm not going to mess with these. I'm just going to take them out." She began to unwind one of her braids, but Sloan reached up and stopped her.

"Let me do it," Sloan said softly. "Please."

"Okay, if you want to. But I warn you, they are a mess to undo."

Sloan started slowly, working her fingers through each golden silky section, pulling them down in ever-lengthening strands. First one then the other was unwoven and allowed to fall in shimmering cascades of spun gold. Sloan laced her fingers through the long flowing ribbons of hair. The satiny smooth texture was like honey flowing through her fingers.

Paris knew it was self-indulgent, but the sensuous feel of Sloan's fingers through her hair was more than she cared to stop.

"Your hair is just as soft as it was when we were kids," Sloan said, her fingers combing through the braid marks.

"I've always loved that you taught me to braid," Paris said.

"I taught you to braid the willow branches. Your grandmother's the one who braided your hair."

"Remember when I talked you into letting Grandmother braid your hair?"

Sloan threw her head back and laughed.

"God, yes. It was terrible. I wouldn't sit still, and by the time she was finished I looked like a cavewoman."

"When she tried to take them out you had a fit," Paris teased. "It hurts, it hurts," she squealed in a childish voice, trying to re-create Sloan's misery.

"Well, it did. Those things were torture. When the Romans ran out of lions to throw the Christians to they just braided and unbraided their hair," Sloan scoffed.

"Oh, stop it. It wasn't that bad, you big baby," Paris admonished and gave Sloan's arm a rub.

"Hey, I don't wear my hair short for nothing. No one's going to braid me."

They both laughed. Paris tossed her hair unconsciously and sent a tingle racing through Sloan's body.

"Come on. I'll give you a ride back." Sloan scrambled off the rock as if she desperately needed something to do or she would have her hands in Paris's hair again. She offered Paris a hand up and led the way through the trees to where she had left the mare.

"Where's the saddle?" Paris asked cautiously.

"Saddles are for city slickers," she replied with a drawl.

"One city slicker, right here," Paris announced, raising her hand. "I haven't ridden a horse in over twenty years, unless you count riding in a carriage around Central Park."

"You'll be fine," Sloan said reassuringly. "I won't let you fall off."

Sloan held the reins in one hand and threw her leg over the mare's broad back.

"Give me your left hand," she ordered.

Paris took Sloan's hand and looked up at where she was to ride.

"Now what? Can you lower a ladder or something?"

"Come on now. Throw your leg over, and I'll pull you up. Grab onto my waistband with your other hand."

Paris made an attempt at getting her leg over but only succeeded in kicking the horse in the rear. The mare gave a disgruntled snort and crow hopped.

"Easy girl," Sloan said in a soothing voice as she pulled at the reins.

Paris jumped out of the way.

"I better walk back. You go ahead," she urged.

"No way. Come over here," Sloan insisted as she steered the horse beside an old stump. "Stand up there and give me your hand again."

Paris did as she was told.

"Now throw your leg over," Sloan offered, holding the reins tightly.

Paris swung her leg up behind Sloan and scrambled into place.

"Hold on."

"Okay. I'm ready," Paris advised, grabbing a belt loop on each side of Sloan's jeans.

"If you just hold onto my belt loops you're going to end up on the ground with denim loops on your fingers. Hold on tight around my waist."

Paris wrapped her arms around Sloan's waist and pulled herself tightly against her back.

Sloan guided the mare away from the trees and headed across the pasture at a slow walk.

"You okay?" Sloan asked, feeling Paris fidgeting behind her.

"Yes. I'm just not used to such a wide seat," Paris replied as she adjusted her legs.

"Bend your knees and press them up behind mine. It will be more comfortable if you have your legs forward instead of just spread straight out."

Paris spooned her legs up to Sloan's, their legs nested together around the mare's stomach.

"How's that?" Sloan asked.

"Much better."

Sloan urged the horse up into a soft trot. She could hear Paris's giggle of excitement as they moved across the field.

"Still okay?" Sloan asked.

"Yes," Paris replied happily. "It's wonderful."

"More?"

"Sure."

Sloan pressed her feet into the horse's flanks and urged the reins forward against her neck. The mare immediately responded with an effortless gallop. Paris's long hair flagged out behind her in a golden plume as they raced toward the corral. She pulled herself tighter against Sloan, her body molded to her back.

Sloan could feel Paris's breasts against her back and the inside of her thighs rubbing her bottom. She wanted to turn the big mare around and ride back across the pasture just to keep Paris's body close to hers, but she eased back on the reins and slowed to a walk as they entered the corral.

"That was fun," Paris said, nearly breathless from the ride.

Sloan looked back and saw a broad grin across her face.

"You look just like you did that first time you rode Snitch with me. You were grinning from ear to ear back then," Sloan said, smiling at her.

"I remember Snitch. He was your birthday present. You taught me how to ride a horse that summer."

"I couldn't wait to show you my horse."

Paris and Sloan exchanged a reflective smile as they each relived the summer Paris learned to ride. Sloan helped Paris down then dismounted.

"No more tears," Sloan said as she brushed Paris's hair back over her shoulders. "You are with family, and we all love you."

"Thank you for the ride and for listening."

"Anytime," Sloan replied softly. "Anytime at all." She stroked Paris's face tenderly then took her hand as they rejoined the crowd.

CHAPTER 13

Sloan thrashed under the covers until six-thirty then sprang out of bed and into a hot shower. Afterward she pulled on a pair of jeans and a sweatshirt. The screen door slammed as she took the two steps in one long stride and headed for her work truck. It was a 1951 Chevy stepside with oxidized blue paint. She had built a rack for the bed of the truck to carry bundled twigs, logs and the completed rustic furniture. It was unattractive but useful. She had a nearly new Toyota Camry in the garage with barely five thousand miles on it. It was air conditioned, comfortable and show-room fresh—all the things the truck was not. But she preferred to drive her trusty old pickup. When it rumbled across cattle guards and mud ruts, the frame and rack shook and clattered noisily. Occasionally the passenger door would fly open without warning, a result of a repair job gone awry. The knob on the floor shifter was made from a piece of burnished mahogany. A miniature twig chair dangled from the rearview mirror on a piece of leather lacing.

Sloan roared around the curves and into her parent's side yard just as her father was pulling out on his way to town. He stuck his head out of the window of his truck and waved.

"Hey, daughter. Better get in there. Your mother's making waffles for Dev."

"I didn't know Devon was coming over."

"He needed some paint for his new apartment."

"Is he moving again?" Sloan teased.

Charlie shrugged and gave a good-bye wave.

Sloan pulled her truck next to Devon's VW Jetta. As she stepped onto the back porch her mother opened the door and waved her in.

"Hello, honey. Do you want strawberries or blueberries on your waffle?" Shirley asked as she pointed to the place already set at the kitchen table. "I saw you pull in the yard."

"Hi, Mom," she said, giving her mother a kiss on the cheek. "Strawberries, please."

"Hey, Dev," she said, ruffling her brother's hair as he carefully ate a small bite. He quickly smoothed his hair back into place and waved her off.

"Hey, Sis," he said, after swallowing the bite.

"Are you moving again?" she asked as she hitched her chair in and poured a glass of juice.

"It's in the same building but a three-bedroom unit with a fireplace," he answered, gloating over this news.

"Three bedrooms? What do you need three bedrooms for? Are you p.g.?" she joked, knowing her mother would reply.

"Sloan!" Shirley shot at her critically.

"No, I am not," he said with a coquettish wiggle. "James is." They both laughed as Shirley smirked at them and shook her head.

"How is good old Jim Bob?" Sloan asked.

"He's fine. I was planning a big party for his fortieth birthday next month, but he surprised me with cruise tickets." Devon took another polite bite.

"Where you off to this time?" Sloan dipped her finger in his strawberry glaze.

"We fly to Miami then board ship and cruise through the Panama Canal then up the West Coast to San Francisco." He made a dreamy expression. "Nine days of sun and tropical breezes and James in a swimsuit."

"Please don't tell me you two wear Speedos. It's a concept I do *not* want to consider."

Devon gave a husky laugh and raised his eyebrows wickedly.

"Gag me," Sloan replied.

"So how is your love life, sis? Any sweet young things on your horizon?"

"How is Paris?" Shirley asked, releasing the fresh waffle from the waffle iron. "She's such a pretty thing. So perky and polite."

Sloan and Devon smiled at each other.

"She doesn't understand what that word perky means," Devon whispered to Sloan. "But she's right. Perky, perky, perky." He pursed his lips then winked at her.

"She's fine, I guess," Sloan replied.

"You guess?" he snipped. He looked at Sloan with a curious stare. "You guess?" he repeated with more curiosity.

"What?" Sloan asked. She heaped a ladle of strawberries on her waffle then began applying an artistic ribbon of maple syrup.

The ringing telephone saved Sloan from a reply.

"Hello," Shirley said in her usual cheery nature. She smirked at the voice on the other end of the line. "Just a minute. Let me look." She let the receiver dangle by the cord as she hurried down the hall and into the bedroom. Within a minute she was back holding a well-worn man's wallet.

"Yes. It's here," she said then grimaced at Sloan and Devon with a look of resignation. "I'll be there in thirty minutes, Charlie. Charles. All right, twenty minutes. Good-bye." She hung up and heaved a disgusted sigh. "Your father forgot his wallet." She unplugged the waffle iron and washed her hands. "You two eat your breakfast. I'll be right back."

"I'll take it, Mom," Devon offered.

"No. I'll do it. I need a couple of things at Safeway anyway. You two set your dishes in the sink, and I'll take care of them later." She took the shopping list from the pad and dropped it in her purse. She kissed Devon and Sloan on the cheek then went out to the car.

"Is Dad getting forgetful?" Sloan asked.

"He had his wallet when he was ready to leave. I saw him put it in his pocket. But Mom convinced him to change his pants. He was going to wear those terrible elastic waist green golf pants." Devon wrinkled his nose at the thought. He stuck his finger in his mouth mimicking a gag.

"As I remember, you gave him those pants for Christmas."

"Yeah. But that was ten years ago. Give me a break. I thought green was a color of importance back then." Devon got up and poured them each more coffee. He rinsed his dishes and filled the dishwasher.

Sloan finished her waffle then rinsed the plate and stacked it in the dishwasher. She sat with her coffee cup, swirling it slowly. Devon sat down across from her and stared at her intently.

"What is it?" he asked.

Sloan was deep in thought but finally realized he was looking at her.

"Huh?" she mumbled.

"Sloan, what is wrong?" Devon asked again with compassionate eyes. "And don't you dare say nothing," he continued. "It's got something to do with Paris, doesn't it?" Devon looked at Sloan with an intuition only a brother could have.

"Why do you say that?"

"Oh, sweetie," he began, resting his hand on her forearm. "I saw you look at her at the barbecue. And so did everyone else. I don't think I've ever seen you look at anyone like that before. It took my breath away. It was a look of love."

Sloan didn't know what to say. He was right even though those inner feelings had been well hidden, or so she thought.

"And honey," he continued. "She had the same look."

Sloan studied his face for verification.

"I don't know about that." Sloan took her coffee cup to the dishwasher.

"What's going on?"

Sloan leaned against the sink as if she couldn't decide if she should tell him.

"Come on. Let's have it." He went to stand next to her. "Let me guess, she has someone else?" he offered cautiously.

Sloan crossed her arms and nodded.

"Can't you fight for her? How great can this other woman be? It is a woman, isn't it?"

"Yes, it's a woman. But I'm afraid this is someone I can't fight."

"No one's perfect Sloan," Devon warned. "Not even you."

"In Paris's heart she is. When you hear Paris talk about her, Gabriella was as close to perfect as anyone wants."

"Oh, come on," Devon groaned. "No one is that great. Even gay people have a few faults." He winked at her.

Sloan shook her head. "Not Gabriella Buttichi. She will forever be the perfect partner, the wonder woman in Paris's life." Sloan turned and fixed Devon with a serious stare. "They were together eight years. She died."

"Sweet Jesus," he gasped and clutched at his throat. "That's terrible. Poor Paris."

"How do I fight a perfect memory?"

Devon looked at Sloan with deep concern. "How long has she been gone?"

"I'm not sure, but several years I think. She doesn't talk about it much."

"It sounds like she has carried that grief long enough. She needs to get past it."

Sloan nodded in agreement.

"Sometimes she is open and emotionally available. Then she suddenly changes and shuts me out. It's like the difference between night and day. She becomes a completely different person. I have known her for over thirty years, but sometimes it's like I don't know her at all."

"Sloan, you and Paris knew each other thirty years ago. That isn't the same as knowing someone for thirty years. People change. She may not be the same person you remember from way back then."

124

"I know, Dev. Sure she's changed. And so have I, but . . ." Sloan stared at Devon. "She's even better than I remember."

Devon studied Sloan's eyes then allowed a slow smile to draw across his face.

"Sweetie," he said, rubbing her back and smiling proudly. "You show Paris how wonderful you are. Show her your romantic side. No one can stack up to my little sister. I have all the faith in the world in you. How could Paris possibly pass up such a sweet person as you?"

"I wish that were true," she muttered, staring at the floor.

"Sloan, is she the one?" he asked softly after studying her face. "Is Paris the one you have been waiting for?"

"Yes," she replied softly, then let a small smile pull across her face.

He gave her a hug.

"I wish I could stay and talk to you about it, honey," Devon said, checking his watch. "But I have to be back by noon. I'm on the air one to five today."

"I thought you worked in the evening."

"A DJ's work is never done." He gave a dramatic sigh. "I'm filling in for Davy. His wife had a baby last night."

"He's the one that plays that rap crap, isn't he?"

"God, yes. And I have to also. His listeners would have a cow if I played anything with a melody." Devon rolled his eyes. "Take care, Sis. Come up and have lunch with me. I'll take you to Hemmingway's at the Bass Pro Shop. They have boiled shrimp on the lunch buffet. Bring Paris along. The four of us can make a double date out of it."

"We aren't dating, Dev." Sloan frowned.

He reached for the doorknob then looked back at her.

"But I have a feeling you will be," he stated with a shrewd look.

Sloan threw the kitchen towel at the door as he closed it.

CHAPTER 14

Paris had spent Sunday working around the house and was enjoying the bright summer day when she rushed into the kitchen and grabbed her cell phone on the third ring.

"Hello, Sloan," she said cheerfully, recognizing the number.

"Are you busy?" Sloan asked breathlessly, the unmistakable sound of her truck engine starting rumbled in the background.

"I was just about to change into my work clothes and put a second coat of paint on the bathroom cabinet."

"Paint tomorrow. Wash your hands and comb your hair. I'll be there in three minutes. Hurry up." Sloan sounded frantic.

"Why? Where are we going?" Paris asked.

"This is important. See you in a few."

Sloan's call ended abruptly, leaving Paris staring at her phone. Paris was used to hasty telephone calls. Cardiologists learned to receive alarming phone calls and immediately assess the problem. But Sloan hadn't told her what the problem was. Her brain began scanning a danger list for possibilities. The more she thought about it, the more concerned she became. Someone could be sick, maybe a heart attack. Perhaps one of her parents. Or a car accident. That could be it. The gruesome possibilities seemed to quicken her preparation. She hurried out onto the front porch just as Sloan roared into the drive, a plume of dust following her truck up to the edge of the sidewalk.

"You ready?" Sloan called, leaning out the window. She hadn't turned off the engine.

"Yes," Paris replied, climbing in. "Let's go."

Sloan spun a U-turn in the drive and headed for town. Paris noticed her anxious eyes and tiny beads of sweat on her upper lip.

"What is it, Sloan? What happened? Is it an accident?" Paris braced herself for the worse.

"What accident? There's no accident." Sloan furrowed her brow at Paris.

"What's wrong then? Is someone sick?"

"Not that I know of. Are you sick?"

"I'm fine. But why the rush? What's so important it couldn't wait?"

"We have to be one of the first hundred people to buy a ticket to get the CD." Sloan slowed at the intersection, looked both ways, and then darted across.

"A CD?" Paris turned in her seat and stared squarely at Sloan.

"Yeah. They're showing that new movie *Charming Web* at the Mall Cinema Six. I just heard on the radio the first one hundred people to buy a ticket for the five o'clock show get a free soundtrack CD. It has some great music on it. k.d. lang, Melissa Etheridge, Jeannie Shaw." She whizzed around the curves and rattled over the metal bridge, her eyes riveted on the road. "What time is it?"

"You rousted me out of my house for a CD?"

"A two-CD box set," Sloan justified.

"Sloan McKinley!"

"Don't you want a free CD?"

"You scared me shitless. I thought something was wrong. Hurry. Get ready. It's important," Paris scoffed, imitating Sloan's phone call.

"It is important. We have to be one of the first hundred in line."

Paris was relieved no one was sick or injured. After the initial shock wore off, she wasn't all that annoyed at Sloan's surprise odyssey. The outing became unexpectedly exciting.

"Damn, we aren't going to make it," Sloan muttered as she entered town. "Look at all this traffic."

"Cut down Elm to Stouffer then take Fourteenth," Paris offered, suddenly consumed with purpose.

"Good idea."

Sloan pulled up to the ticket window and dropped off Paris to get in line while she went to park. By the time Sloan found a parking spot and joined Paris, they were next in line to buy tickets.

"Two please for *Charming Web*," Paris said.

The girl behind the window took the money and slid two tickets and two CD boxes under the glass.

"Great! We made it. We are one of the first one hundred." Sloan beamed broadly.

"Actually you are number seven and eight," the girl related. She pointed to the nearly full case of CDs on the floor next to her. "I heard the movie isn't very good."

"Here you go, Richard Petty," Paris teased, handing Sloan her ticket and her CD.

"At least we got them," she muttered, following Paris inside the lobby.

"Theater four at the end of the hall," announced the young man taking ticket stubs.

"That's the little one," Sloan said.

She held the door for Paris, and they stepped into the darkened theater. They stood inside the door as their eyes became accustomed to the dim light. Just as the girl at the ticket window said, there were only six other people in the theater, two young couples and a pair of teenaged boys. The boys were sprawled out in the second row with a seat between them, their legs propped up on the seat backs in front of them. One of the couples was sitting dead center, sharing a huge tub of popcorn and a jumbo soft drink. The other couple was still roaming up and down the aisle in search of the perfect seats.

"Where do you like to sit?" Sloan whispered. "Front, back or in the middle?"

"To be honest with you, I haven't been to a movie in years so I'm not sure," Paris whispered back.

"Really? I don't come very often myself. When I hear about a movie I want to see, by the time I get around to it, I can rent it and watch it at home."

"What is this movie about? I've never heard of *Charming Web*." Paris looked up and down the rows of the small theater.

"I have no idea. Something about a woman falling in love with a stranger, I think." Sloan followed Paris to the fourth row from the top. "So I'm the first one to get you out to a movie in a long time, huh?"

"Yes, you are. Are you proud of yourself?" Paris settled into her seat.

"I most certainly am," she replied, polishing her nails on her chest. "I have accomplished what seven million New Yorkers couldn't do. Get Paris to a movie."

"But you tricked me."

"No I didn't. I told you it was important. And it was." Sloan tried to read the back of the CD case in the dim light.

"You were afraid I'd say no if you told me what you really wanted to do, weren't you?"

"Would you have come?"

Paris leaned over and whispered in Sloan's ear just as the fanfare for the movie began. "Yes, I would have."

Sloan smiled contentedly.

Two more couples fumbled their way into seats as the previews rolled.

"Do you want some popcorn or something?" Sloan asked.

"No. I'm fine. Movie popcorn is loaded with cholesterol. There's more fat in a bag of popcorn than in . . ."

"Hush," Sloan interrupted. "Don't tell me that. I love movie popcorn. If I only have it once a year it won't kill me."

"True," Paris added.

By the time the film had established a plot Paris had noticed one of the young couples off to her side had begun kissing. Innocently at first, they exchanged little pecks and smooches of affection. Paris propped her elbow on the arm of her seat and leaned on her hand, trying to ignore the couple as their kisses became longer and lustier. Soon they were exchanging long French kisses and fondling each other. If the movie had been the slightest bit interesting she might have been able to keep her eyes on the screen and not on them. She fidgeted in her seat as the young man caressed the girl's breasts between kisses.

"Are you okay?" Sloan asked, noticing her nervousness. Paris looked at Sloan then traced her eyes over to the couple. Sloan's eyes followed Paris's lead. Sloan smiled a half smile and raised her eyebrows then went back to watching the movie. Paris looked away, but the sound of the girl's soft moan drew her attention back again. There was something in the tender way he touched her and kissed her that held an unmistakable attraction.

"Does that bother you?" Sloan whispered, noticing Paris's gaze returning to the young couple.

"No," she replied quietly.

"Making out in a movie is like a rite of passage for teenagers. All couples do it."

"No, they don't," Paris stated softly.

"Sure they do. Didn't you when you were a teenager?" Sloan argued in a whisper.

"No."

Sloan turned and looked at her to see if she was kidding.

"I can't believe you never went to the movies to make out."

"We went to the movies to watch the movie," she said defensively. "Why pay good money just to go kiss when you can do that someplace else for free?"

"Do you mean to tell me you have never kissed someone in the back of a dark theater before?"

Paris scowled back at her, a defensive set to her jaw. "No, I have not. So what?"

Sloan heaved a determined sigh and looked over her shoulder to see if anyone was behind them. No one was and those in the rows in front of them were engrossed in the gory action scene. Sloan wet her lips and turned back to Paris. Before Paris could see it coming, Sloan had pulled her close and planted a deep full-mouthed kiss on her.

Paris's eyes widened in surprise, and she glowered at her.

"Sloan!" she gasped in a whisper. "What are you doing?" She looked around to see if anyone was watching them. Between the stabbing and the shooting on the screen, no one had seen anything. Sloan gave a wry smile and slowly leaned in for another kiss. Paris didn't pull away. She sat stiffly as Sloan's lips touched hers, this time tenderly. Paris closed her eyes as Sloan pressed her soft lips to hers, parting them and allowing her tongue to invade Paris's mouth. Paris had never felt such soft lips before.

Sloan cupped her hand at the back of Paris's head. Paris leaned into the kiss, her hand finding Sloan's knee and folding over it as Sloan's tongue delved deeper and more inquisitively into her mouth. Paris's mind was a wild mix of emotions, both urgency to enjoy more of Sloan's taste and touch, and guilt for doing it in a public place. Urgency was winning out, and there was nothing she could do about it. She moaned quietly and tugged at the front of Sloan's shirt, pulling her closer. Sloan's nimble fingers unbuttoned Paris's blouse and slipped inside, her fingertips tracing the soft skin of her cleavage. Just as Sloan's fingers were about to creep inside her bra and find her hardening nipple Paris pulled back and pushed her away.

"Stop," she whispered, rebuttoning her blouse but wishing

Sloan's hand had found its target. Her breasts throbbed at what might have been.

"Now you can say you've kissed at the movies," Sloan whispered and winked at her.

Paris looked around to see if anyone had noticed. No one had paid any attention to them. She looked over at Sloan and smiled shyly.

"I guess I can."

"Want to try for making out, too?" Sloan asked in a low, husky voice.

"No," she replied, looking around to see if anyone was listening to Sloan's lusty suggestion.

"This is a participatory sport, you know." Sloan discreetly motioned toward the young couple now engaged in some serious French kissing and groping.

"Yes, I know. But not here, it isn't." Paris feigned her attention toward the screen, but she could feel Sloan's eyes still watching her.

"Where then?" Sloan asked as Paris looked back at her. She gave another quick peck on her cheek and placed her hand on Paris's thigh.

Paris looked back at the screen and narrowed her eyes. "This isn't much of a movie, is it?"

"Who cares?" Sloan muttered as she placed a trail of kisses up Paris's neck.

"Sloan," she whispered sternly, pressing her fingertips against Sloan's mouth. "Someone will see us. Now behave and watch the movie."

"I didn't want to see the movie," Sloan argued.

Paris stared at her in disbelief.

"I didn't," Sloan continued. "I just wanted the CD set. It was twenty-eight-ninety-five at the store. The movie was only six bucks. You do the math." Sloan grinned proudly.

"Then why are we sitting here watching a movie about a man having sex with a woman he is about to stab to death?"

"So we can kiss in the movie." Sloan gave a coy look. "I was creating a milestone for you."

"Can we go then? This movie is getting very gross."

Sloan led the way up the aisle and out into the lobby.

"Oh my God!" she said with panic-stricken eyes. "I forgot the CDs." She turned to go back down the hall, but Paris grabbed her arm.

"You mean these?" She waved the CD cases coyly. "You made such a big deal out of them, how could you forget them?"

"I was preoccupied with something else." Sloan offered a wink. "Come on. I'll treat you to a chocolate dip cone."

"They still make those?" Paris asked, her eyes bright at the thought.

"Absolutely. Nothing is too good for my date."

A warm contentment consumed Paris at the thought of being Sloan's date. She realized Sloan had created a subtle flame of desire deep within her, a flame that threatened to erupt into a firestorm of passion at any moment. Paris had felt these emotions growing from that first moment she recognized Sloan and hugged her beneath the willow tree. As much as she tried, it was one of those forces of nature she couldn't ignore. Sloan was tightly woven into the fabric of her life, filling it with joy, contentment and love. That was all she needed to know for now.

CHAPTER 15

Sloan ordered two dip cones, and they sat at the picnic tables outside the Dairy Queen laughing about the movie, the CDs and the couple making out in the theater. The evening was warm and the sky was full of stars. It was far too pleasant to just call it a night and go home.

"That was a fun evening," Paris declared, looking up at the star-filled sky as they walked back to the truck.

"So it wasn't so terrible that I took you away from painting the bathroom cabinet?" Sloan asked, looking over at her contented smile. She opened the passenger's side door and waited for Paris to slide in.

"No. I'm glad you did," Paris replied as Sloan closed the door then climbed in her side. "It's surprising how an evening of free CDs and ice cream can be more exciting and satisfying than a night on the town in Manhattan. I really truly loved it, Sloan. Thank you." Paris released her seat belt and leaned over to kiss Sloan on the cheek.

Before she could move back and buckle up again Sloan placed her hand on Paris's knee.

"Wait," she said softly. "Use this one." She pulled the middle seatbelt out of the cushion and folded it across Paris's lap.

"Okay," Paris replied. She hadn't sat next to anyone like this since college. It was a comforting feeling to be so close to Sloan, their legs touching. Paris could feel Sloan's muscles flex as she worked the pedals. Sloan tried to casually drape her right arm over Paris's shoulder, but she constantly had to pull it down to shift the gears.

"Is this a standard H?" Paris asked, watching Sloan shift through the gears.

"Yes. Just an old regular three-speed," Sloan replied, pleased that Paris knew about such things.

"Here, let me do it," Paris offered, covering Sloan's hand with hers. "I love your truck. It is a real classic. What year is it? Fifty-one?"

"Yes." Sloan smiled at her. "How did you know?"

Paris returned her smile. "We city girls like classic vehicles, too, you know."

"I almost drove my Toyota Camry tonight. I'm glad I didn't. It's nearly new, but I hardly ever drive it."

"You made a good choice. Camrys are nice, but this is way better."

"I'm glad you think so." Sloan allowed her fingertips to stroke the back of Paris's neck as they drove along.

"Why are we going this way?" Paris asked as Sloan turned north at the highway instead of south.

"I want to show you something."

"What is it?"

"You'll see."

Sloan turned off the highway onto a winding road and followed it as it narrowed to single lane dirt trail. Her truck rattling along over the ruts as they climbed through the trees and hills north of Banyon. She carefully steered around potholes and downed logs. After a last hairpin turn, she headed for a small clearing, switching off the headlights as they eased to a stop.

135

"Here we are," Sloan announced as she shut off the engine.

"Where is here? Looks like a nature trail," Paris offered, peering into the darkness.

"It's Lace Hill," she said proudly.

"What did you want to show me?"

"That," Sloan pointed out Paris's side window.

Paris gave a quick look, not expecting to see much. She did a double take, her mouth open at the surprise.

"Lace Hill," Sloan repeated.

The lights from Banyon were stretched out in the valley below visible through the leaves on the thick stand of trees.

"You can't see this in the daylight. Only at night when the lights are on in town. That's how this place got its name. The lights through the trees look like lace, don't they?"

"It's incredible. You're right. The lights twinkling through the leaves look just like lace. It's gorgeous." Paris leaned back against Sloan's side and admired the view. "This is prettier than the lights in the New York skyline." She pulled Sloan's arm around her and rested her head against it as they watched the lights. That couple should have come here," Paris said.

"What couple?"

"The one in the theater. The couple sucking face. They could have had this lovely view instead of doing what they were doing in a movie theater."

"No," Sloan whispered as she wrapped her other arm around Paris and pulled her close. "This is for us. No one else." Sloan kissed Paris on the temple.

Paris snuggled against Sloan's arm. A quiet serenity flowed over Paris as Sloan held her. Paris could feel Sloan's heart beating against her back and the calm rise and fall of her chest.

"Paris, I'm not dating anyone. I want you to know that," Sloan said softly.

"I believe you."

"How about you? Are you seeing anyone?" Sloan asked cautiously.

"No. I'm not dating anyone."

Paris couldn't see the relieved smile on Sloan's face as she admitted being unattached. But she could feel Sloan's arms fold tighter around her, and it pleased her.

"I must admit no one makes me laugh like you do," Paris remarked.

"That's it? I just make you laugh?"

"You didn't let me finish. You also make me feel comfortable."

"Like old slippers?" Sloan asked softly, then chuckled.

"No, like a warm blanket, a fuzzy warm blanket on a snowy night," Paris said, pulling Sloan's arm over her as if she was pulling covers around her.

"A fuzzy blanket, eh?"

"With soft satin binding," Paris added with a snicker.

"And what color blanket am I?"

"Let's see," Paris thought a moment. "Baby blue."

"So I'm a baby blue fuzzy blanket with a satin binding."

"Yes. Warm and protective and comforting." Paris heaved a contented sigh. They sat quietly listening to the sounds of the night.

"Listen to the locusts," Sloan whispered. "That's the sound of summertime in the Ozarks."

"I had forgotten how nice the summers could be here," Paris said.

"It's nice all year round. My favorite time is in the fall when the leaves change color."

"That must be spectacular."

"Oh, it is," Sloan insisted. "I think you should stay and see it."

"Maybe I can get a weekend off and come back in October."

"No," Sloan whispered. "I mean stay here through the summer and fall. Winter and spring, too." Sloan's voice was soft but heavy with expectation.

"I told you, Sloan. I'm only here for a few weeks."

"If you won't stay a year, why not at least take a few more months, at least through October. We'll have a great time. I'll take you to movies, and you can feed Barney granola bars."

Paris laughed, the idea surprisingly appealing, though out of the question.

"Please," Sloan added in barely a whisper.

"I can't! I wish I could, but I can't." Paris could feel Sloan sink back slightly.

"I'll be your own personal baby blue fuzzy blanket with satin binding," Sloan teased.

"I know you would." Paris placed a kiss on Sloan's arm.

"I could keep you warm and comfortable," she added. "We could go camping. I could be your blanket there, too," Sloan offered, intent on coming up with a justification for Paris to stay.

Paris sat up and turned around to face her.

"You aren't going to drop this, are you?"

"Do you need a demonstration of how good a blanket I can be?" Sloan asked grinning broadly.

"No, I do not," Paris ordered, pushing against Sloan's chest playfully as she leaned for her.

"Yes, you do." Sloan knelt on the seat, her hands walking toward Paris.

Paris giggled and scooted back across the seat as Sloan crawled ominously closer, whispering in a lusty voice. "I'm a baby blue fuzzy blanket with satin binding. I'm a baby blue fuzzy blanket with satin binding." Sloan lowered herself, nuzzling her mouth against Paris's neck and making snorting sounds.

Paris laughed wildly as Sloan's hot breath tickled her neck.

"Okay, okay. You are a blanket," Paris giggled.

Sloan looked down at Paris, her face just a few inches above hers. Instead of continuing the playful antics over Paris's body, she slowly lowered herself again, holding her weight on her elbows and knees.

"Am I hurting you?" Sloan whispered as she stared adoringly into Paris's eyes.

The dashboard lights were the only illumination inside the cab of the truck, but it was enough to see the softness in Sloan's eyes. Paris eased her hands around Sloan's waist.

"No," she replied in a whisper.

Sloan ever so slowly lowered her lips to Paris's in a brief but firm kiss. She could feel Paris's hands tighten around her waist. When she pulled away she saw Paris's eyes still closed and poised from the kiss. Again she lowered her lips to Paris's, this time parting them, their tongues tasting each other cautiously.

Paris arched herself up to Sloan's touch, her arms pulling her tightly to her. Sloan pressed herself onto Paris, devouring her mouth with a deep kiss. Paris opened her mouth, welcoming Sloan's tongue and exploration. Sloan eased her knee between Paris's thighs and pressed against her pubic bone. The more Sloan massaged Paris's crotch with her leg, the deeper Paris dug her nails into Sloan's back. Sloan slipped her hand into the warm area between Paris's legs and worked the seam of her slacks against the moisture she could feel through the fabric. Paris groaned and pulled her legs apart as Sloan continued a slow rhythmic massage. Sloan eased down the zipper and slid her hand inside. She pushed past Paris's panties and cupped her hand over her patch of curly hair.

"Yes, Sloan," Paris gasped, her eyes closed, her breath rapid. She folded her legs around Sloan. Sloan's mouth traced her hot breath down Paris's neck, kissing and nibbling at her soft skin.

Sloan felt Paris's nails scratching at her back through her shirt. But the pain only urged her on. She wanted to unbutton Paris's shirt and taste the soft skin in her cleavage, but she needed her other arm to hold herself up to keep from smashing Paris. She pulled her hand out of Paris's pants and quickly unbuttoned her shirt. Paris grabbed at her hand and pushed it back inside her panties.

"Wait a second," Sloan whispered as she pulled Paris's bra up, releasing her breasts. She took one of her hard nipples in her mouth, floating her tongue over it in rapid flicks. She pushed her hand back into Paris's panties and slid two fingers down beside her clit, gently massaging the hardening nub.

"Yes, Sloan, yes," Paris urged. Her hands skated down and grabbed at Sloan's buttocks, pulling her hips tightly against her. She threw her head back, biting down on her lip as Sloan moved from one breast to the other, sucking the nipples to hard erections.

Her nails dug into Sloan's ass, her jeans no match for Paris's passion-driven grip. She pressed herself up into Sloan's hand, reaching for more.

"Harder. Please, harder. Yes. Yes, like that. Don't stop," Paris gasped through clenched teeth.

Sloan responded to Paris's command and quickened her rhythmic massage, pressing harder at the hot demand of Paris's need. Sloan wanted to replace her hand with her tongue, tasting Paris's wetness and the musky richness of her womanhood, but Paris held tightly to her, ready to explode with ecstasy.

"Yes, yes," Paris screamed, holding Sloan so tight she could barely breathe. "Oh my God, yes," Paris yelled, her body stiffening then falling back on the seat, shuddering deeply. She released Sloan with breathless exhaustion, going limp under her. Sloan cupped her hand firmly over Paris's pubic bone and held it as the ecstasy flowed over her. She watched Paris's face as she rested quietly, her eyes closed with satisfaction.

Sloan sat up and pulled Paris to her, stroking her hair and kissing her temple. She held her in her arms listening to her breathing. The sound of the summer night again filled the truck as if it were acknowledging the passion they had shared. It was a long time before anything was said.

Paris started to say something, but Sloan stopped her.

"Shhh," Sloan whispered. Her eyes were closed. There was a serenity she wanted to preserve. This was the moment she had dreamed of for years. She had made love to Paris, the woman she had always loved, and it was wonderful, so wonderful that tears began to fill her eyes.

Paris heaved a contented sigh and pulled herself closer to Sloan. She felt the complications in her life growing by the second. Sloan's kiss in the theater and now this were all screaming out to her that this was more than just a passing tryst, more than just two old friends sharing an evening. She knew Sloan's intentions were a matter to be taken seriously. She couldn't ignore the feelings Sloan had for her any more than she could ignore her own feelings for

Sloan. These feelings were welcome and satisfying. But Paris also knew the distance between them was going to be a problem. But none of that mattered right now. She couldn't bring herself to find anything wrong with this perfect moment. The practical woman Paris prided herself in being was losing out to the deep soul-consuming emotions of a woman in love. She snuggled her face into Sloan's neck and kissed the soft skin behind her ear.

"I could stay here with you in my arms all night," Sloan said tenderly.

"I know."

"How can I let you go back to New York City?" Sloan asked with a catch in her voice.

It was Paris's turn to hush Sloan from spoiling the moment. It was a quiet ride home with Paris snuggled against Sloan's side. Sloan pulled into Paris's driveway, eased up beside Paris's car and turned off the engine. They sat in the darkness for a long moment.

"I had a wonderful time tonight," Paris said finally then placed her hand on Sloan's. "All of it."

"I did, too." She turned to face Paris. "Every single second of it." She kissed her softly then opened the door for Paris to slide out. She walked her to her car and opened the door for her. She waited while Paris slid in.

"A very wonderful time," Paris added, reaching up and touching Sloan's face tenderly.

Sloan kissed the palm of Paris's hand then closed the door.

Paris watched her return to her truck and start the engine.

"I can't get serious about you, Sloan," she whispered to herself as Sloan pulled away. "I'm leaving in two weeks." She closed her eyes and sighed. "Good night, my sweet."

CHAPTER 16

Paris gave several toots on the horn as she drove around to Sloan's shop. Barney trotted over to the fence and stuck his head through the rails. He gave a welcoming nicker and bobbed his head as Paris climbed out of her car. The shop door was open and the lights were on, but Sloan was nowhere to be found.

"Sloan," Paris called, checking the shop then returning to the driveway. "Anybody here?" When no one answered, she headed for the kitchen door. She knocked several times to no avail. "Sloan," she yelled across the pasture. The sound of giggling voices came floating down from above. "Who's up there?" Paris perched her hands on her hips and smiled up at the big cotton-wood tree. "I hear voices in the treehouse."

"No you don't," replied one of the twins.

"There's no one up here," the other one added.

Their two heads popped out the back window, and they smiled down at her.

"I see there's no one up there." Paris smiled back. "I suppose Aunt Sloan isn't up there either."

"Nope, she isn't," Sloan replied, her head popping out between the girls. "We are not up here."

"Too bad," Paris insisted, shaking her head. She retrieved a bakery box from the front seat of the car and held it up. "Because I have four chocolate cupcakes with sprinkles on top. They are special treehouse cupcakes. But if no one is up there, I guess I'll take them home with me." She peeked inside the box and scraped off a fingertip full of frosting. She licked it off then headed back to the car.

"Cupcakes?" Lori squealed. "We're up here, Paris. Really we are."

"See," Lucy added, waving her arm out the window.

"We were just pretending," Lori admitted seriously.

"Come on up," Sloan called. "And don't drop my cupcake."

"You could come down," Paris suggested, smiling up at the three faces.

"But you said they were treehouse cupcakes. We have to eat them up here in the treehouse," Lori explained.

"She's got you there," Sloan chided and waved Paris toward the ladder.

"How am I going to climb the ladder with this box in my hand? I'm not a monkey like you all."

"Put it in the basket and we'll pull it up," Sloan said lowering the rope with a basket tied to the end.

The twins carefully pulled the basket of cupcakes up as Paris climbed the ladder. The girls opened the box and arranged the goodies on a tiny table. It was a cramped fit, but the four of them sat on the floor around the short table.

"Look," Lori said, pointing to the script letter on top of each one. "There are letters on the frosting."

"Can you read them?" Sloan asked, leaning back against the corner.

"I can. I can," each one said. "L, L, S and P."

"What are the letters for?" Lucy asked.

Sloan smiled over at Paris. "I don't know. Do you have any idea?"

The girls studied the cupcake decorations for a long moment. Paris moved the one with an S in front of Sloan and the P in front of herself then let the girls study them again. The sudden revelation of the initials came to both of them at almost the same second.

"S is for Sloan," Lori said proudly.

"P is for Paris," her sister added with the same expression of accomplishment.

"L is for Lori and the other L is for Lucy."

"Right." Paris stroked each one on the cheek and grinned. "You are very smart. How old are you two again? Eighteen?"

"No," Lori laughed. "We're not eighteen. We're eight. But I'm older."

"Only three minutes," Lucy quipped with a frown. "You're only three minutes older."

"But I *am* older," Lori declared.

"It was very nice of you to allow Lori to be born first, Lucy." Paris offered to the disappointed twin. "You are a very considerate sister."

Paris's statement seemed to brighten the younger girl's spirit, and she sat up straight and glared at her sibling. "Yeah, I let you go first. So there."

Sloan laughed loudly and ruffled both girls' hair.

"You two argue about everything. Eat your cupcakes."

The girls peeled back the paper and dug in. It didn't take long before there was nothing left but four cupcake papers and a few crumbs. Sloan wiped the frosting off Lori's chin and Paris did the same for Lucy.

"What do you say for the treats?" Sloan asked.

"Thank you," they both said with bright smiles.

"You're welcome," Paris replied. She collected the empty papers and brushed off the crumbs. "Now you can play up here, but I'm going down."

"I'll come with you," Sloan offered. "You two remember the rules. No hanging out the window. Okay?"

"Okay," Lucy replied, moving the table aside so they could spread out their coloring books on the floor.

Paris and Sloan climbed down and headed into Sloan's shop.

"That was nice of you to bring the goodies," Sloan said.

"When you said you were babysitting today I thought you could use some distraction. Why is this piece of driftwood on the pedestal?" Paris asked circling a gnarly length of wood that nature had scrubbed clean of its bark.

"Inspiration," Sloan replied, sorting some tools into their proper bins.

Paris kept slowly circling, squinting at the grotesque shape.

"That old pedestal used to be in a church. It was part of the pulpit. I found it at an estate sale, and I use it to hold some of the really unique pieces of wood I find. I'm waiting for the inspiration of just what I should make out of that old hunk of driftwood."

"You put every piece of driftwood on this pedestal?"

"Heavens, no. I'd never get anything made. But once in a while I find something special, something so unique in character that I want it to become a—" Sloan hesitated as she thought of the right word.

"Work of art?" Paris offered.

"Something like that."

"What do you have in mind for this one?"

"I don't know. Maybe a settee or table. I haven't decided yet."

Paris examined it again, her eyes narrowing.

"The way it flows along in a waving motion it reminds me of something tranquil," she said, running her hand over the smoothness. "Like a headboard for a bed."

"Yeah. Like a headboard for a bed," Sloan agreed.

Sloan stood next to Paris squinting at it.

"Very good, Paris. A headboard for a bed." Sloan smiled and wrapped her arm around Paris's waist giving her a grateful hug. "I should have had you look at the beast."

"The beast?"

"Yeah. It was this huge root ball I dragged home last year and spent months trying to decide what to make out of it." Sloan grimaced as she remembered the folly.

"What did you make out of it?"

"The most hideous pedestal table you ever saw. It looked like something a dinosaur coughed up."

"What did you do with it?" Paris asked, looking around the shop for the strange creation.

"I sold it. A lady in L.A. bought it for her beach house. And she paid a pretty penny for it, I must say." Sloan laughed. "She thought it was magnificent."

"Then it couldn't have been all that bad."

"Oh yes it was," Sloan insisted defiantly. She went to the bulletin board and unpinned a photograph. After blowing off the shop dust she handed it to Paris. "See what I mean. Dinosaur hairball."

Paris studied the picture then turned it upside down. When that didn't help she handed it back to Sloan.

"It does have a singular uniqueness," Paris offered diplomatically.

"Uh-huh."

"It couldn't be all that bad if that lady bought it for her home," Paris justified.

"The lady wore a dog collar and had tattoos of spiders up and down both arms."

They both laughed loudly.

Their laughing was cut short by the sound of crying and screaming outside the shop. Sloan was out the door like a shot, Paris close on her heels. Lucy and Lori were standing inside the corral by the gate. Lucy was crying and holding her thigh with both hands. Lori stood next to her screaming for Sloan and watching the blood running down her sister's leg.

"What happened?" Sloan said sticking her head through the railing of the fence. As soon as she saw the rip in Lucy's flesh and the pulsing stream of blood she gasped and scrambled through the fence. Paris had come through the gate and knelt next to the crying child. She wrapped an arm around her waist and held her tightly as she examined the wound. Sloan dropped to her knees and grimaced at the blood, the color draining from her face. With shaky hands, she reached for the leg.

"Don't touch it," Lucy screamed. "It hurts." She looked up at Sloan with tear-swollen eyes. She continued to cry inconsolably, the salty tears running down her face and mixing with the blood as they splashed onto her thigh.

Sloan flinched and pulled back, not sure what to do next.

"I know sweetie," Paris cooed, kissing her forehead. "It hurts real bad. I know. And you are so brave to let me look at it. But I won't touch it. I promise." Paris brushed the hair from Lucy's face and smiled reassuringly at her.

"Okay," Lucy said through her tears. "But don't touch it. You promise?"

"I promise," Paris said emphatically. She kept her arm firmly around Lucy's waist as she looked at the gash. "This is a very unique wound, Lucy. Did you know that? It is very unusual," Paris offered.

Lucy continued to cry, but the news from Paris distracted her enough to quiet the screaming sobs. She leaned over to see the uniqueness of her wound, even though she didn't know what unique meant.

"No one in all of Banyon has one just like it, I'm sure. I'm a doctor back in New York, you know." Paris continued to examine and talk.

"You are a doctor?" Sloan asked, her eyes instantly widened at the revelation.

Paris nodded but kept her attention on Lucy's wound.

"I can't tell for sure, but I bet no one in all of Missouri has a cut just like this," she said, smiling warmly at the child.

Lucy lifted her thigh slightly so she could see whatever it was Paris saw. That was just what Paris wanted her to do, move her leg.

"But it depends on how you got it. That will make it really special."

"She got it on the fence," Lori said, pointing to the top railing near the gate hinge.

147

"Were you climbing on the fence?" Sloan asked, trying to divert her eyes from the blood and ripped flesh.

Lori nodded and lowered her eyes, well aware they had done something they shouldn't.

Sloan studied her with a scolding stare. "I've told you a million times no climbing on the fence. It is taller than you are." Sloan was visibly guilt-ridden for allowing her niece to be injured while on her watch.

Paris went to the fence and searched the spot where Lori had pointed. A rusty bolt head protruded from the fence post where the hinge was attached.

"Is this where you cut yourself, sweetie?" Paris asked, touching the bolt.

Lucy nodded, the memory of it bringing on a new round of sobs.

Paris scooped Lucy up in her arms and carried her to the house. Sloan and Lori followed behind like sheep following the flock.

"Do you know if Lucy has had a recent tetanus immunization?" Paris asked, gently sitting Lucy on the counter by the kitchen sink.

Sloan shrugged, her face still pale. "I don't know. Doctor Cameron's office here in town would know. That's where Stacy has always taken them."

"Call the office and find out," Paris ordered. "Then get me some tape, gauze and some antiseptic. You've got those don't you?"

Sloan nodded as she dialed Doctor Cameron's number. While Sloan called the doctor's office, Paris wrapped some ice cubes in a clean kitchen towel, broke the ice with a meat tenderizer, then handed it to Lucy to hold over her wound.

"Hold this on it gently, sweetie and it won't hurt as much," Paris said, wiping Lucy's tears away.

Lucy looked skeptical but did as she was told. "Is this what you do to aneak cuts?" she asked, trying to suppress her tears.

"Aneak?"

"You said my cut is aneak."

"Oh, unique. Yes, this is exactly what you do to unique cuts." Paris stroked the child's cheek tenderly. "You are very brave."

148

"Not since she was eighteen months old," Sloan said as she hung up.

"Then she needs one," Paris said quietly in Sloan's direction.

Sloan's mouth dropped. "A shot?" she whispered in stark terror.

Paris noticed Sloan's pale complexion and wide-eyed stare.

"She'll be all right," Paris said softly, trying to reassure her.

"Are they going to sew it up?" Lori asked, standing next to her twin and touching the blood trail that ran down to her ankle. "Daddy had a big cut on his leg and they sewed it up with a needle and thread. He let us see it. And I touched it."

"No, Lucy doesn't need stitches. It has almost stopped bleeding. Keep that ice on it." Paris checked under the ice pack then replaced it.

Sloan opened the cabinet under the sink and pulled out a first aid kit. Her hands were so shaky she couldn't operate the simple latch to open the case.

"Are you okay?" Paris asked, opening the kit and taking out what she needed.

"Yeah, I'm fine." Sloan's voice was thin and distant.

"Look, Sloan," Lori announced. "Lucy has pink stuff in the cut. Wanna see?" The girls were peeking under the towel at the J-shaped cut that stood open, a quarter inch wide and an inch long. Lucy had stopped crying and joined her sister in examining the inner workings of the wound.

"Look, I can make it bleed." Lucy stretched her thigh slightly and watched a pillow of blood swell up in the crevice then spill out and run down her leg. "See?"

Sloan looked but quickly diverted her eyes as the red liquid pulsed out of the little girl's leg. Sloan swallowed hard and placed a hand on the counter to steady herself as the room spun around her.

"Sloan, are you okay? Maybe you should call Stacy. Tell her what happened, but tell her the cut isn't very deep and doesn't require sutures." Paris rubbed a hand down Sloan's back. "I'll take care of this."

"Yeah, I'll call Stacy."

Sloan moved to the telephone and punched the memory button next to her sister's name. Stacy was in Springfield with her husband at an RV show. From one side of the conversation, Paris could tell Stacy hadn't freaked out about the mishap and was perfectly confident with their ability to handle it. She had also granted permission for Lucy to get a tetanus shot. It also sounded like one for Lori might be a good idea as well. Stacy would call Doctor Cameron's office and tell them it was okay for Sloan to bring them in.

"Did you tell mommy I have a unique cut?" Lucy asked proudly.

"Yes, I did," Sloan replied, looking only slightly less than nauseous.

"Did you tell her I can make it bleed if I want to?"

"It would be better if you didn't make it bleed," Paris said gently, realizing Sloan was having trouble with the gruesomeness of it.

"Why?" Lucy said, producing another trickle of blood.

"Because you might let all your sweetness run out. Then you would be all stale and ugly."

"Oh," Lucy gasped, pressing the ice down on it again.

"If I get a big cut I'm going to make it bleed a whole lot," Lori advised, seemingly disappointed the blood trail was over. "I'm going to let it bleed and bleed and bleed, all over my shoes and onto the floor and everywhere." She threw her arms out dramatically. "Gallons and buckets of it."

"I could too," Lucy added. "But I don't want to be stale and ugly. I could make it bleed gallons and buckets if I wanted. Couldn't I, Sloan?"

Sloan tried to smile, but the room was a blur of faces and smells. The sound of the twin's voices floated in and out of her ears like red waves. Sweat began to form on her upper lip, and her knees became rubbery.

"Sloan," Paris said. "Why don't you sit down?" Paris had begun cleaning the blood from the wound and applying antiseptic.

Sloan didn't say anything as she turned toward the kitchen table. She took one hesitant step and reached out for the chair, but it was too late. She crumbled to the floor with a thud, her face white as a sheet.

"Sloan. Sloan." Paris's voice was like a faint sound through the fog, growing louder as Sloan opened her eyes.

Sloan could feel something cool and wet on her forehead. The room slowly stopped spinning as Paris dabbed the cloth down Sloan's face and across her neck.

"There you are," Paris said with a worried expression. She combed her fingers through Sloan's hair with soft strokes. Her eyes conveyed her tender concern as she cradled Sloan's head in her lap. In spite of Paris's strong professionalism and medical experience she felt an overwhelming need to smother Sloan with attention and sympathy.

"What happened?" Sloan asked hesitantly as she regained her senses.

"You fainted."

"Oh, God. I didn't, did I?" Sloan winced at the thought.

"Yes. It seems your nieces have a stronger constitution than you do."

Sloan began to sit up, but Paris held her shoulders against her legs.

"Not so fast. Just lie here a minute," Paris admonished. Sloan's head nestled in her lap became more than a wise medical idea. It was a comforting sensation and one she didn't want to hurry.

"Lucy. What about Lucy?" Sloan asked as the memory of the child's wound returned to her.

"She's fine. I bandaged her leg and put the two of them in front of the TV to watch cartoons. When you're up to it we'll take her to the doctor. But there's no hurry. How are you feeling?"

"I feel like an idiot, that's how I feel." Sloan slowly sat up and rubbed the back of her head.

"Is your head okay? It took a pretty good whack."

"The only thing wounded is my pride. Fainting, what a stupid thing to do."

"Actually it is your body's way of protecting you. In this case it was protecting you from the shock of seeing Lucy's blood."

Sloan grimaced at the thought.

"I've cut myself before, and I never fainted at the sight of my blood," Sloan argued.

"It isn't unusual. I've seen two-hundred-and-fifty-pound men pass out like a tree falling in the forest when they see their children hurt."

"I've never done this before. I swear it."

"Have you ever had one of your nieces or nephews injured in front of you before?"

"Well, no. I guess not."

"There you go. You wanted to protect Lucy from being hurt and you couldn't. It was difficult for you to see her in pain and not be able to take it away, so voila, you fainted."

"No shit," Sloan declared.

"Maybe it would be better if I take her in the exam room while she gets the shot."

"I hate to sound like a terrible aunt but that would be wonderful if you would do that."

"No problem. Are you sure you're okay?" Paris looked at her with concern.

"I'm fine. Let's get Lucy to the doctor. I've got bad news for Lori, too. But I'm not telling her now. Stacy wants them both to get a tetanus booster."

"And I bet I get to be the bad guy for that too, huh?"

"Yes, please," Sloan replied with a relieved sigh.

"Okay. I'm up to it. But you better come up with something as a reward for afterward."

Sloan gave a mischievous grin. "I think I can think of something as a reward."

"Not for me, silly. For the twins." Paris went to the living room to call the girls then looked back at Sloan. "But don't abandon that idea," she said with a wink.

They all piled into Sloan's truck and headed for town.

"Why didn't you tell me you were a doctor?" Sloan asked.

"Don't pick that tape off, Lucy," Paris said, noticing her curiosity getting the best of the little girl. "Let's keep it covered so it won't get dirty and start bleeding again."

"Okay," Lucy replied.

"Paris, why?" Sloan asked again.

Paris lowered her eyes. "Because I never tell anyone I'm a doctor when I'm on vacation. I'm a cardiologist in Manhattan. It's my business, but I want to keep it in the office. If people know I'm a doctor everybody has an ache or a pain. Everyone wants an instant diagnosis and first thing you know my vacation is one big clinic." She gave Sloan an understanding smile. "But you are right, I should have told you. I'm sorry. It is just habit, I guess."

"Wow, a doctor. Damn!" Sloan shook her head in disbelief then grinned broadly. "A cardiologist even."

Paris watched as Sloan digested the news.

"A doctor," Sloan repeated loudly, as if the fact needed more exclamation.

Paris chuckled at her.

"I guess I shouldn't be surprised," Sloan offered. "When we were kids you always had a genuine sympathy for anyone who got hurt."

"I did?" Paris asked.

"Sure." Sloan reached over and patted Paris arm. "You were always taking care of me."

Paris smiled at Sloan's declaration. She may have been right. The memory of the summer Sloan broke her wrist wafted across Paris's mind and came into focus.

"What happened to your arm?" Paris asked, studying the cast and the crayon decorations as Sloan joined her on the island.

"Broke my wrist," Sloan replied with cautious pride. "Playing softball. I did it going for a foul ball. I tripped over the bat rack."

"Gosh! Did it hurt real bad? Did you cry?"

"Naw, it didn't hurt too bad." Pinocchio's nose was growing. "But I can't play softball for the rest of the summer."

"Well, your arm is more important than any old softball game."

"But I was the catcher. No one can play that position like me. Coach

has Melody Creepy catching now, and she can't stop anything. She closes her eyes when anyone swings at the ball. Then she has to run to the backstop and pick it up."

"Melody Creepy? Is that her real name?" Paris asked skeptically.

"No, but it ought to be. She has fat ankles and this one eye that goes crossed when she looks at you." Sloan made a grotesque face to make her point. They both laughed.

"That isn't very nice to talk about anyone like that," Paris added quietly.

Sloan grimaced and looked down at her cast.

"Yeah, I know. But I wanted to play." She kept her eyes diverted, hoping Paris wouldn't notice how close she was to crying. "Darn old bat rack anyway," she muttered, kicking at a dandelion puff ball.

Paris didn't reply. She realized how important it was to Sloan and how much she missed getting to play. She kicked a dandelion, too.

"Can I write on your cast?"

"Sure. But I get it off next week," Sloan said, seemingly pleased with Paris's interest.

The following Wednesday morning Sloan's mother telephoned Paris's grandmother and asked if Paris would like to accompany them to Springfield where Sloan had a doctor's appointment to have the cast removed. Paris, forewarned about the call, awaited the decision from the top of the stairs where she hung on every word.

"Paris?" Grandmother called from the hall telephone.

"Yes, Grandma. Can I go, please?" Paris blurted out as she scrambled down the stairs.

"She'll be ready in ten minutes, Shirley," her grandmother said into the receiver with a chuckle then hung up.

"You go change into that pretty pink shorts set. I washed it yesterday and ironed it. Then wash your face, and I'll run a brush through your hair." She waved her hands at Paris, shooing her up the stairs to get ready.

Sloan was taken right in at the doctor's office. Within ten minutes she was out, rubbing her wrist and beaming her relief to be free of the cumbersome cast. As soon as Shirley stopped the car in Paris's driveway, the two girls were out the door and skipping off toward the pond.

"Thank you for inviting me, Mrs. McKinley," Paris called politely then ran to catch up with Sloan.

"You both have good clothes on," Shirley yelled to the fleeing girls.

"We'll be careful," Paris called back.

"You be careful, Sloan. That wrist is still weak. I don't want you breaking it again. You heard what the doctor said." She yelled louder as if knowing her admonishment was falling on deaf ears.

When Paris caught up with Sloan, she was waiting at the bridge. They crossed the bridge and flopped down in grass under the tree.

"Does your arm hurt?" Paris asked, watching Sloan rub it.

"No." Sloan rotated it. "Well, maybe just a little."

Paris watched as Sloan examined the spot where the bone had snapped. It was now a pea-size lump surrounded by the last faded shades of a large bruise.

"Want to touch it?" Sloan asked, holding out her arm.

"Okay." Paris touched the lump carefully then rubbed her finger up and down the arm. "I can feel it."

"Listen," Sloan said, rotating it back and forth, a popping sound counting each rotation. "It snaps when I turn it. Isn't that neat-o?" Sloan grinned at the discovery. "Now I make noise when I move."

"Grandma makes noise when she walks, too," Paris added. "I think it is her knee. She said Arthur Itis makes her do it."

"Who's Arthur Itis?"

"I don't know. But he must be someone at church. Grandma says he comes to visit her when she sits too long in the church pew."

"How's your wrist?" Paris asked, returning to reality and the ride to town.

"Fine, why?" Sloan said looking over at her.

"I was just thinking about that summer you broke it."

Sloan looked down at her wrist and rotated it. "I hadn't thought about that in years. You have a tremendous memory."

"Melody Creepy," Paris said after a moment.

Sloan laughed and nodded, acknowledging Paris's accurate recollection.

"Good old Melody Creepy. Worst eleven-year-old softball player in history."

Sloan pulled into the parking lot at the clinic. Lucy was wide-eyed at the idea of going to the doctor so the word shot was not used until they were in the waiting room. Lori was happily playing with the toys in the kiddy corner until Sloan broke the news she would be getting a booster shot as well.

"You two have to decide where we are going after the doctor's office," Sloan offered with her best diplomacy. "Mickey D's for ice cream, Grandpa's store for candy bars or the truck stop for pie."

"Ice cream," Lucy said immediately.

"Grandpa's," Lori added almost simultaneously.

Paris laughed at Sloan, knowing an agreement was going to be hard to achieve. The girls argued back and forth while Sloan rolled her eyes.

"Too many good choices," Paris said.

"Any suggestions?" Sloan asked Paris.

"Hey, girls. I have an idea. How about we get ice cream and get an extra one to take to your Grandpa Charlie? Then you can have candy, too." Paris spoke with the voice of a deliberator.

"Okay," the twins agreed happily, realizing that was a far better deal.

"Thank you," Sloan said in Paris's direction.

"Lucy, Lori," the nurse called from the open door. "Hi girls. Would you like to come with me?"

"Oh, God," Sloan whispered.

Paris patted Sloan's leg and stood up, ready to be the martyr and take the twins through the door to the awaiting shots. "Relax. You aren't throwing Christians to the lions," she said.

"Tell that to the flip-flopping in my stomach. I feel terrible about all this." Sloan looked up at Paris with a pained expression.

"It's not your fault. Accidents happen. If this is the worst thing that ever happens to them, their life will be a breeze." Paris gave a mothering smile. "Don't worry."

Before Sloan could pace the waiting room twice and gulp down a couple of swigs from the water fountain the door reopened. Lucy and Lori emerged with a sucker in each hand and Barbie doll Band-Aids on their thighs. Paris was playfully licking a sucker as well.

"Mine is cherry. What's yours, Lucy?" Paris asked cheerfully.

"Grape. And I got a root beer, too." She didn't seem the worse for wear.

"I got pink and strawberry," Lori added. "What is pink?"

"Watermelon, I bet," Paris offered.

"I got watermelon and strawberry," she corrected. She ran over to Sloan and hugged her waist. "If you are good, maybe you'll get a sucker, too."

"But I'm not getting a shot, sweet pea," Sloan said rubbing her back affectionately. The nurse looked at Paris with curious eyes. Sloan noticed the silent communication between the nurse, Paris and the twins. There was something going on, and she began to suspect it wasn't good.

"What?" she asked finally, convinced there was a plot afoot. "Naomi?" she said in the nurse's direction.

"Sloan McKinley," the gray-haired nurse announced, scanning a folder. "It has been eight years and four months since you had a tetanus shot. And that is way too long in your line of work. Who knows what kind of old rusty stuff you handle."

"Come on, Sloan," Paris urged. "It'll just take a second. She has it all ready." Paris nodded her head toward the exam room.

"Is this a conspiracy or what?" Sloan frowned at the group.

"Do you want me to go in with you, Aunt Sloan?" Lucy said, her eyes full of empathy as she took Sloan's hand. "It won't hurt much. You just look at the bug poster and count the butterflies. Then you won't feel it. Well, maybe a little." Lucy pulled Sloan toward the nurse.

Sloan gave a heavy sigh, as if realizing her fate was sealed.

"Thanks, but I can do this alone." Sloan looked down at her and pinched Lucy's nose softly.

"Want me to go in with you?" Paris asked quietly.

Sloan straightened her posture and adjusted her shirt collar.

"No. I will go alone." She was being as dramatic possible, acting like a martyr headed for the guillotine. "If I don't return," she followed the nurse through the door then stuck her head back around the corner, "I leave my sucker to the three of you." She closed the door slowly.

Before Paris got comfortable in a chair she heard the muffled sound of Sloan yelling a cuss word.

"I think she's finished, girls," Paris remarked.

CHAPTER 17

The next morning was the end of Paris's patience. She had arrived in Banyon a week ago and was tired of Malcolm's slow progress on the repairs he had so strongly suggested be done. She also had a growing suspicion about his business practices. She made some telephone calls and did some investigative work then headed for Aurora and a serious chat with him.

Paris pulled into the parking lot next to Malcolm's office. It was a metal building with brick veneer across the front. The windows were littered with placards and stickups promoting everything from Pilates classes to the Rotary Club. A buzzer sounded as she opened the front door and stepped inside. A girl in her late twenties hurried back to the front office and greeted her with a tentative smile.

"Can I help you?"

"I would like to see Malcolm Vetch, please." Paris spoke in a purposeful tone.

"I think he's on the phone. You want to wait?" she said indifferently.

"Could you please see if he's free? I need to talk with him now." Paris fixed the girl with a deliberate gaze, unimpressed with her lack of professionalism.

The girl smirked and started for the hall. She looked back at Paris before opening an office door.

"Can I tell him who is here to see him?" she asked.

"He'll know who it is," Paris replied, then crossed her arms. She didn't want to give her name and run the risk Malcolm would duck out the back door.

The girl disappeared inside the office. After only a minute she returned to the front, her face flush and distraught.

"He'll be right with you, ma'am," she muttered then sat down and went to work on her computer.

The longer Paris stood waiting the deeper the furrows wrinkled her brow. She had all the ammunition she needed, and Malcolm Vetch was about to reap Paris's fury.

His office door opened and he came striding down the hall toward her, a wide smile on his face. Paris instantly thought if he only knew why she was here he wouldn't be smiling.

"Ah, Paris," he said, offering her his hand. "It's good to see you again. Did you have any trouble finding the office? We moved a few months ago so most folks aren't used to this new place." He kept smiling and shaking Paris's hand as he talked. "You're looking good, Paris. Missouri weather seems to agree with you."

"Thank you. I need to talk with you, Malcolm," she said, pulling her hand away and discreetly wiping the residue of his sweaty palm on her pant leg.

"Sure, sure. Any time at all. Come on in my office." He motioned down the hall, but Paris waited for him to lead the way.

"Marsha, be sure and let me know if that call comes in." He gave her a knowing nod then headed down the hall.

Paris started to follow then went back to the receptionist's desk. She leaned over and spoke quietly so only Marsha could hear her.

"Marsha, let me give you some good advice. Don't put any calls through to Malcolm right now." Paris gave her a hard stare before following Malcolm into his office and closing the door.

He held a chair for Paris to sit then took his place behind his big desk. It was covered with paperwork and a laptop computer. Before he could do anymore sweet-talking, Paris took a newspaper clipping from her purse and placed it on his desk.

"I think we need to talk," she declared, then leaned back in the chair.

His smile melted as he eyed the clipping advertising Paris's property to be rented for weddings, reunions and parties.

"What's this?" he said, trying to act innocent.

"I think you know what this is, Malcolm. In fact, according to the advertising department at the newspaper office, you've had this same ad in the *Monett Times* for six years. It's bigger than the one you used to have in the *Springfield News-Leader* or the *Banyon Gazette*. But since your sister works at the *Monett Times* you get a reduced rate. But then there are the posters you have in the bridal shop. Oh, and there's one in the tuxedo and formal attire rental shop as well. They make up for taking the ad out of the other papers I guess. Oh, yes. There's also the ad in the Southwest Missouri State University *Standard*."

"Let me explain, Paris," he started, attempting to laugh it off.

"There is more, Malcolm," Paris continued over his interruption. "Like Kathy and Ryan." She pulled one of the wedding napkins from her pocket and tossed it on the desk. "I found this along with the rest of the leftover wedding decorations on my island."

"Paris," he cajoled. "If anything, your property is more valuable because of my extra efforts. I'm sure you noticed the new bridge over to the island. It is wider and much safer with the handrails. I had it made especially for your property. It keeps the graceful Victorian theme of the house. I'm sure I have the invoice and work order here somewhere." He began digging through his papers. "Marsha isn't much on filing, but I'm sure she'll be able to find it for you."

"It's funny you should bring up the bridge. I've been doing

some checking. Did you know there is a manufacturer's label and UPC code stapled to the bottom of the bridge? You have to be in the water to see it, but it is there, plain as day."

Paris dug in her purse again and pulled out a photocopy of a receipt from the lumber yard. "And speaking of invoices, I have one here from Meeks Lumber. Is this what you meant?" She held it up for him to see then read it out loud. "One white arched garden bridge, delivered to route three, box eighteen, Banyon, Missouri. Received by Malcolm Vetch. Discount applied, no warranty, display model, damaged posts, three hundred dollars. It is dated April fifth."

Malcolm didn't reply. He swallowed hard, the corner of his moustache twitching nervously.

"And on my monthly statement for that particular April I have an interesting item." She read from another photocopy. "April fourth, one hundred fifty dollars, dismantle and haul away unsafe and damaged bridge over pond. April fifth, construction of new replacement bridge, one thousand five hundred dollars, including lumber, paint and labor. Amounts deducted from April and May rent receipts." Paris looked up and gave Malcolm a moment to digest what she was saying.

"Captain Ferguson of the Banyon rural fire department told me he remembers conducting a practice for the new members of the department at my farm. He said you contacted them about burning an old wooden bridge. They agreed to burn it for free in exchange for using it as a training fire."

Malcolm sat dumbfounded as Paris continued.

"Let's see. What else was there?" Paris frowned and tugged at her ear as she thought. "Oh, yes. Shall we discuss the backhoe rental? You charged me four hundred eighty dollars to dredge the pond saying that the pasture was having a flooding problem. Turns out it was right after Melinda Mathews dropped a certain diamond ring in the pond. There's only one backhoe service in Banyon, Malcolm. And the owner has a very good memory." Paris stopped and narrowed her eyes at Malcolm. "Did you have to resize the ring for your wife?" She gave him a cutting stare.

162

"Then there's Foley's Antique and Collectibles out on the highway," she continued. "They have had some interesting Victorian accessories for sale. It seems you sold them a lovely dining room chandelier, some mahogany molding, and, oh yes, a cast iron ball and claw footed bathtub. And would you know anything about some timbers that were neatly cut in the basement ceiling under my mudroom so the floor would creak and bounce like it was rotting? And how about charging Sloan McKinley five hundred dollars a year to harvest and trim my trees? Would you like me to go on Malcolm?"

"Paris, let me explain. This can all be explained," he said nervously.

"Malcolm," Paris said quietly and with restraint. "You have exactly three minutes to find my contract, write on it that it is canceled and sign it. I am firing your ass, Malcolm. And your brother's and anyone else you hired to do my repairs. If you ever set foot on my property again I will have you arrested for trespassing and prosecute you for theft, fraud and anything else I can think of. My lawyers in Manhattan would love to prosecute a two-bit crook like you. Do I make myself clear, Malcolm? And by the way, if you have contracted for any other weddings or anything else on my property, I suggest you call them and give their money back or I will have the Barry County sheriff knocking on your door with so many warrants you will have to hire a helper for Marsha just to read them." Paris sat back and crossed her arms.

Malcolm furrowed his brow as he took a slow deep breath as if formulating his defense. He gave a weak smile, the twitching still pulling at his moustache.

"Malcolm," Paris said softly, with a smile.

"Yes, Paris," he replied, still sitting at his desk.

"You have two-and-one-half minutes left," she warned as she pulled her cell phone from her purse.

He wanted to say something but seemed to think better of it. He went to the file cabinet and found Paris's contract.

"Both copies, Malcolm," she added without looking up. "I signed two."

He pulled the other contract out of her folder. He did the paperwork Paris requested and signed it. She signed it as well.

"Notarize it, Malcolm," she ordered.

"I'm not—" he started.

She stared coldly at him and pointed to the notary sign on his desk. He grunted and affixed the stamp to the forms. Paris took the papers from his hand and collected her stack of photocopies. She opened the office door then turned back to him.

"You are a crook, Malcolm. A conniving, thieving, money-grubbing crook. But that's just my opinion. I'm sure there are folks who admire those qualities."

She walked out and slammed the door. Marsha hurried back to her desk from where she had obviously been eavesdropping.

"You can put his calls through now, Marsha." Paris took one of the peppermints from the candy dish on her desk and left.

CHAPTER 18

The next morning Paris pulled into Sloan's driveway just before eight, worried she was too early to find her up, but Sloan was already puttering outside her shop.

"You're up early," Paris offered.

"Early bird gets the wormy wood," Sloan replied as she dropped some rope in the back of her truck.

"Oh? Where's the wormy wood?"

"Estate sale in Mount Vernon. Supposed to be old tools, lumber, lots of goodies. Want to go with me?" Sloan asked eagerly.

"I don't think I need any lumber or tools. What I need is a table and chairs for my kitchen and maybe a couch for the living room. I was hoping you could tell me where there's a furniture store near here."

"Furniture? What do you need furniture for?" Sloan gave a frown that quickly changed to a smile of revelation. "Are you moving into the house?"

"I think so, at least temporarily. I decided why should I be paying for a motel for two more weeks when I own the house? But all I have so far is a bed. I think I found one I like at Mattress World in Springfield. I don't need a lot but a small table and a couple of chairs would be nice or I'll be eating my meals standing up."

"That's a great idea," Sloan said, obviously thrilled to hear Paris was establishing a degree of attachment for the house. "First of all, don't buy a frame for the bed. Just buy a mattress and box spring. I have a log-framed bed for you. It is double size, if that's okay. And I won't take no for an answer. For the other stuff, I wish I had some tables and chairs ready for you, but I don't. I delivered the ones I had. All my stuff is special order right now. But why not go with me to the estate sale? The auction listing in the newspaper included lots of household stuff. A four-bedroom farmhouse full. Tables, chairs, dressers, couch, dishes, lamps, appliances. You name it. You might find something you could use. The prices are usually pretty good unless they're antiques. Mom got a twenty-cubic-foot chest freezer, almost new, for sixty-five dollars at an auction in Pierce City last fall. And I found a Jenny Lind walnut headboard for my sister for eight bucks."

"Really?" Paris looked genuinely interested.

"Yeah. Auctions are fun. Great way to furnish a house. Sometimes you have to compete with the antique dealers and collectors, but they aren't usually looking for the basic household stuff."

"But I bet they don't deliver."

"They don't, but I do," Sloan replied, patting the side of her truck. "Come on. Go with me, and I'll haul it home for you." Sloan gave an encouraging look.

Paris thought it over and found no reason to refuse. Even though she had never been to a rural estate sale, the idea of finding a few pieces of furniture at a reasonable rate and Sloan volunteering to haul them seemed like a perfect solution to how she could live in Maybelline while overseeing the repairs. The idea of spending the day with Sloan seemed just as appealing.

Paris parked her BMW next to the shop and locked it. Sloan took more skeins of rope from the peg and dropped them in the truck as Paris climbed in the cab.

Sloan was dressed for an outdoor auction. She wore faded Levi's, a white T-shirt under an open bright yellow nylon vest and a pair of sneakers. Paris, however, was dressed for an outing at the mall or an afternoon luncheon in town. Her tan linen slacks had a crisp crease down the leg and an alligator belt. Her turquoise short sleeve sweater fit her figure perfectly and was smoothly tucked in the waistband of her slacks. Her sandals showed off a silver toe ring. She wore a thin gold bracelet that matched the gold chain around her neck. A pair of tiny gold hoops dangled from her earlobes.

Sloan pulled onto the highway, the rack in the back of the truck rattling as she rumbled over the cattle guard.

"So, tell me about estate sale auctions," Paris asked slipping her sunglasses tightly against the bridge of her nose. "Do we sit in a barn or something?"

"No. They put all the stuff out on flatbed trailers or in the yard. You wander around before the auction starts to see what you want to bid on. The auctioneer wears a microphone and goes from trailer to trailer, hawking the prices as his helpers hold up the items. Near the end they sell whole boxes of stuff for a dollar or two. But early on they'll milk stuff for every penny they can get. The people running this one are nice folks. Harlan and June Goodpasture. You'll recognize him. He'll be the one with the handlebar moustache and white Stetson hat. June is the bookkeeper and gives out the numbers. She also tells Harlan when he's talking too fast."

"So I need a number to bid?"

"Yes. You give them your name and address and show some I.D. They'll give you a card with your number on it. When you win something, hold up the number."

"Do I hold up the card so he'll know I want to bid on something?"

"You don't have to. Some of these dealers have a little nod or

167

twitch they use to let him know they're bidding. There's a lady from Branson, Virginia Beal, who has an antique shop that specializes in porcelain and ceramics. She goes to all these estate sales and bids like crazy on figurines and dishes. All she does to bid is wink at the auctioneer."

"You're kidding? What if he doesn't see her?" Paris asked with a chuckle.

"Virginia is hard to miss. In fact, I'll bet when we get there you'll know who she is without me telling you."

"Oh really?" Paris was skeptical.

"Yep, bet you two bits."

"What's two bits?"

"Quarter."

"Oh, big gambler." Paris smiled over at Sloan. "Okay, you're on."

"I hope you find some great stuff today."

"All I want is a couple of chairs and a little table where I can sit to eat my meals."

"Okay."

"Maybe a chair for the living room."

"Uh-huh."

"And a little end table."

Sloan nodded.

"And a lamp."

Sloan smiled to herself, glad her truck was a long bed.

By the time they pulled onto the farm road, it was already lined with cars, trucks and a few RV's. They walked the quarter mile up to the house where a large crowd was milling around the flatbed trailers of household possessions. They waited in line and secured their bidding numbers. Sloan knew it was going to be a big sale with lots of eager bidders since their numbers were two hundred sixteen and two hundred seventeen.

"We've got thirty minutes before they start so we can look around," Sloan said, leading Paris through the crowd to where the furniture was arranged in the front yard. "Why don't you look around here while I take a look at the tools and wood?" Sloan checked her watch. "Meet you in front of the concession stand in twenty-five minutes, and I'll buy you a cup of coffee."

"Okay," Paris agreed as she caught sight of a small tile-topped kitchen table. She went to work examining the furniture as Sloan headed off toward the tool shed full of rusty goodies. She was relieved most of the lookers were concentrating on the mechanical and farm tools. The small crowd around the woodworking tools seemed mostly interested in the table saw, band saw and drill press—things Sloan already had. She squatted beside a long wooden bin of old hand tools, most covered in years of rust, grease and cobwebs. She poked through the bin, occasionally pulling out a tool worthy of closer examination.

She walked through the rows of stacked lumber, sorted by condition and general type. Most were oak, probably cut and rough sawn from the farmer's acreage. A small stack of dark gray wood drew her attention. The boards were well aged, rough cut and had been painted across the ends with green paint. She knew this meant someone had wanted to protect the boards from splitting. She opened her single-blade pocket knife and shaved a sliver off the corner. She couldn't be certain without an exposed cut, but the tight grain and tiny swirled dots looked like maple, and not just any maple but bird's eye maple. This was exquisite cabinet-quality wood. Sloan mentally measured the good wood in the stack. A few boards were split slightly and one was warped beyond use but there were at least one hundred feet of lumber with distinctive character and usable dimension. She would just have to wait and see how many other woodcrafters had an eye on this stack.

She continued to check out the tools and equipment, occasionally looking across the yard where Paris was giving the household items close scrutiny. Sloan finished her perusal in the barn and headed for the concession stand. By the time she had made her way through the crowd, Paris was already in line at the beverage window.

"Over here, Sloan," she called. "Cream and sugar, right?"

"Yes. Thank you. You find anything you can use?" Sloan asked, blowing across the top of the cup.

"I think so. There's a cute tiled table and although there's no matching chairs I found three old wooden chairs I think will work."

"Good."

"Testing, testing," a man called as his microphone squealed. "Testing, one, two, three. Okay, ladies and gentlemen. Let's get started." A tall, thin middle-aged man with a white cowboy hat and a heavily waxed handlebar moustache adjusted the microphone on his headset. "Are we set? You all have your numbers out there?"

"Harlan?" Paris asked Sloan quietly.

Sloan nodded.

"Was June the lady at the table where we signed in and got the number?"

"Uh-huh." Sloan looked around then smiled discreetly. "Have you spotted Virginia Beal yet?"

Paris sipped her coffee as she scanned the crowd. No one jumped out as Virginia material. Just as she was about to say no, a woman standing at the far corner of one of the flatbed trailers turned around. Paris did a double take and choked slightly on her coffee. The woman was large. All of her features were large, from her profusely ratted tomato red hair and exaggerated bright red lipsticked-mouth to her lemon yellow pantsuit stretched tightly over her ample hips. She wore white sneakers with rolled down white anklets. Paris tried not to stare, but it was impossible not to study the enormity of the woman's physical being. She may have only been marginally overweight, but her nearly fluorescent hair and clothing combination made it seem like she was standing under a blinking light. She was talking to another woman of smaller stature, her booming voice rolling across the yard in waves. When she finished having her say, she threw her head back and laughed robustly, her large bosom bouncing over her chest. If that weren't enough to suggest she was surely a Virginia Beal candidate, her mascara-heavy lashes were the clincher.

170

"Don't tell me," Paris muttered behind her cup, trying to hide a snicker. "It can't be her."

"You owe me a quarter," Sloan whispered.

"Okay, we're ready to start over here with the appliances," Harlan announced. He stood on the back porch and pointed his carnival cane at the row of white kitchen appliances.

"First we've got a twenty-cubic-foot frost-free refrigerator. It's a ninety-six model, and it works perfectly. We've got it plugged in, and June filled the ice cube trays so it's all set to go. And what am I bid for this refrigerator? Who'll give me a hundred dollar bill to start us off?"

Several number cards went up and stayed there until he took the bid and eased it up in twenty dollar increments. As the price went up, cards went down until two bidders dueled over the last five dollars Harlan could extract from them. "Sold for one hundred eighty-five dollars to number sixty-one." He pointed to the man at the back with the card held over his head.

June followed along with a clipboard, keeping track of the item, price and the winning bidder's number. After each page of sold items was completed, the page was delivered to the accountant's table where it was transferred to the bidder's running account. In spite of the noise and confusion, the choreography of the sale moved smoothly. Harlan moved down the line of appliances, giving the pertinent information for anyone who hadn't gotten a look before the sale. A young couple won the washer and dryer. The man who bought the refrigerator also won the stove and dishwasher. The chest freezer went to a man who looked like Grizzly Adams. Sloan and Paris both assumed he was going to fill it with venison.

Paris watched the various procedures for bidding and raising. Some bidders waved their arm wildly like a child needing to be excused for the bathroom. Others used hand signals for whole bids or half increment bids. Virginia Beal had not yet performed the wink so Paris assumed she didn't need appliances. Since Malcolm had suggested she provide a refrigerator, stove and washer and dryer to help with renting the house, she didn't need them either. After noticing the prices, she wished Malcolm had thought of getting Maybelline's appliances at an estate sale like this.

"Okay, we're going to sell what's on this first trailer now. We've got some good stuff over here so wake up your husbands ladies and drag 'em on over," Harlan joked as he climbed up on the trailer and stood at the end overlooking the crowd. "We got some nice sets of dishes here, ladies. We're going to start with the set of Jadeite by Fire King."

As soon as he announced the highly collectible dishes, Virginia Beal muscled her way through the dense crowd and took a position at the corner of the trailer where she could see the entire array of merchandise. Paris and Sloan smiled at each other and moved over a few feet so they could see Virginia's face. As soon as Harlan asked for the first bid she gave a deliberate wink. When he didn't pick up on her bid quickly enough, she cleared her throat loudly and winked again.

"We've got fifty down here in the corner," he said, pointing to her finally. "And we've got sixty dollars from the man in the red hat," he added, pointing to another bidder. Virginia quickly gave another wink.

"Seventy down here," Harlan caught her bid immediately. The bidding continued between Virginia and several other bidders until she gave a final winning bid.

"Sold for two hundred and ten dollars to number fourteen. Virginia caught you all napping," Harlan said with a chuckle.

Virginia made an entry in her notebook and slid the pencil back behind her ear where it immediately became lost in her big hairdo.

Paris held up a quarter like holding a cigarette between two fingers.

"I love people who pay their debts." Sloan kissed the quarter and stuck it in her watch pocket. She leaned close and whispered in Paris's ear. "Now think back. Who does she remind you of?"

Paris furrowed her brow in deliberation.

"Um," she dug deep into her memory bank. Suddenly a bright look came over her. "Oh, yes. She was grandmother's friend from

172

church. What was her name? Calvin, Calloway." She looked at Sloan and pointed dramatically. "Annabelle Calhoun."

Sloan nodded decisively.

"Remember those God-awful swimsuits she made for us that one summer," Sloan said, frowning and shivering deliberately at the memory.

Paris wrinkled her nose and nodded.

"They were terrible. They had pleats on the skirts and were made from that hideous green and pink flowered material." Sloan smirked. "She was so proud of those things."

"They looked like something right out of the Victorian era. They covered everything from our necks to our knees." Paris laughed quietly as she remembered it.

"Your grandmother fawned over them, saying how beautiful they were." Sloan began to giggle too.

"And we both stared at them like they were the ugliest things we ever saw."

"They were so bad, Paris, *so* bad," Sloan continued, giving a deliberate shudder. "What was it I said about them?" she asked only half listening to Harlan taking bids on a pair of ugly lime green table lamps.

"You said they looked like your grandmother's wallpaper," Paris said, then laughed even louder. She quickly covered her mouth and the loud outburst with her hand, the hand that held the bidding card.

"We have twenty-four," Harlan announced, pointing to Paris. "Sold for twenty-four dollars, number two sixteen."

"No," Paris gasped, looking up at the pair of lamps she had just purchased. "Those are hideous," she added with chagrin.

"They may be, but now they're yours." Sloan laughed and applauded.

Several people joined Sloan in teasing and laughing at Paris's mistaken bid.

"Little lady, we've got a matching floor lamp if you want to open the bidding with a twenty-dollar bill," Harlan continued.

When the auction ended Sloan waited her turn then backed the truck into the yard to load their purchases. She finished securing the ropes over the load as Paris loaded the last cushion from the sofa. The pair of lime green table lamps was wedged between the cushions. Sloan's experience loading furniture had been tested to the limit to load a sofa, an end table, a kitchen table with three chairs, a small bookcase, a three-drawer dresser, two area rugs, a microwave, two lamps and a box of kitchen doodads into her pickup along with her own purchases of lumber and hand tools.

"Miss DeMont," called one of the auction workers. He was trotting across the yard carrying the lime green floor lamp. "Harlan said to give this to you. The winning bidder paid for it but decided she didn't want it." He proudly stood the lamp next to the truck and straightened the tilting shade. "It's free," he beamed then returned to his work, as if escaping before she refused to take it.

Sloan suppressed a snicker as she searched the load for a hole to slide in the gift.

"Thank you," Paris replied as he hurried away. She examined the monstrosity with a smirk. "The best thing you can say about this lamp is . . ." Paris said, then hesitated and gave the lamp shade a slight adjustment.

"What's that?" Sloan asked, making room for it.

"It matches the table lamps," Paris added, raising her eyebrows.

"A dubious honor at best," Sloan said, wedging it into the last corner available.

"Maybe I could paint them."

"Or break them."

"Now, now. Don't talk that way about my new lamp ensemble." Paris chuckled at the ugly lamps. "You never know. I may be going for a retro look."

Paris climbed in the truck and buckled her seat belt. Sloan gave the rope a snap then climbed in as well. She adjusted the rearview mirror so she could see around the big load.

"Did you have fun?" she asked, shifting through the gears as she pulled out onto the road.

"Yes." Paris rolled down her window and leaned her arm on the opening. She closed her eyes and took in a deep relaxing breath. "I had a great time. I got everything I needed." She looked over at Sloan. "And a few extras. Thank you. It was a super idea. And I got everything for less than it would cost for a couple nights at the hotel."

"Good," Sloan replied with a nod. "And I like the lamps," she teased. "Nice bidding technique. I think Virginia Beal was jealous." Sloan gave a cockeyed smile.

Paris blushed. "It was an accident." She scowled at Sloan playfully.

"I remember that look. Your grandmother would use it and tell us," Sloan furrowed her brow in a thought. "What was it she'd say? *You're being bad eggs, girls. Now stop that this instant.*"

Paris nodded happily. "We were always either bad eggs or good eggs. That's how grandmother would differentiate our action."

"Were we ever rotten eggs?" Sloan asked, thinking back.

"I don't think we were ever that bad."

"How about when we chased the pigs? No, I know when we were really rotten." Sloan narrowed her eyes in thought. "We were about ten. It had been raining all week. We had wanted to go camping, but no one would let us. So we pretended we were camping in the barn. Remember?" Sloan shook her head as the memory crystallized in her thoughts.

"Oh yes." Paris covered her face with her hands and hunched her shoulders as she too remembered the event. "That was so bad, Sloan. We were worse than rotten eggs."

"The camping wasn't bad," Sloan offered carefully.

"But building a campfire inside the barn was." Paris peeked over at Sloan through her fingers. "Can you believe we did that? It's a wonder we didn't burn down the barn."

"Did you get in big trouble over that?" Sloan asked.

"Grandmother made me go to bed without my supper, and I had to clean the kitchen floor with a sponge."

"That's all?" Sloan said with a doubtful glance. "My dad took me out to the barn and gave me such a spanking. Then my mother gave me a couple more whacks with her hairbrush." Sloan wiggled in her seat at the thought.

"You didn't tell me that." Paris looked over at her sympathetically. "I'm sorry."

"Hey, we deserved it. For months after that my dad told me every time he drove down the road and saw your grandma's barn he wanted to tan my hide all over again. For a year just seeing a box of matches made my ass hurt."

They laughed, Sloan wiggled in her seat again.

"Aw, poor baby," Paris cooed. "Did the whipping leave any marks on your poor little bottom?"

"I don't think so. But I try not to look at my ass, if I don't have to." The vision of Paris's perfect fitting slacks and the way they hung over her hips and ass flashed across Sloan's mind. She needed to wiggle in the seat again.

A strong wind buffeted the truck and its oversized load as a semi-trailer whizzed past. Sloan gripped the steering wheel tightly as several more trucks roared by in a convoy of big rigs. An SUV and a big sedan followed the line of trucks, weaving in and out, passing whenever a few feet became available. "There's an accident just waiting to happen," Sloan muttered.

"No kidding," Paris added. "They're driving like New Yorkers."

"Please don't tell me you drive like that, Paris." Sloan gave her a parental frown. "I don't want to have to worry about you in that little sports car."

"Not me," she quickly stated. "But in New York if you leave a few feet of space between you and the car in front of you, someone will change lanes and cut you off."

Sloan backed the truck up to Paris's front porch. It didn't take them long to unload and arrange the furniture from the estate sale. The full truckload didn't make much of a dent in the wide open spaces of the big house, but at least Paris had a place to sit and a place to eat. When Paris leaned over to move the end table next to the couch, the gold chain around her neck fell forward and out of her shirt, a watch face dangling from it. It had once been a wrist-watch but the prongs that held the pin for the watchband were missing from one side and bent on the other. A gold jump ring had been added to suspend it from the gold necklace. She grabbed it with her free hand and dropped it back inside her shirt, pressing it against her chest while she adjusted the table.

"Okay, I have to ask," Sloan said, noticing Paris's maneuver to protect the contents of the chain. "What's with the two watches? Isn't one enough?"

"What two watches?" Paris asked with genuine innocence.

Sloan pointed to her wrist then to the chain around her neck.

"Oh," Paris replied with a shy smile, patting her chest softly. "This isn't really a watch. It doesn't work anymore."

"Can I see it?" Sloan asked curiously.

"It's just an old wristwatch," Paris replied with reservation.

Sloan studied Paris's face as she carefully pulled the chain out of her shirt. The case was thin and hexagonally shaped. The crystal had a jagged crack across the middle and the stem was missing. The hands were stopped and mashed at ten twenty-nine. Sloan squinted at the inscription on the back, rubbing her thumb over the part that was practically unreadable.

"Looks like your name, but it is hard to read," Sloan said.

Paris nodded.

"Ten twenty-nine, huh?" Sloan said, looking at the face.

"Yes. It was Gabby's." Paris pulled away and dropped it back inside her shirt.

Sloan noticed the distant and hollow look in Paris's eyes when she mentioned Gabby's name.

"So Gabriella was a paramedic?" Sloan asked carefully.

"Yes, with the New York City Fire Department."

"Wow! That sounds exciting."

"She loved it. She was very good at it, too."

"Tell me what she looked like," Sloan said softly, not wanting to rush it.

"She was tall. She had the biggest brown eyes you ever saw. Her hair was thick and brown. It was short in the front and long in the back, but she usually wore it in a ponytail. She had gorgeous skin and a laugh that turned heads. She was a bundle of energy." Paris sighed and smiled to herself. "She was just Gabby."

"She sounds wonderful," Sloan offered, watching Paris's eyes light up as she spoke about her.

"She was. But she wasn't perfect. She had a temper. I saw her about tear a guy's head off once."

"Damn! Why?" Sloan asked with a furrowed brow.

"He was in line ahead of us at the grocery store with his little boy who was about three or so. Real cute little towheaded kid with big blue eyes and eyelashes to die for. He was playing peek-a-boo with Gabby around his daddy's leg. She loved little kids. She had a way about her that attracted them. Anyway, when the line moved, the guy pushed his basket forward and the little boy tripped over the wheel and fell down. He wasn't seriously injured but it hurt, I'm sure. He bumped his head and whacked his elbow. He started to cry. His father laughed at him and called him clumsy. That was bad enough, but when he kept crying and rubbing his head the son-of-a-bitch slapped him right across the face. He told the little boy to suck it up and act like a man. That made him cry all the more. When he told the boy to shut up, he was giving him a headache I thought Gabby was going to drop the guy right where he stood. She worked out to stay in shape for her job so she was a strong woman. She gave him this vicious look and called him some names even I've never used before. He pointed his finger right in Gabby's face and told her to keep her nose out of his business or he'd give her some of the same. Then he gave her a shove." Paris shook her head and laughed. "That was exactly the wrong thing to say and do to Gabby. She kneed him in the crotch and pushed him into the magazine rack. Then she flashed her badge, which looks like a police badge, and threatened to arrest the guy for child abuse."

"What happened next?" Sloan asked, following Paris out onto the porch.

"The store security caught it all on video and had already called the cops. Turned out he had a warrant out for his arrest for domestic violence. He was also on parole for assault."

"So he had it coming. Gabby did the right thing."

"Yes, but she almost got suspended for attacking him like that. The fire department takes a dim view of kneeing people in the crotch in a grocery store."

"Hey, I'd have done the same thing, I think."

"Gabby was always trying to save someone. It was second nature to her."

"Like a knight in shining armor riding in on a white horse?"

"Yes, something like that," Paris said with reflection.

"Okay. Here's the million dollar question," Sloan announced with a lighthearted wink. She felt the need for some humor.

"What's that?" Paris asked.

A grin slowly pulled across Sloan's face.

"Gabby may have been all those wonderful things, but was she a good lover?"

Paris laughed out loud and looked away, a blush shooting up over her face. When she looked back there was a twinkle in her eyes.

"Yes, she was," Paris said softly.

"Sounds like I have some big shoes to fill," Sloan replied, stroking Paris's face tenderly. She gathered Paris into her arms and kissed her. It was a long kiss, one filled with all the devotion and reassurance Sloan could convey. It was also one full of serenity and contentment for Paris.

"Look!" Sloan exclaimed, pointing upward. "A shooting star! Quick, make a wish."

Paris closed her eyes. She tried to make a wish, but the torment of her choices was stronger than her will to decide. She wanted to wish for happiness and a life with Sloan, but the practical professional in her resisted. She wanted to also wish for guidance on what to do with Maybelline and the farm, but her grandmother's voice echoed through her mind, making an objective decision impossible.

Sloan's wish came from deep inside her soul. It was immediate and absolute. All she wanted, all she ever wished for was Paris back in her life. It had been her one and only wish since their last plaintive meeting as children. Her wish had come true. The question of how long was the uncertainty she wanted to ignore.

"I made mine," Sloan declared.

"Me, too," Paris replied, having spent her wish on general happiness and good health for everyone she knew.

Paris wrapped her arms around Sloan and held on tight. The turmoil of what to do about their relationship was growing by the second.

Sloan took Paris back to her house to collect her car.

"Want to come in? I'll make you some dinner," Sloan suggested as she pulled into the driveway. "We can watch some television, or take a walk in the meadow. Anything you want, sweetheart."

"I'd love to, but it is late, and I'd fall asleep before you even got dinner made," Paris replied, her eyes heavy. "I think I'll go home and melt into a hot bath."

Sloan followed Paris to her car and held the door for her. She leaned in and kissed her.

"Drive carefully, sweetheart," she declared.

"You, too. And thank you for inviting me to the estate sale. I had a wonderful time."

"You did all right, for a city girl," she added with a grin then kissed her again. "Goodnight."

Paris waved out the window as she pulled away.

CHAPTER 19

Within two days and with Sloan's help, Paris found a carpenter to complete the repairs to Maybelline. She was pleasantly surprised to find they weren't as severe as Malcolm had claimed. Replacing the cut timbers, correctly wiring the new light fixtures and repairing the plumbing leaks seemed to be the major items. At last Maybelline was coming together as Paris had hoped.

Paris picked out the light fixtures from McKinley's Hardware store then stopped at the gas station. She finished filling her tank and replaced the handle onto the gas pump. As she waited for the machine to print out her receipt she noticed a gray-haired man in an SUV watching her intently. It was hard to ignore his persistent stare. Against her better New York judgment, she offered a small smile and a nod in his direction. He touched his ball cap and returned her smile.

"You Paris DeMont?" he asked just as she was about to climb in her car.

"Yes."

"Doctor DeMont?"

"Yes," she answered reticently.

"I'm Seth Cameron, Doctor Seth Cameron," he offered.

"Oh, hello Doctor Cameron," Paris replied, recognizing his name.

"Call me Seth. You were in my office with Sloan and the twins the other day, right?"

"Yes. Poor little girls had to get shots."

He laughed. "I hear Sloan finally got her tetanus booster, too."

"Yes, she did. I think the twins were braver about it than she was." Paris chuckled.

"I've been chasing her to get that thing for three years. Congratulations on talking her into it. You must be a pretty good doctor."

Paris blushed at his compliment.

"Thank you, but I think she knew she was cornered and had no choice," Paris replied.

"I hear you're a cardiologist back in New York City. That must be hectic."

"It keeps me busy. I imagine your practice here in Banyon keeps you busy, too."

"Hell, yes. Too busy sometimes. I'm getting too old for this. I'd rather be hunting or fishing. I've been treating folks in these parts for over thirty years."

"Wow! Thirty years," Paris said in amazement. "You don't look that old, Seth."

He gave a gruff laugh and took off his cap to show his balding head and nearly white hair.

"The hell I don't. But thank you for saying so, Doctor DeMont. I'll tell my wife she's wrong. I don't look eighty. But I think she tells me that so I'll hurry up and retire. She wants to take a vacation to Europe for a month or some such time." He shook his head and grimaced as if the idea was cutting him right down to the bone.

"There's some very beautiful scenery in Europe. You could go fishing in Scotland or go hunting in the Black Forest."

182

"You sound like a travel agent."

"I've been to Europe a couple of times," she confessed.

"So how do you like Banyon? Pretty dull, huh?" he asked.

"No. Banyon isn't dull. It's quiet. The people are very friendly."

"Aren't people in New York friendly."

"It's just different. Everyone is busy."

"How long are you going to be in town?"

"Just another week."

"Too bad. Ever thought about family practice?"

The question caught Paris off guard. She gave a nervous laugh, knowing full well what he was leading up to.

"I never gave it much thought. Family practice doctors in New York are way overworked and underpaid."

"That's the way it is everywhere. But I can't complain. I've done okay. I can refer my patients to specialists in Springfield or Joplin so I've got good coverage. I even have a pretty fair number of heart patients I have to send off to cardiologists. Now someone like you would have an advantage in family practice. You would be able to treat a lot of those patients yourself. Bet you'd save some lives." He spoke encouragingly, a convincing twinkle in his eye. "Yep. Bet you'd make a damn good country doctor. Damn good." He smiled slowly, realizing he had Paris's attention. "Cardiologist doing family practice. Right smart idea, if I do say so myself."

Paris didn't want to be impolite and tell him her practice in Manhattan was plenty satisfying for her.

"You might want to give it some thought Doctor DeMont. I've heard some good things about you. Seems like you have a fan club around Banyon, especially with the McKinleys."

As much as her conscious mind told her Seth's idea was completely out of the question, her subconscious was drinking in every word.

"Timing would be pretty good, too," he added, starting his engine. "I'll be around for a few months before I hang up my stethoscope and take up full-time fishing. Come on by if you want to talk about it. I've got a turnkey operation and a fair price for the right person." He nodded and waved a salute before slowly pulling out. He had a mischievous smile on his face, seeing he had raised Paris's interest.

She stood watching until he was well down the street.

"Don't even consider it, Doctor DeMont," she muttered to herself. "Don't even." She climbed in her car and started the engine. She sat staring out the window, unable to ignore Seth's offer or the seed he had planted in her mind. A sign hanging outside the clinic in Banyon that read *Doctor Paris E. DeMont, Cardiology and Family Practice* flashed across her mind. "Forget it. Just forget it," she ordered herself and pulled out on the street.

She headed out of town, mulling over what Seth had said in spite of her attempt to put it out of her mind.

The next day Sloan came over bright and early. She insisted on doing some window caulking in the attic for Paris. The small round Victorian windows were hard to reach and didn't open but were desperately in need of caulk to stop the leaking onto the attic floor. Paris wanted to help, but Sloan wouldn't hear of it.

"If you won't let me help I'm going to town to get groceries so I can make us a super special dinner," Paris said, sticking her head through the opening to the attic. "Do you need anything, babe?"

"Nope," Sloan replied. She was crouching in the far corner of the attic running a bead of caulk around one of the windows. "I'm fine."

It was a hot sweaty job.

"Are you sure you don't need me to stay and help you?" Paris asked, concerned over the rising heat and cramped quarters. "I still think you should let the carpenter do that. There are too many windows, and it is sweltering up here."

"No. I've got this under control. Besides, you promised to cook dinner for me, woman." She grinned over at Paris. "So go. Shop. Cook."

"Do you like red wine or white wine?"

"Are you trying to get me drunk so you can have your way with me?" Sloan teased, giving her a wink.

184

"You never know," Paris replied with a long gaze.

"Get both then." Sloan had a twinkle in her eye.

"Be back shortly." Paris ducked down out of sight.

"Hey sweetheart," Sloan called.

Paris's head popped back up.

"Yes?"

Sloan crawled over and gave her a kiss.

"Nothing. I just wanted to do that." She stroked Paris's cheek. "We need to talk you know."

"I know," Paris replied, knowing Sloan meant they needed to talk about her returning to New York and when they would see each other again.

Sloan crawled back into the corner and continued caulking.

Paris went to the grocery store and liquor store, carefully selecting all the elements for a perfect dinner. She planned their quiet evening to include candlelight, wine, the best steaks Banyon, Missouri had to offer and most of all, Sloan's bright face across the table from her. It was such a captivating image she nearly missed the turn off the highway. The thought of Sloan's soft eyes brought a smile to Paris's face. The thought of Sloan's body against her all through the night made her sigh. But Sloan was right, they needed to talk. How would they find time together? What would Paris do with Maybelline? The closer she and Sloan became, the greater the miles between Missouri and New York seemed. How could she possibly say good-bye to her next week? She headed home from town, her mind busy with thoughts of Sloan. The memory of their last good-bye when they were fourteen flashed across her mind like a painfully cold wind, floating around her and stinging her soul.

It was a chilly late winter afternoon. Marcus and Liz DeMont were busy inside Grandmother's house, sorting and packing. Paris went out the back door and across the yard to the fence. The house that held so many warm memories had gone cold for her. She didn't want to help her parents sift through Grandmother's personal possessions. She didn't want to drape sheets over the furniture. It seemed too final, too heartless. Surely Grandmother would get better and come home soon. A stroke and broken hip couldn't be as bad as they said. Grandmother couldn't be helpless and bedridden. She had to be back home by summer. How was Paris going to come and stay with her like she always did if she was in a nursing home? Paris kicked a stone in disgust. Why did Grandmother have to go and fall like that? Why did she have to spoil the routine Paris had grown to count on every summer? When would she ever see Sloan again?

Paris closed the pasture gate behind her and headed for the pond. She stood on the bridge, tossing pebbles into the water. She could hear the faint sounds of a car pulling into the drive. It must be another well-wisher coming by to give out hugs and hear the story of how Grandmother had fallen off her stepstool while cleaning the top of the refrigerator and was now confined to a bed at Valley Vista Nursing Home in Aurora. Paris could retell the story in her sleep. She had heard all the sympathetic replies and all the medical jargon, even if she didn't understand it. She wished everyone would just go away and stop talking about it. Grandmother was going to be all right. She had to. Paris threw the rest of her pebbles into the water in frustration.

"Hey Paris," Sloan called from the top of the hill. She waved at Paris then ran down the slope and onto the bridge. During the six months since they had last seen each other both girls had grown. Paris was stretching out with long legs and willowy arms. Her hair was still blond and long, but her figure was changing. The nubbins she and Sloan had teased each other about were growing into well-defined breasts.

Sloan was growing taller as well, though more gangly. Her hair was beginning to darken from bright crimson red to a softer auburn. Her figure was growing, but her athletic physique hid her growing bustline.

"Hi," Paris replied, equally happy to see her. She gave Sloan a hug, surprised at how tightly Sloan held her, something she hadn't done in the past.

"I heard you were back," Sloan said cautiously, as if testing Paris's emotional status over what had happened to her grandmother. "I'm sorry about Grandma West," she added quietly.

Paris shrugged and lowered her eyes, feeling a lump rise in her throat.

"Are you and your parents moving into the house?" she asked, her voice full of hope.

"No," Paris answered dejectedly. "They are getting some of her stuff to take to the nursing home. She wanted her own quilt and a table to have by the bed. I told Daddy to take her rocking chair. She liked sitting in it. But he said she can't get out of bed by herself. I think he should take it anyway," she added under her breath.

"When will she get to come home?"

"I don't know. I heard Mom tell someone on the phone she had a stroke, and she is paralyzed on her whole left side. They think the stroke made her fall off the stool."

"What the heck is a stroke?" Sloan asked.

"I'm not sure. Something like a heart attack, I think. But I think it is in her head. Daddy said something about a rupture in her brain." Paris stared out across the pond, narrowing her eyes as tears began to fill them.

Sloan noticed how difficult it was for Paris to talk about and didn't ask anymore questions.

"I won't get to come to Banyon this summer," Paris said after a long silence. She looked at Sloan for a response.

It was obvious Sloan had already contemplated that idea as disappointment flooded her face. She swallowed hard but didn't reply. They looked at one another for a long moment then both turned to stare out over the water.

Sloan heaved a deep sigh and walked onto the island, as if the realization of Paris's news was more than she wanted to accept. Paris followed, equally sad over the news.

Sloan stood silently braiding and unbraiding some branches of the willow. Paris sat against the trunk and watched, deep in thought.

"I sure wish you were coming back this summer," Sloan said finally, disappointment still etched on her face.

"Me, too."

"I wish your grandma didn't have a stupid old stroke." Sloan looked up, seemingly aware that sounded selfish and cruel. "I like your grandma. She's okay, for an old person."

Sloan sat down next to Paris and joined her in plucking off blades of grass.

"Do you think we'll ever get to spend a summer together again?" Sloan asked.

Paris shrugged her shoulders. "I don't know. I'm going to miss you."

Sloan looked deep into Paris's eyes, trying to communicate her feelings and stop the tears that threatened to fill her eyes. The realization that this might be their last time together for a long time was like a knife plunging deep into Sloan's stomach. The color drained from her face, and she fought back the urge to cry.

"I'm really going to miss you, too. Really," Sloan replied.

For whatever reason, the deep sense of separation, the finality of this visit, or Paris's soft and vulnerable eyes, Sloan couldn't help herself. She leaned over and kissed Paris on the mouth. It was awkward, brief and a little off-center, but it was as complete an explanation of her feeling as she could manage. She pulled away as if shocked by her own actions. She studied Paris to see if she had made a colossal mistake, but Paris's eyes told her it was okay.

"Why did you do that?" Paris asked softly, touching her own lips.

" 'Cause," Sloan replied. She looked down, then back at Paris. "Was it okay?"

"Yes," Paris said as a blush pinked her cheeks.

"Can I do it again? That one wasn't very good," Sloan stated with eager eyes.

Paris nodded shyly and turned her head to receive another one. Sloan leaned over and kissed her again. This one was on target. And to both their relief, it was longer as well, even though it was tight-lipped and dry. For these fourteen-year-olds it was wonderful and perfect.

They sat stiffly, pressing their lips together without touching any other part of their bodies. Paris opened her eyes to find Sloan's eyes staring back at her. She pulled away and scowled at Sloan.

"You're supposed to close your eyes, silly," she admonished.

"I was."

"No, you weren't. You were looking at me."

"How did you know? You didn't have your eyes closed either."

"I just opened them for a second," Paris argued.

"So did I," Sloan replied, trying to redeem her honor.

"Don't press so hard. It makes my lips hurt," Paris said quietly.

"Okay," Sloan replied, ready to try again.

This time Paris tilted her head, closed her eyes, and pursed her lips, waiting for the next kiss. Sloan obliged, this time using soft pressure. They both immediately felt the wisdom of a soft touch. Sloan placed her hand on Paris's shoulder and leaned closer, suddenly wanting to be against Paris's body. It was as if the kiss had opened secrets neither of them had imagined. They both felt the confusing emotions rising from deep inside their young womanhood.

Sloan leaned away and released her hold on Paris's shoulder. They looked at one another cautiously, trying to understand their own feelings.

"I love you, Paris," Sloan said softly, then looked away as if she wasn't sure how Paris would receive the announcement.

Paris touched Sloan on the hand and waited for her to look back at her. Before she could reply, a car horn tooted out a beckoning call to Sloan. She jumped to her feet, seemingly relieved at the interruption.

"I have to go," she said starting for the bridge. She stopped and looked back with wide eyes. "I forgot. I have a present for you." Sloan dug in her jeans pocket and pulled out her new pocket knife, the one she had used to carve their initials on the tree. She held it out to Paris.

"That's your new one. The one you got for your birthday," Paris said in amazement. She stood up and studied the knife without touching it. "You shouldn't give away a birthday present."

"It's mine, isn't it," Sloan replied with a shrug. "I can do anything I want with it. Besides, I don't need it. I have my old one. It works okay."

"I don't know," Paris said with a measure of caution.

"Don't you want it?"

"Yeah," Paris quickly answered. "You won't get in trouble will you?"

"No," Sloan replied proudly. "They won't care." She shoved the knife into Paris's hand.

Paris closed her hand tightly around the knife and swallowed hard. "Thanks." Paris smiled warmly then gave Sloan a quick kiss on the cheek.

"Be careful when you use it. It's real sharp," Sloan admonished as she touched her cheek where Paris had kissed her.

"I will. I promise." Paris crossed her heart and held up her hand to seal the promise.

The car honked again followed by the faint sound of Sloan's mother calling her name. Sloan started across the narrow bridge with Paris following along behind. Sloan stopped at the end of the bridge and looked back at Paris.

"Don't come," she said her eyes reddening. "Stay here, Paris."

"Why?" Paris pleaded.

Sloan walked back to her and looked deeply into her eyes.

"Because I want to remember you here by our tree." She pointed to the spot where they had sat beneath the willow and kissed.

Paris looked over at the place they shared, the grass still matted from their bodies.

"Okay," she said quietly. "Will you write to me, Sloan?"

"Sure," she replied stoically.

"Come on, Sloan," Shirley called from the gate. "It's time to go."

"Coming," Sloan yelled. She smiled at Paris then turned and ran up the hill as fast as her legs would carry her. She closed the gate and headed for the car, never looking back for fear Paris would see her tears.

Paris smiled at the childhood memory. She didn't remember ever feeling so close to Sloan as she was that moment.

CHAPTER 20

Paris rolled down the car windows and allowed the fresh warm breeze to stir her hair. She drew in a deep breath. The scent of recently cut clover thrilled her senses. She slowed to a crawl and checked to make sure no one was following her then leaned her head as far out the window as she could reach. Like a dog sniffing the wind, she drove along with the wind blowing her hair and whistling around her sunglasses. A broad smile panned her face. There was nothing in New York to compare with how completely contented she felt.

Paris had just rounded the corner by the creek bridge when the screeching sounds of sirens in the distance caught her attention. The sounds grew louder and soon the flashing lights were in her rearview mirror. She pulled to the side of the road to allow the sheriff's car, fire trucks and a parade of vehicles roar past.

"Somebody's got trouble," she said to herself as the last pickup truck with a portable emergency light on the roof sped around the curve and out of sight.

Paris pulled back onto the road and continued around the lazy curves and rolling hills. As she crested the long hill that overlooked the valley that held Maybelline, she could see billows of angry black smoke filtering up above the thickly treed expanse.

Her hands froze on the steering wheel as she slammed on her brakes, skidding to a stop. She couldn't see the house from this distance, but she knew the smoke was on her property, it had to be. She also knew it wasn't a grass or wood fire. That would be gray smoke. This was black, inky black. Gabby had explained in great detail how black smoke meant a petrochemical fire—plastics, synthetics, furniture, carpeting and paint—a house fire.

"Oh, God!" Paris could hardly speak. She ripped the sunglasses from her face and stared motionless at the growing black smoke. She mashed down on the accelerator and careened around the curves toward home.

"It has to be the barn. God, make it the barn. Not the house. It has to be the barn." By repeating it, her mind hoped to will it so. "Make it the barn." The thought of Sloan working in the attic grated through her. Fires go up. The attic is on the top floor. Fires work their way right up through the attic. Just like 9/11. Just like the World Trade Center. The fire goes upward.

"Make it the barn. No one is in the barn. I don't need the barn. I can live without that old thing." Paris was making elaborate deals with God, trying to trade Sloan's safety for the barn. She pictured the barn totally consumed by fire and collapsing into a pile of smoldering ashes while the firemen and Sloan stood safely by, watching. She mentally framed that thought and concentrated on it as she rounded the last curve and sped up the lane toward her property. But as she turned in her drive, her image melted into desperation as she saw the flames and smoke shooting from the second story windows of the house.

A volunteer fireman quickly waved her to a stop and motioned her away from the fire trucks and working crews. Paris screeched to a stop next to Sloan's ATV and flew out of the car.

"This is my house," she screamed as she raced past him.

"Please, miss. Stay back," the young man warned as he followed her. "Is there anyone home? Anybody inside?"

"Yes. Sloan McKinley. She's working in the attic." Paris's mind was spinning as her fears grew. "At the front. Near that window." Paris pointed to the small gabled window high above the front porch.

The firemen had stretched their hoses all around the house and were training a stream of water into the upper windows. The man relayed Paris's news to the captain in the white helmet. Two pairs of firemen had already donned air tanks and were ready to make their way inside. One team pushed their way in the front door allowing smoke to billow out onto the porch. The other team entered the back door that was standing open, where small puffs of smoke belched out as well. The chief was on the radio relating the incident status to the dispatcher.

"We've got a three-story wood frame structure fully involved, flames showing on the second floor. I repeat we have a three-story working structure fire."

One of the firemen, a woman with a steeled expression, carried a clipboard and kept track of who was inside and who was outside the house. Within two minutes three more fire trucks arrived. Paris had overheard enough of Gabby's slang to understand the house was completely involved. She also knew the firemen were having trouble getting up the stairs. The flames and thick smoke were beating them back.

"Get back, miss," the captain yelled to Paris as she paced back and forth in front of the porch, staring up at the top floor and the tiny attic window.

With a crack, the glass suddenly blew out, and flames shot out like golden daggers. The captain grabbed Paris's arm and pulled her out of the way as the shards of broken glass floated to the ground.

"You have to get up there. Sloan is in the attic way back in the

193

corner. She's caulking the windows." Paris spoke frantically, her eyes wide with desperation. "You need to send someone up there to get her out. She won't be able to see with all that smoke."

"We're trying to get up there, miss," the captain said plaintively. "Why don't you move back over there by the barn. We don't want you to get hurt."

"No, I'm all right," Paris said, her eyes hollow and pained.

"I can see someone moving around in there, Captain," a man yelled from atop the truck-mounted ladder where he was aiming a water-cannon down into an upper floor window.

His announcement brought all free hands to that side of the house where several streams of water were concentrated on the corner window. The force of the water quickly broke in the remaining pieces of glass and began a hissing steam rising from the opening.

The captain talked to his crews inside the house on walkie-talkies but frowned at the news that the stairwell was fully ablaze. A team of firemen came out onto the porch, surrounded by the billowing angry smoke. One of the firemen retrieved an infrared camera from the cab of the fire truck. Paris knew that meant they couldn't see their hand in front of their face and would rely on the camera to detect Sloan's location. They pointed and gave an update to the captain then returned inside. Just after they disappeared through the smoke, a thunderous crash shook the house followed by a shower of sparks that shot out the front bedroom window. He immediately called to his inside teams for a status report.

"The attic floor has fallen through," reported a garbled voice over the walkie talkie.

"Can you see anyone near the front corner room?"

"We can't see shit. And there's too much fire to use the infrared camera."

"Can you get past the stairs?"

"No. The stairs are cut off. Top two steps are gone and the rest of them are going to collapse any minute."

"Come on out. I don't want anyone hurt when that ceiling goes. Both teams, out now." The captain glanced over at Paris as he released the key to his walkie-talkie.

"I'm sorry, miss," he said with deep regret.

Paris stared back in disbelief, the reality of his words slapping her across the face. It couldn't be happening to her again. It couldn't.

"We'll try from the outside," he added.

A ladder was placed against the side of the house, but the fragile heat-damaged siding soon gave way and crumbled under the weight of the ascending fireman. He quickly slid down and stepped clear as the extension ladder fell through the side of the house and into the flames. The hole in the side only added to the intense black smoke filling the driveway and yard. Those without air tanks and respirators were forced back as the heat and choking smoke were swirled by the wind. The house seemed to glow as the flames licked at every corner, popping and crackling as the contents succumbed to the power and anger of the fire. The flames extended high above the surrounding trees tops, blackening everything they touched.

Paris stared helplessly as the firefighters did battle with the relentlessly growing fire. But she had not given up hope. Sloan had to have found an air pocket, a safe corner somewhere inside. She had to. She couldn't have been trapped by the thick smoke and intense heat. She couldn't have. Paris couldn't allow herself to admit she had lost another person to a vicious holocaust. The shock of it was too much for her to accept. The pain of losing Sloan to a fire was more than even the most hardened professional could bear. As the sections of the house collapsed onto themselves, sending sparks and flames skyward, Paris felt her knees weaken and the blood drain from her head. The pit of her stomach began to churn, her breakfast announcing itself in spasms and grinding cramps. She bent over, grabbing her knees, expecting her stomach to purge itself at any moment. The firemen trained all their water pressure on the remaining front corner of the second floor, desperately trying to knock down the flames and find any survivors still alive, as unlikely as that had become.

As the roof over the front porch fell into the yard, Paris felt her stomach rise. She looked away, trying to swallow back and resist the need to vomit. Out of the corner of her eye she caught the distant figure of someone on a dead run across the pasture, past the pond and up toward the house. Paris gasped and dropped to her knees, her hands clutching at her stomach. It was Sloan on an all-out run toward her, panic etched across her face. Paris began to cry and smile at the same moment, relief so deep that her mind could not focus. She held her stomach and cried, rocking back and forth on her knees, afraid to look up. Afraid it was a mirage.

Sloan raced to Paris's side, pulled her to her feet and held her in her arms. Paris hid her face in Sloan's sweaty shirt, her sobs deep and soulful. Sloan was so out of breath from the run across the field, she could not speak. She held Paris tightly, allowing her tears to flow.

Finally Paris looked up and stroked Sloan's face, needing to touch her to fully accept that she was truly there and safe. She grinned with a childish exuberance so wide it squeezed the last tears from her eyes and sent them racing down the wet trails on her cheeks. She then threw her arms around Sloan's neck and hugged her so tight she could hear her gasp for air.

"Are you all right?" Sloan asked, finally catching her breath.

"Yes. Are you?" Paris whispered, her voice weak from panic. "They said they saw someone inside."

"I'm fine. What happened?"

"I don't know. The fire department was already here when I got home." Paris looked over at the house and tears again began to fall. "Thank God you are all right."

"I left right after you did. Dad called me on your cell phone and told me one of my customers was in town to pick up a table. I was on my way back across the pasture when I saw the smoke."

"But your four-wheeler is still here," Paris exclaimed, pointing to where it was parked next to the barn.

"It was a nice day so I walked across the pasture." Sloan stopped suddenly and turned toward the house, her eyes wide. "Barney," she gasped. "Barney was out here in the yard when I left. Where is he? He didn't follow me home."

"I haven't seen him. But I haven't been looking for him," Paris replied. Then her eyes widened as she put two and two together. "Oh, no! It couldn't be."

"Was the back door open? He can push a door open if it isn't closed tight," Sloan said through her fear.

"Yes, I think so. The firemen didn't break it down like they did the front."

The hissing steam and whitening smoke marked the turning point for the firefighters. It took several hours, but finally the flames had subsided, leaving a pile of remains barely recognizable as a house. Paris and Sloan stood under a tree with an arm around each other watching as the last flickers were extinguished and squirts of water cooled the fallen timbers. One of the firemen had hooked a blackened metal box with his pole and pulled it from the smoldering ashes.

"Hey, captain," he called. "You ought to come see this."

The captain and the sheriff examined the partially melted electrical box.

Sloan looked over the captain's shoulder as he pried open the door with his pocket knife. The metal was too hot to touch, but the blackened fan-shaped patterns radiating from the breaker panel were clear evidence that this was an electrical fire. The captain pointed to the culprit and gave an accusatory whistle. He looked up at Paris and shook his head.

"This is most likely where it started. Right here in the breaker box," he said. "Looks like one of those cheap pieces of crap they sell over at that railroad salvage place in Aurora. UL bare minimum, nothing more."

"It didn't start upstairs?" Paris asked, remembering the flames she had seen shooting from the bedroom windows when she drove in.

"I'd say it started here and moved up the wall to the second floor. You probably had more flammable material in the bed-rooms—linens, mattress, clothing and that gave it all the fuel it needed. These old frame houses are like a box of matches, just waiting for a spark to set them off. I'm sorry, miss. We didn't stand much of a chance."

"I know you did your best. I appreciate it," Paris said, swallowing a lump in her throat.

"At least no one was inside," he continued. "Glad you're okay Sloan." He gave a relieved laugh. "I'd hate to have to tell your folks we lost one of their youngins."

"Thanks, Bill. But I think we might have lost someone after all."

Bill stood up and gave her a frantic glare.

"Who?" he snapped.

"Barney."

"That old pony of yours?"

"Yeah." Sloan's face melted at the thought. "You know how he loved to go inside an open door."

"Captain?" A female firefighter called from near the front porch. "Got something."

The group who had been examining the electrical box moved to the front yard and the spot where the woman was pointing. She had a grimaced look on her face.

"Got a crispy one over here," she said before noticing Paris and Sloan following along. She immediately frowned, realizing her insensitivity.

"What you got, Rene?" The captain drew a gasp as he looked where she was pointing. "Son of a bitch." He looked back at Sloan. "Looks like good ol' Barney." He took off his helmet and wiped his forehead.

Sloan took a deep breath and flinched at the sight. Barney's body was partially hidden by a charred section of the fallen stair-case. His eyes were open, his legs stiff, his tail and mane had been singed to the skin.

"Looks like smoke got him, Sloan. That's what kills most people in a house. Smoke. Not the fire."

"Oh, Sloan," Paris gasped, tears once again filling her eyes. "Poor Barney." Her hands clasped over her mouth.

Sloan didn't speak as the muscles in her cheek rippled. One tear welled in her eye then spilled out and ran down her cheek.

"Let's cover him up, Rene," the captain said quietly as Sloan and Paris moved away.

"Are you all right?" Paris asked, walking beside Sloan and linking her arm through hers.

Sloan walked along, her eyes lowered, her face pale and pained.

"I'm so very sorry, sweetheart," Paris added. "Barney was so gentle and loving. All he wanted was to be near people and be loved."

"The whole family will miss him. He was everyone's pet." Sloan looked out across the pasture, as if remembering the last carefree trot that he had taken. "I left half a donut on the kitchen counter. I bet he smelled it and—"

"This was *not* your fault Sloan. Not Barney, not the fire," Paris quickly interrupted. "It was just one of those things. I'm insured." Paris gripped Sloan's arm tightly and shook it. "You remember that. It's not your fault. I'm just glad it wasn't you lying under that staircase. That may sound heartless, but it is deep down true."

Sloan looked over at Paris and smiled softly.

"And I'm glad you are safe, too. You have no idea what kind of torture I was going through as I ran across that field, seeing the house in flames and not knowing where you were. I was about crazy with fear by the time I saw you standing there. When you went down on your knees I thought you were hurt. I almost lost my mind. Nothing, not one thing in the whole world, is as important to me as you are, Paris. You remember that." Sloan pulled her close. "Nothing," she whispered. "Nothing."

Sloan's strong arms held Paris tightly as if shielding her from any danger or fear. Paris remained safely in Sloan's warm embrace, content to block out the horror of the fire and its aftermath.

The firemen finished hosing down the last smoldering embers and collected their equipment. The fire marshal sifted through the ashes and worked on his report. Barney was pulled from the debris, wrapped in a plastic tarp and loaded in a pickup to be delivered to Sloan's parent's farm for burial. Sloan called Charlie and gave him the grim news. Within a few hours the news of the fire had spread across Banyon and Paris had dozens of offers for everything from clothing and furniture to free meals and accommodation. She was gripped with a mix of emotions that took her from fear to relief and back again.

Paris's insurance agent, Janet Dawson, a stocky woman in her fifties, arrived and began taking pictures of the damage. She talked with the firemen about the possible cause of the fire. She also interviewed the passing farmer who had first noticed the smoke and called the fire department.

"Do you need a place to stay tonight, Paris?" Janet asked as she made notes in a folder. "I can have a room reserved for you at the Best Western."

"She's staying with me," Sloan offered.

Paris gave a weak smile and nodded in agreement, tears still occasionally filling her eyes and spilling out.

"I'm so sorry about all this, Paris. It's a real shame this had to happen when you were restoring it." Janet looked at her sympathetically.

"Thank you," Paris replied, staring blankly at the blackened rubble. She sat down on the bumper of her car and allowed the breeze to stir her hair. Her face was pale and expressionless. The house and its contents seemed almost meaningless to her, coldly insignificant. The memories of her childhood had not been damaged and the possessions she had placed inside were few and minor. She realized the house had changed over the years from Grandmother's warm home and sanctuary to an aging rundown house. Rebuilding it seemed like a fruitless task, and she didn't understand why she had taken it on. Sitting there in the waning hours of a summer day she felt empty and abandoned. It was the same feelings that had washed over her after Gabby's memorial service when she opened the mailbox to find Gabby's mail. She looked over at Sloan poking through the ashes. A shiver shot up her back and made her shudder.

"It will be all right, Paris," Janet said reassuringly as she noticed the tears welling up in Paris's eyes. "You will be able to rebuild. You have great coverage. You'll end up with a wonderful new home with modern amenities and just the way you want it. Don't cry. We'll get you fixed up like nothing happened."

Paris stared at Janet silently. This woman couldn't possibly understand how much this had changed her, and there was no way to explain how this fire had scorched her down to her soul.

"I need to get back to the office and file this paperwork. I'll call you tomorrow." She patted Paris on the arm and headed to her car.

"You doing okay?" Sloan asked quietly.

Paris nodded then her eyes drifted away.

Sloan continued sifting through the remains, looking for anything salvageable. If she got out of sight, Paris would frantically call for her as if being able to see Sloan was a necessary reassurance.

"Looks like you have another nosy neighbor coming to see what happened." Sloan pointed to the vehicle roaring up the road.

The SUV pulled in the drive and stopped in the front yard. Doctor Cameron climbed out and headed for Paris with a concerned look on his face.

"Are you two all right, Paris?" he asked with a sense of urgency. "I heard about the fire."

"Yes, we're fine, Seth." Paris offered a small smile at his concern.

"What happened?" he asked. "Do you know yet?"

"Firemen think it was electrical. Wiring was too old and the breaker box was too small."

"I'm so sorry." Seth shook his head sympathetically. "This was such a grand old place. One of the real historic homes in Barry County. Did you know Eisenhower spent the night here during his campaigns for presidency?"

"No. I didn't know that."

201

"Yep, he was on his way to a campaign rally in Springfield and there was a real bad thunderstorm that flooded the road. He had to stay in Banyon overnight. My dad told me about it. He said his entire entourage had to be put up in private homes. He slept in the front bedroom right up there." He pointed to the front corner of the pile of ashes. "Pauline West made him grits and ham for breakfast. And she burned the grits." He laughed.

"Grandmother?" Paris gasped. "She burned grits for President Dwight D. Eisenhower?" Paris chuckled, not imagining her grandmother had ever burned anything.

"She was teased about that for years. People used to send packages of grits to her with instructions written in great big letters. She'd get bags and bags of the stuff."

"She never told me that story," Paris replied.

Sloan had come over to listen to the tale.

"Wow, Paris. You are the granddaughter of the famous Banyon grit burner." Sloan smiled proudly.

"No wonder I don't like grits."

They had a small laugh about it.

"Anyway, I sure am sorry about this, Paris. I just had to come out and make sure you were okay. Can I do anything for you? Do you need a place to stay?" he asked.

"Thank you, Seth. I appreciate it."

"She's staying with me, Seth," Sloan offered.

"I figured as much. But don't be afraid to ask if you need something. I'll be out of town tomorrow, but I'll be back in the afternoon. My wife is going to visit her sister in San Diego, and I have to take her to the airport in Springfield. If you need anything, anything at all, you call me, Paris." He wrapped his arm around her shoulder and gave a reassuring hug. "Banyon folks take care of their own. And you are one of us." He gave her a knowing wink.

"Thank you."

"Paris is a strong woman," he said to Sloan as she walked him to his truck. "But the shock of a house fire can be devastating, even for a doctor. If she needs anything you call me, Sloan." He fixed her with a serious stare and gave a nod in punctuation. "Come by the office sometime. I'll take you two for coffee." He patted Sloan on the back and climbed in his truck. "Take care of her, Sloan."

"I will, Seth."

He waved and headed home.

CHAPTER 21

Paris couldn't sift through the ashes and remnants of Maybelline any longer. There was nothing she wanted buried beneath the charred beams and collapsed walls. In that one instant Maybelline had changed from her home to an empty piece of property. A strange ache gripped her deep in her soul. For one fleeting second she hated her grandmother for leaving Maybelline to her. If the house had been sold when she went into the nursing home or when she passed away then Paris's heart wouldn't be breaking all over again. Just as tears welled up in her eyes, ready to spill out, Paris noticed Sloan pulling something from the ashes.

"Paris, look!" she called with a cockeyed grin. "Your lamps survived, sort of." She held up one of the blackened but unbroken lime green table lamps. The shade had been melted to the wire frame. As Paris watched Sloan's discovery, the irony of the grotesque survivor of the holocaust brought on new mix of laughter and tears flowing freely down her face. Sloan dug out the mate to the lamp, also charred but unbroken. She held them up triumphantly. Paris continued laughing uncontrollably.

"I can clean them up and rewire them. You can get new lamp shades and they'll be just like new," Sloan offered, trying to find some solace in the devastation.

"How did those things survive?" Paris scoffed.

"Too ugly to die."

"Miss DeMont," a man in a fire department hat said as he finished signing his clipboard. "Can I get your signature on this?" He handed her the clipboard and a pen. "You'll get an official letter in the mail, but I can tell you right now you shouldn't have any trouble with your insurance about the cause of the fire. There's no doubt in my mind an electrical short in the breaker box caused this. The age of the house didn't help either. The insulation around old wire can get pretty brittle with age. I'm really sorry Miss DeMont. It's such a shame when we lose one of the nice old homes in the county. We don't have that many historic places left."

She signed and returned the document.

"My report will be mailed out by first of the week so you can get going on rebuilding right away." He nodded encouragingly then walked to his truck.

Paris took a glimpse of the rubble then let her eyes drift across the pasture, a faraway look on her face.

"Thanks," Sloan replied in his direction then turned to Paris. She saw a change in Paris's eyes and in her voice.

The late afternoon sun painted a plaintive glow around Paris as she ambled down the pasture. Sloan strolled along with her, quietly watching the tall grass around the pond waving in the breeze. Sloan could feel Paris's anguish, but respected her silence. They circled the pond then crossed the bridge onto the island. Sloan sat down under the willow and leaned against its trunk as Paris strolled the water's edge, pushing stones in the pond with her toe. Finally she turned to Sloan, forcing a small smile.

"Thank you," Paris said softly.

"For what?"

"For everything."

"All I did was find your ugly lamps and walk the fire marshal to his truck."

"Thank you for being here with me and," Paris looked away, "for being safe."

"I try to always be safe, Paris."

"It scared me so much to think you might have been inside the house." Paris's eyes glistened with emotion. "You have no idea what thoughts were racing through my mind when the fireman said he saw someone moving around upstairs and they couldn't get to them."

"Poor old Barney," Sloan said painfully and shook her head.

Paris knelt down in front of Sloan and fixed her with a solemn expression.

"It could have been you," Paris said, then closed her eyes as if the thought of it was too much to reconcile.

"But it wasn't me, Paris. I'm fine." Sloan sat up and extended a hand to Paris. "It wasn't me in that fire. Touch my hand. Feel that I'm still here. I'm just sorry you lost your house."

"Screw the house. God forgive me, but screw Barney, too. I almost lost you." Paris spoke as if yelling at Sloan would ease the shock and pain. "I almost lost everything again." Tears began to roll down Paris's cheeks. "I just don't think I could have survived that again. Losing Gabby was like a knife through my heart. Losing you would have been a knife through my heart and my soul."

Sloan gripped Paris's shoulders and looked deep into her eyes.

"You didn't lose me, Paris."

Paris nodded feebly as her chin began to quiver.

"There are no guarantees in this life but as much as I can promise, I'll always be right here for you," Sloan declared.

Paris stroked Sloan's face, still convincing herself she was indeed alive and not a mirage. Paris couldn't hold back the tears any longer. She buried her face in her hands and wept as she rocked back and forth on her knees. Sloan wrapped her arms around her and pulled her close, allowing Paris time to cleanse her need to cry.

"I love you, Paris. I truly love you. I would never do anything to hurt you. If that means being extra careful, I promise I will. If it means looking both ways before crossing the street, then I will look each way twice," Sloan whispered then kissed Paris's temple. "I promise," Sloan replied, wiping the tears from Paris's cheeks.

They walked back up to Paris's car, Sloan's arm around her protectively. There was nothing else they could do with the remains of Maybelline today. Paris looked at the house key on her key ring, the one Charlie had made for her.

"Strange," she offered.

"What's that, sweetheart?"

"This key still looks brand new. But now it doesn't open anything."

"Throw it away."

"But I feel like I should keep it for some reason."

Sloan didn't argue with her. She saw the remnants of some unresolved feelings on Paris's face. The house key seemed important to her somehow.

"I'll meet you at my house in a few minutes. I want to take the four-wheeler home. I'll ride it across the field. It's faster than on the road." Sloan started the ATV and headed across the pasture.

Paris hesitated at the end of the driveway, ready to pull out onto the road. As she adjusted her rearview mirror she caught a glimpse of the blackened pile that was once her Maybelline. The brick chimney stood at the side of the debris like a tombstone marking the fallen majesty that was once a four bedroom Victorian home. It was amazing how such a large house could be reduced to such a small heap of broken and charred beams. Another twinge of panic rippled though her.

"Oh, God, Sloan," she whispered to herself. She shuddered at the memory of the burning house. She closed her eyes and tried to block it out. She pushed the rearview mirror to the side and roared out onto the road. The image of what might have happened seemed to be everywhere around her and closing in fast. She needed to be someplace else, away from this farm, away from the fear it represented. She sped around the curves, her eyes narrowed and riveted to the road. She wished the fresh scent of grass didn't remind her of the farm. She also wished the trees waving in the wind didn't remind her of Sloan and her skillful hands crafting rustic furniture. Just after she crossed the metal bridge over the creek she noticed the remains of a burned-out shed next to a farmhouse. She knew it had been there, but it had never screamed out to her before today. The blackened roof with its gaping hole seemed to be illuminated with a thousand spotlights.

She pressed the gas pedal harder, roaring down the hill and up the other side. At the curve in the road, a willow tree waved its tentacles as if reaching out for Paris. She careened around the curve, escaping the beckoning tree. She gripped the steering wheel until her knuckles turned white. She was not going to think about the fire. She was not going to think about what could have happened. She was not. The more she tried to ignore the painful memories of the fire the harder she pressed on the gas pedal. The trees became a blur. A cloud of dirt blew up behind her each time a tire drifted off the pavement. The bends and curves of the road came faster and faster. Even the agile handling BMW swayed and squealed as she maneuvered the last curve before Sloan's driveway. She skidded around the corner and rattled over the cattle guard before screeching to a halt. A cloud of dust floated over the car obscuring her view. When it settled, Paris could see Sloan sitting on the four-wheeler, giving her an accusatory stare.

"Are you okay?" Sloan asked, walking over to the car. "I could hear you ripping up the road since you turned the corner."

Paris lowered her eyes and sat motionless for a moment hoping her mind would settle as fast as the dust settled. Sloan squatted down and draped her hands over the open driver's side window.

"Paris," she started cautiously. "What is it? Why are you driving like a maniac? This isn't like you."

"I'm sorry. It's nothing. I forgot I wasn't on the interstate." Paris looked up and gave a weak smile.

"Come on," Sloan said, opening her door and taking her by the hand. "Let's go inside and find some dinner. It's almost seven."

Sloan made dinner and ate ravenously, but Paris only pushed hers around the plate. As much as she tried, Paris couldn't ignore an image of Sloan being trapped in the burning house. The agonizing possibility of what could have happened was far more powerful than the reality of Sloan sitting across the table from her, safe and sound.

"The bed," Paris said suddenly looking up with wide eyes. "The bed you gave me, it's gone. It didn't survive. I'm so sorry, Sloan." She reached across and touched Sloan's hand as if offering comfort for a long lost relative.

"Don't worry about it," Sloan replied. "I'll make you another one."

"But it was such a beautiful bed." Paris's face veritably dripped with regret.

"When you get the house rebuilt I'll make you a bed for every room," Sloan stated as she squeezed Paris's hand. "And tables and chairs. I'll make you a whole house full of furniture." Sloan stroked Paris's face tenderly. "I'll make anything you want."

"But," Paris started.

"It was just a bed, a piece of wood, Paris. So what if it burned. I don't care. You are all right. I'm all right. And Barney is at peace."

Paris carried her plate to the sink then turned to Sloan. "I didn't mean what I said about Barney. I am so sorry about what happened to him." She sighed softly. "He will be missed."

"I know you didn't mean it." Sloan took her plate to the sink and gave Paris a kiss on the cheek. When she tried to give her a kiss on the mouth Paris moved away, trying to act busy washing the dishes. Sloan didn't force the issue. She allowed Paris the space and time she needed to be alone with her thoughts.

After they finished the dinner dishes, Paris made a few calls about the house and the insurance. Sloan selected some clothes from her closet and spread them out on the bed for Paris.

"That's all right, Sloan. I can go shopping tomorrow."

"Please, Paris. Let me help. They aren't Saks Fifth Avenue, but I think they will fit you. Here's a sleeper shirt for tonight." Sloan held up a white T-shirt with frogs hopping across the front. "Cute, huh?"

"Yes. Cute," Paris replied with a half-hearted chuckle. "Is it okay if I take a shower?"

"You don't have to ask, Paris. Make yourself at home." Sloan went into the bathroom and took out fresh towels. She opened a new bar of soap and checked the shower drain for hair then pulled her towel off the shower pole. It's all set. You can take a long bath if you want."

"Just a shower would be great."

"There's shampoo and conditioner on the side of the tub. There's a package of new razors and moisturizer there, too. Help yourself. Anything else?"

"I don't think so. You have thought of everything." She patted Sloan's arm then closed the bathroom door.

Sloan stood outside the door for a moment listening for sounds that Paris was all right. Something about her had changed. Something in the way she looked, something in the way she acted. Sloan couldn't put her finger on it, but Paris seemed different, distant. She decided it had to be the trauma of losing her house to a fire. Sloan went about closing up the house and turning out the lights. When Paris finished in the bathroom Sloan took a quick shower. By the time she had towel dried her hair and turned off the bathroom light she assumed Paris would be in bed if not already asleep. The bedroom was dark, but Paris wasn't in bed. Just as Sloan was about to go search for her she caught a glimpse of a silhouette against the bedroom window. Paris was sitting on the blanket chest in front of the window staring out at the moonlit night. Sloan stood behind her, gently stroking her hair.

"Here, I have something for you," Sloan said pressing the spare key into Paris's hand. "My house is your house, sweetheart. You make yourself at home."

Paris looked at the key as if she wasn't sure she should take it. Sloan closed Paris's hand around it. "It's a beautiful night, isn't it?" Sloan whispered.

"The nights are so clear and simple here. They aren't cluttered with bright lights and loud noises," Paris replied.

"Banyon isn't Manhattan, that's for sure," Sloan added.

"In so many ways it's better than Manhattan." Paris looked up at Sloan tenderly. Her eyes widened as she realized Sloan was naked. "Sloan, where are your pajamas?"

"I don't wear any. Never have. Nothing but a smile and a little baby oil." She grinned broadly and turned slowly to show off her full profile. "What do you think?"

"Very nice," Paris replied after doing a slow sweep from her toes upward.

"Thank you. Thank you," she replied, bowing deeply so her breasts bounced.

Paris laughed happily, something she hadn't done all day. Sloan did another pirouette and gave a ballet-type leap across the room. Her well-toned body moved gracefully as she turned and jumped for Paris's amusement. Paris continued to laugh and applaud as Sloan leaped back to her. She pulled Paris to her feet and wrapped her arms around her, dancing her playfully around the room. It was the first time since the fire Sloan felt like the real Paris was with her. They swayed, waltzed and dipped from one side of the bed to the other. Paris grinned and hugged Sloan tightly as they floated along in the darkness. Sloan finally turned Paris in a dizzying spin then tumbled onto the bed. They continued to laugh as they caught their breath, still locked in each other's arms. Sloan felt Paris's body against hers, warm and supple. This was her Paris. This was the woman she loved. This was the one person she wanted in her life from the time she was a teenager. Sloan kissed her deeply and emphatically. Their tongues entwined as the kiss grew deeper. Paris pulled herself toward Sloan's embrace. Sloan wrapped a leg over Paris and slid her foot along her calf. Paris cupped her hands over Sloan's smooth bottom and pulled her tightly to her. The lighthearted dancing had suddenly become a nearly frantic embrace. Sloan gripped Paris's hair in her two hands and orchestrated an urgent kiss. Her body stiffened against Paris, their mounds rubbing and massaging each other into arousal. Sloan rolled on top of Paris and urgently pressed her knee up between Paris's legs. Even through Paris's panties Sloan could feel the warm moisture of her valley against her leg.

Sloan ripped Paris's T-shirt as she pulled at it trying to get it over her head. Her panties suffered the same fate as Sloan tugged at the waistband. Paris bent her knee and pressed it hard against Sloan's crotch. Even with the summer breeze blowing across the bed, their bodies glistened with sweat. Sloan traced kisses down Paris's body, nipping at her breasts and inner thighs. Paris moaned at each gentle bite and pressed against Sloan's exploring tongue as it moved across her moist skin.

As Sloan moved back up over her breasts to her neck, Paris felt her growing passion consume her. She rolled over on top of Sloan and grabbed handfuls of her hair. As if a wild tiger had been unleashed, Paris devoured Sloan's mouth, her body pressing and gliding insistently against Sloan's. Paris's heart pounded in her chest. Her hands skittered down Sloan's abdomen and plunged into her moist crotch.

Sloan realized she had relinquished control and willingly allowed Paris's burning passion to guide them. With her fingers pressing deep inside Sloan, Paris moved her body against Sloan's, her own wetness leaving a trail down Sloan's thigh. Sloan rode the intense waves of ecstasy as Paris pressed harder and deeper. She gripped the sheet and arched her back, screaming out as the white-hot orgasm seared itself deep within her.

"Don't stop. Don't stop," Sloan gasped as she threw her head back and pulled at the sheet until it ripped on both sides.

Paris plunged deeper inside Sloan, feeling the rhythmic contractions of her orgasm. Just as Sloan passed her peak and fell exhausted against the pillow, Paris looked down at her, a single tear welling up in her eye and dropping onto Sloan's sweaty chest. Paris smiled bravely and wiped the second tear away before it could fall. She collapsed across Sloan's spent body drinking in the musky scent of her perspiration and sex. Nearly breathless, Sloan wrapped her arms around Paris and kissed her on the forehead.

"Don't say anything," Paris whispered.

"I wasn't going to," Sloan replied softly.

As the night breeze cooled their sweaty bodies, Sloan pulled the sheet over them and they drifted off to sleep in each other's arms. Sloan hadn't slept well for worrying over Paris. She awoke just before dawn to find Paris still clinging to her side as she slept, the tracks of tears staining her face. Sloan wanted to wake her and tell her there was no need to cry, that she would take care of her. Instead Sloan folded her arms gently over Paris and let her sleep.

When Sloan awakened again it was after nine. Paris was already up, dressed and gone. Sloan knew she must be busy with insurance and other matters about the house fire. Sloan dressed and went into the kitchen to make coffee, sorry she hadn't gotten up to fix breakfast for Paris. She dropped some toast in the toaster and reached for the telephone to call Paris. She gave a smirk and hung up as she remembered her cell phone had melted in the fire. She went to the refrigerator for the carton of orange juice. As she reached for the door handle she was stopped by an envelope with her name on it taped to the refrigerator. She recognized Paris's handwriting. Sloan felt her heart rise into her throat as she ripped open the envelope.

My dearest Sloan, I know you are wondering why I left this letter instead of talking to you face to face. Believe me, it was hard to leave without saying good-bye but this way I can explain why I had to go back to New York City without you arguing with me to stay. Don't laugh. I know you would try to talk me out of this.

I know this seems sudden and hard for you to understand, but I can't stay in Banyon. I just can't. There's no sense prolonging the inevitable. With Maybelline gone now, it seemed like the right time to go. I found an afternoon flight out of Springfield and Seth Cameron graciously agreed to give me a ride to the airport since he was going that way anyway. He is also going to store my car for me as it was easier to fly home and worry about the car later. I couldn't face that long drive in the hot summer.

Please don't think me uncaring, Sloan. My decision to go back to Manhattan was not, I repeat, not an easy one. It is the most difficult decision I ever had to make. For so many reasons I can't explain, I just had to go. Don't worry if you don't hear from me right away. I'll be inundated with work for a while. It always happens after I have been out of town.

Please take care of yourself, sweetheart. I just couldn't stand it if something happened to you. You are very precious to me, baby. I will be in touch. Love always, Paris

Sloan stood staring at Paris's handwriting, too stunned to blink. A sinking feeling gripped her soul, as she slowly lowered the letter. She noticed the key she had given Paris was hanging on the peg next to the telephone.

CHAPTER 22

Sloan rested her foot on the frame of the baggage return and waited for the conveyor to begin spitting out suitcases. She wished she had just brought a carry-on so this tedium could be avoided. To her surprise, her bag was the first one down the chute. With her New York City map in hand, she made her way to the subway. The rush hour traffic seemed even more ominous than she wanted to confront so she walked to the taxi stand and hailed a cab.

Sloan had attended a furniture convention at Madison Square Garden six years ago and vowed never to set foot in the Big Apple again. She always considered herself a woman of the world, hardened by the experiences of life, business, relationships and emotions, but New York City brought out the worst in her. She became defensive, moody and judgmental. No one smiled and waited for someone else to go first. No one picked a piece of merchandise up from the counter and returned it to the same place. There was no grass and no birds. The pigeons on the street lights didn't count. Sloan was sure millions of people loved the hustle and bustle, but she wasn't one of them. Visiting New York during the convention had been a chore, not a pleasure. But now Paris was here somewhere in the vast, smelly, noisy brick pile. And for Paris, Sloan knew she would walk on hot coals, something she was proving by riding a taxi through Manhattan during rush hour on a Friday evening.

If Paris wasn't home, Plan B was anyone's guess. But it was after seven, and surely she was home by now. The cab driver turned the corner at Lexington and Seventy-Fourth then pulled up in front of the apartment building. Sloan paid him and climbed out.

The doorman to the building was just as Paris had described him, short with a big moustache and a slight limp. She was right. His eyes did look like black jelly beans.

"May I help you, miss?" he asked politely, closing the taxi door.

"Paris DeMont's apartment?" Sloan asked.

"Nine fourteen," he said. "But . . ."

"Let me guess, she isn't in," Sloan said with a heavy sigh.

"Oh, she's in, I think. I haven't seen her today. We try to keep track of our tenants. I don't know if she went in to the hospital today. She hasn't been feeling well. Ever since she got back from her trip she's been under the weather. Minnesota must not have agreed with her."

"Missouri," Sloan corrected.

"Are you from Missouri, miss? Never been there myself. Never been out of New York. No, I take that back. Been to Jersey and New Haven once. Nothing worth seeing there."

"Nothing worth seeing in New Haven?" Sloan speculated.

"Nothing worth seeing in Connecticut," he replied, then took Sloan's suitcase and held the door for her.

"You said Paris is sick?"

"I'm not sure, but she sure hasn't been herself. Must be the flu. Some of those viruses hang on for weeks. I had one last October that kept me running for a month. Seems like since she's a doctor she'd be able to take something for it."

216

"Yeah, you'd think so," Sloan offered, instantly increasing her worry about Paris.

"Let me see if she's home." He placed her case next to an arm chair in the lobby. Sloan remained standing while the doorman called and talked to Paris. He cupped his hand over the mouthpiece giving the conversation a measure of privacy.

"Doctor DeMont said to send you up. You're Sloan McKinley, I assume." He pressed the button on the elevator and held it open for her then slid her suitcase inside. He tipped his hat as the door started to close.

"Tell Doctor DeMont I hope she's feeling better."

The door closed before Sloan could reply. It opened again to gold tapestry wallpaper with small sconce light fixtures dimly lighting the hall. Sloan set her suitcase down and was ready to knock on Paris's door just as it opened.

"Hi," Paris said cheerfully, hugging Sloan like nothing unusual had happened. "Come on in."

"Hi, yourself," Sloan replied as Paris pulled her suitcase inside and closed the door.

"This is a surprise," Paris said as she led the way into the living room.

"I was in the neighborhood," Sloan offered.

"Let me guess, it took American Airlines and the New York Transit to get you into the neighborhood," Paris replied with a slight smile.

"Delta."

"Have you eaten?"

"Sure. Two bags of pretzel sticks and a cranberry juice on the plane, a box of Milk Duds in the cab and a breath mint on way up in the elevator."

"Come in the kitchen. I haven't eaten either so we can look together."

Paris opened the refrigerator and examined the nearly bare shelves.

"We can have blackberry jam on Ritz crackers. An English

muffin or maybe limp celery stalks with a generous coating of low fat ranch dressing." Paris smirked at her sparse pantry then at Sloan. "Sorry I don't have much on hand. If I'd known you were coming I could have stocked up."

"If you knew I was coming you might not have been here," Sloan replied smugly as she leaned against the counter, her arms folded across her chest.

Paris ignored her and checked the cabinets. Suddenly she shifted into a brighter mood and smiled broadly.

"Tell you what. Grab your hat. I'm taking you to Selkey's Delicatessen for the best pastrami sandwich in New York City. Well, at least the best in Manhattan, and it's only three blocks away." Paris brushed past Sloan and collected her wallet, keys and jacket.

Sloan reluctantly followed her to the door then stopped Paris with a gentle hand on her arm.

"We don't have to go out. I'm okay."

"I need food and so do you. Traveling is hungry work." Paris tried to move away from Sloan's touch.

Sloan moved closer, trapping her in the corner by the front door. She placed a hand on the wall on either side of Paris and looked deeply into her eyes. Slowly she leaned in, her lips only inches from Paris's. Paris stood stiffly like a trapped animal. Sloan slowly pressed a kiss onto her lips then pulled back to see Paris's reaction.

Paris's eyes were closed, her lips still receptive. Sloan kissed her again, her arms enfolding her. Pairs slipped her arms around Sloan's neck and hugged her tightly as their tongues greeted each other in a passionate exchange. As if the delight over Sloan's unexpected arrival could no longer be restrained, Paris hungrily devoured her mouth, pressing her body against Sloan's. Sloan responded with an eager tongue and warm arms, holding Paris securely and protectively. Just as quickly as Paris gave herself to Sloan's embrace she pulled away, nervously fumbling with her keys.

"We better go. I'm starved."

"What's wrong?" Sloan asked with a frown, studying Paris's sudden change in character.

"Nothing," Paris insisted, giving an artificial smile and holding the apartment door open for Sloan. "Come on. Let's eat."

Paris hurried ahead and pushed the elevator button. She checked her hair in the mirror and adjusted her blouse uneasily. Sloan didn't say anything. She just watched Paris's behavior with growing concern.

"How was your flight?" Paris asked, noticing Sloan's eyes on her.

"Paris," Sloan said in a clear voice. "Do you want me to get a hotel room? I can if you want me to."

"Heaven's no. Why would I want you to do that?" Paris rushed into the elevator, pushed the lobby button and held the door as Sloan stepped in.

The elevator reopened and Paris led the way onto the street. The doorman smiled at them and tipped his hat as he flagged a cab for another tenant. Paris took Sloan's arm as if she were escorting an old sorority sister off to swap rumors. They hurried along exchanging small talk and news about Sloan's family. Paris laughed and joked about each bit of news from Banyon.

"Here we are," Paris pointed to a small establishment with darkened windows and a steady stream of customers going in and out. Inside was noisy with the heady smell of garlic and strong coffee.

"Hey, Paris," called a large man behind the counter. His accent was definitely New York, but his cheery wave and jolly eyes were right out of the Midwest. "Long time, no see."

"Hi, George," she replied with a wave as she searched the dimly lit room for a table.

"I think there's one for you upstairs," he advised.

Paris led the way through the crowded tables to the narrow stairs that led to the balcony. It was small and accommodated eight cozy tables. Paris found one near the railing that looked out over the main floor and deli counter.

"Can you see the menu? It's on the wall behind the counter," Paris asked.

"No. But you can tell me what's good."

"The pastrami is great. Excellent Rueben sandwiches if you like sauerkraut. Roast beef on rye is out of this world. They are huge. They also have salads and homemade soups. I think Friday is clam chowder or chicken with wild rice. The usual deli stuff."

"What are you having?" Sloan asked, studying Paris's face.

"Oh, gee. I don't know. The sandwiches are so big, I don't know if I can eat a whole one tonight. Maybe I'll just have some soup."

"What can I get you?" asked a gum-chewing teenager with a piercing in each eyebrow and one in her lower lip.

"Go ahead," Paris said, looking across at Sloan.

"We'd like one pastrami on dark rye with Swiss cheese, cut in half on two plates and two cups of soup," Sloan stated, raising her eyebrow to Paris for agreement.

"Sounds great."

"What kind of soup?" the waitress asked as she wrote on her pad and popped her gum.

"Chicken wild rice for me," Paris offered.

"Me, too," Sloan added.

"To drink?"

"Coffee, decaf," Sloan replied, holding up two fingers.

The waitress popped her gum again then sauntered away. Sloan watched the girl until she had descended the stairs.

"Ouch," Sloan laughed, rubbing her eyebrows.

"No kidding," Paris agreed discreetly.

"I wonder if she was aiming for her ears and missed or if she really meant to do that?" They chuckled.

The deli was too noisy and too crowded for Sloan to ask Paris anything personal or important so she decided her curiosity and concern about her sudden departure from Banyon could wait until later. She smiled at Paris and engaged in small talk about Manhattan eateries, restaurant décor and waitresses.

Paris was right. The sandwich was huge and the pastrami was

delicious. They lingered for a second cup of coffee then headed up Seventy-Fifth Street. The night air was heavy over Manhattan. There was a warm, gritty stench hanging over the city, one that New Yorkers referred to as summertime. Sloan wanted to either hold her nose or blow it. She wasn't sure which would clear the odor from her nostrils.

"How do you stand the smell?" she asked, rubbing her nose.

Paris smiled at her. "You get used to it. It's the smell of a bustling big city."

It was after nine by the time they returned to Paris's apartment. Paris put on her nightshirt. Sloan changed into a pair of silk boxer shorts and T-shirt. They sat together on the couch watching the last inning of the Yankees baseball game.

"That's our boys. Take a two-run lead into the ninth inning then give it away," Paris chided. "Can I get you anything? Something to drink? A dish of ice cream?" she asked, turning off the television and hopping up.

"I'm still full from dinner, but thanks," Sloan replied. She patted the couch and waved Paris over. "Come talk with me."

"About what?" Paris asked, taking a place on the couch with a measure of caution.

Sloan leaned back and draped her arm over the back of the couch. She studied Paris for a long minute, hoping a conversation would bubble up on its own. But Paris sat silently waiting for Sloan to pick a topic.

"Well, let's see. How about why you left Banyon in such a hurry without even saying good-bye?" Sloan suggested.

Paris lowered her eyes, not at all surprised by Sloan's choice. She folded her hands in her lap, quietly planning her reply.

"I explained everything in the letter I left for you. Didn't you read it?"

Sloan nodded but remained silent. She wanted this to be Paris's opportunity to talk, not hers. She left the awkward silence for Paris to fill.

"I know it was a shock for you. Maybe I was wrong to just leave like that, but it was the only way I could do it. I had to get away. I just had to." Paris's eyes searched Sloan's face for understanding. She reached over and placed her hand on Sloan's. "I am sorry if I hurt you. I never meant to do that. You have to believe me."

Sloan leaned forward and peered into Paris's eyes. "Was it something I said? Did I do something wrong?"

"No," Paris replied instantly. "It wasn't anything you did. Trust me on that."

"Then why? Why, Paris?" she pleaded.

"Because I love you," Paris said in a whisper. There was a strange calm in the way she said it that caught Sloan off guard.

"I don't understand. I love you, too. With all my heart I love you, Paris. Why is that so terrible that you had to run away?"

"I had to leave before we got too involved. So involved I couldn't leave. I just had no choice. I can't do this again." She looked away.

"Do what? Fall in love with me?" Sloan demanded. "Why is that so terrible? Am I that bad a person?"

"No!" Paris gasped, almost angry Sloan would think such a thing. "You are a wonderful person." Paris smiled tenderly at her. "You are so incredible. You are everything to me. That's why I can't be with you, Sloan. It's because you are so wonderful and funny and gentle and caring that I had to leave Banyon."

Sloan had a blank look on her face as if Paris's explanation made no sense at all.

"I lost one love on Nine Eleven. My Gabby. My wonderful Gabriella." Paris clutched her hand to her chest. "When the house in Banyon burned, and I thought you were in it, I thought I would lose my mind. I thought I had lost my Sloan. I can't explain how deeply it scared me. I felt my heart breaking all over again. It was the worst feeling I ever felt in my entire life."

"But Paris, I'm all right. Nothing happened to me." Sloan eased closer to Paris and stroked her face reassuringly.

"I know," Paris said fighting back the tears. "But I can't take that chance again. I can't take a chance on losing you. It would hurt too much. I love you too much."

The confession confirmed what Sloan feared most. The transformation she had witnessed Paris make after the house fire was still bitterly present. The trauma of the fire had become a harsh reflection of the 9/11 disaster, something with which Paris still had unresolved issues. Sloan also knew they would never have a life together so long as Paris refused to deal with the unfinished business of Gabby's loss.

"I'm sorry," Paris said through a sniffle.

"I wish I knew what to say to you. How do I convince you to give our love a chance? How do I convince you to trust our life together?" Sloan wiped a tear from Paris's cheek.

Paris stiffened and pushed away from Sloan.

"How long will you be in New York?" Paris asked.

"Just two days."

Paris's mouth dropped. "That isn't much of a visit," she declared dismally. "Can you extend it a few days?"

"Sorry. I can't. I have some customers coming in to pick up orders," Sloan reported with a shrug. "But we have tomorrow."

"What would you like to do with your day in the Big Apple?"

"I did have something in mind," she said warily. "Will you take me down there? Please." Sloan took Paris's hand in hers and held it tightly.

"Down where?" Paris asked curiously.

"Ground Zero," Sloan said softly.

Paris took a deep breath and pulled her hand away.

"Sloan, I can't. I just can't." There was an unmistakable tremble in her voice.

"Have you been there since that day?"

"Yes, twice." Paris spoke quietly, holding tight to her emotions. "The day it happened. It was around sunset. The rubble was still burning. And I went down about three weeks later, when they found Gabby's watch." Paris pulled the necklace holding the watch

223

face from inside her nightshirt. "One of the firemen recognized it. He was a friend of Gabby's. He was working on one of the search and rescue crews the night it was found. Her watch stopped at ten twenty-nine. That's when the North Tower came down." She closed her hand around the watch and held it tightly as the cold reality of the statement settled over them.

"That was the first one hit, right?" Sloan asked respectfully.

"Yes. Tower One, the North Tower, was struck at eight forty-eight. Everyone in Manhattan knows where they were and what they were doing at eight forty-eight that morning." There was an agonizing despair in Paris's eyes as she retold the details of that morning.

Sloan reached for the watch. Paris opened her hand so she could see it.

"This is all they found of her. I haven't been back since. There's nothing for me down there."

"I think there is," Sloan said.

Paris shook her head slowly, her eyes lowered.

"Why would I possibly need to go back there?"

"To say good-bye," Sloan offered.

Paris looked up as a tear began its run down her cheek.

"I can't," she whispered, barely able to speak. Her chin trembled as she looked into Sloan's eyes, the look of a terrified child on Paris's face.

"I think you can. And I think you know you have to let go of your past. And what's more, I think deep down inside you want to go there and do this, to say good-bye. I'm not asking you to forget Gabby. I'm not asking you to pretend you never loved her with all your heart and all your soul. She will always be part of you. What happened to Gabby and so many others was unexplainably cruel and gruesome. But now it is time to accept it and time to say good-bye. Time to remember Gabby for the good times and move on with your life."

Paris went to the window and stared out at the city lights. A gentle rain had begun to fall. She touched her fingertip to the pane and traced a raindrop as it meandered down the glass.

"Just when I think I have gotten past it, I see something or smell something or hear something that reminds me of her," Paris said as she continued to watch the rain.

"It will be like that for a long time. You will always love Gabby, and you will always miss her. Be thankful for that. Be thankful you had such a strong relationship and cared so deeply for each other. When you love someone, they become part of you. All the good things they are become woven into your soul." Sloan said softly. "It's okay to cry for her. I don't mind." Sloan stood beside Paris and looked out into the night with her.

"Gabby would be laughing her head off over all these tears. She'd be calling me her silly old goose for crying so much. She loved to laugh and have fun, but she hated to cry. She always wanted to be in control."

"Sounds like she was in control right up to the end."

Paris thought a moment before answering.

"I guess she was. She was doing what she could to help. She made the decision to go inside Tower One even though it was burning. That's the way she was."

Sloan examined the inscription on the back of the watch.

"Part of the inscription was scratched off when the building collapsed," Paris related, looking down at it. "It's supposed to read To Gabby, with all my love, from Paris."

"With all my love Paris," Sloan read. "The way it reads now is like a message. She is telling you she loves you." She stared at the words then looked into Paris's eyes tenderly. "It's like she is saying good-bye to you, Paris."

"No, you see the words are just—" Paris started as she read the words again then stopped with a gasp. She read the inscription over and over to herself, her eyes widening. "My God. You're right. The comma is gone, too. It's as if she is saying that to me, not from me." She looked at Sloan, a lump rising in her throat. "She's saying good-bye to me, isn't she?"

"Yes, sweetheart, she is," Sloan agreed warmly as she wrapped her arm around Paris. Paris leaned into Sloan, clutching the watch in her hand. "Can you do it too?" Sloan asked.

Paris did not answer. She closed her eyes and hugged Sloan tightly. They could feel each other's heart beat as a clap of thunder and a bolt of lightning split the darkness. The rain fell heavier, splattering against the window in angry torrents. The summer thunderstorm dumped its deluge on Manhattan as Paris clung to Sloan and wrestled with her decision. She was a consummate professional in the hospital, but deciding if she had the courage to once again visit lower East Side Drive made Paris weak in the knees and wrapped her stomach in knots.

Sloan held Paris in her arms, silently waiting for her decision, a decision only Paris could make. Sloan kissed Paris's temple and tightened her hug. She said a silent prayer, asking God and Gabby to give Paris the strength she needed and so desperately deserved.

"We can go tomorrow morning," Paris whispered.

"I'll be right with you every second, sweetheart. Every single second," Sloan said softly.

It was a long night for both of them. Paris spent most of the night staring at the ceiling, listening to the rain and wrestling with the decision she had made to return to the World Trade Center site. Sloan lay next to her, occasionally touching Paris's leg or patting her hand in support. Sloan finally fell asleep sometime after three and was snoring quietly as Paris slipped out of bed, showered and dressed. Paris was sipping a cup of tea and working on an English muffin when Sloan wandered out of the bedroom with a sleepy look on her face.

"Good morning," Sloan said through a yawn. "What time is it?"

"Good morning. Eight-fifteen," Paris replied. "Did you sleep all right? I'm sorry if I kept you awake."

"You didn't. It was just one of those nights."

"Would you like coffee or tea? I have both," Paris offered.

"Coffee, please, if it isn't too much trouble."

"It's already in the machine. All I have to do is turn it on. And I have an English muffin with strawberry preserves for you, too."

Sloan showered and dressed while Paris made the coffee and set a place at the table. She used her best linen and the bone china she had inherited from her grandmother. She listened for the bathroom door to open then slid the English muffin under the broiler.

"Breakfast is served," she called.

Sloan came bounding out of the bedroom looking fresh and invigorated.

"Nothing like a cold shower to get the blood flowing," she announced, rubbing her hands together.

"Cold shower? You have to be kidding! Wasn't there any hot water?"

"Yeah, there was. But sometimes I let the cold water run over me for a minute at the end just to wake me up." She flashed one of her big grins.

"Come sit down and have your breakfast."

"You're going to sit with me, aren't you?"

"Yes. Let me get another cup of tea first." Paris went into the kitchen as Sloan took her place at the table.

"I'll wait for you," Sloan called.

"No, don't. Your muffin will get cold," Paris declared.

"My muffin is already cold," Sloan replied with a lilt in her voice.

"Yes, yes. I know exactly what you mean," Paris said from the kitchen.

"Don't you want to come warm my muffin for me?" Sloan said, hoping to lighten the morning with a little of her suggestive humor.

"Eat your breakfast."

When Sloan finished her breakfast they went down to the lobby, and Paris hailed a cab.

"Church and Vesey," she said to the driver after a deep breath.

"Going to see the World Trade Center site, eh?" the driver advised as he pulled out into traffic.

"Yes," Paris said then sat back in the seat and stared out the

227

window. Sloan slid her hand over on the seat and touched Paris's hand without looking at her. Paris nodded slightly as she continued to watch the traffic.

The driver pulled up to the curb on Church Street and stopped behind a delivery truck. Sloan paid him before Paris could reach for her money.

"I've got it," Sloan said and opened the door, holding it for Paris.

They stood on the corner staring at the open space where the World Trade Center used to stand. A fence stretched around the sixteen-acre construction site where the subterranean reconstruction was well under way. All the noise and congestion of a busy Manhattan day couldn't mask the eerie presence that hung in the air. Sloan wasn't sure what to expect, but a sense of reverence was all around them. The enormity of the tragedy was almost greater than Sloan's ability to comprehend it.

Paris stared through the empty space in the skyline where the buildings once stood as if she could see something no one else could see. Her face was pale and emotionless. She slipped her hand in Sloan's for reassurance.

"The World Trade Center was so huge. How can we understand what happened here?" Sloan stared wide-eyed at the screaming gap in the skyline.

"That was the shock for New Yorkers. It was inconceivable that the Twin Towers could be brought down. It meant no one was absolutely safe. We are all accessible and vulnerable." Paris looked away for a moment as if to recapture her thoughts.

"Tell me about that day. Tell me about Gabby," Sloan asked with compassion and tenderness.

"Let's walk." Paris slipped her arm through Sloan's and crossed the street with the light. They strolled along arm in arm. Pedestrians hurried past, seemingly indifferent to the two women.

"Gabby dropped me off at the hospital that morning about seven. She had just gotten off duty from working a double shift, but she was going back to the station house. One of the firemen

228

was turning fifty, and she wanted to be there for the birthday party. She was going to meet me for lunch later. It was the first time in weeks we had been able to have lunch together. Her schedule was as crazy as mine. She made me promise to set aside at least thirty minutes even if we only ate in the hospital cafeteria. I didn't tell her, but I was giddy as a teenager over our plans for lunch. I was really looking forward to it. Anyway, she pulled up to the doctor's entrance of the hospital and gave me a kiss. As I was walking toward the door she rolled down the car window and whistled at me. It was one of those wolf whistles construction workers whistle at passing women. When I turned around to tell her to stop that she had this very cheeky grin on her face. She winked at me and said later, cutie. Then she roared away. That was the last time I ever saw her."

Paris took a deep breath. "She was off duty when the first plane hit, but when the emergency call came in at eight forty-seven she went along with the ambulance crew to help. They told me she was triaging some walking wounded on the sidewalk as they were coming out of the North Tower when the second plane hit the South Tower. As the ambulance was leaving with a load of critically injured for the hospital they saw Gabby going inside the North Tower, Tower One. There were reports of people injured and unable to get out of the building because some doors were locked. She went inside to help get them out. Tower Two collapsed a little before ten. Twenty-five minutes later the North Tower came down." Paris stopped, her eyes searching the construction site.

"Ten twenty-nine. That's the time on her watch, right?"

Paris nodded and clutched at the chain around her neck.

"Thousands of people went to work that morning and just disappeared," Paris added with a soft resolve.

"Did you lose any patients?"

"Three," Paris replied quietly.

"I can't imagine how much courage it took to run inside those burning buildings," Sloan said, transfixed by the image.

"I was very proud of her," Paris whispered. "But I was mad at

229

her, too. For a long time I was furious with her for going inside and putting herself in harm's way, for choosing the people in that building over me. I thought, how dare she put her life in jeopardy like that."

Sloan listened without interrupting.

"I know what you're thinking," Paris added. "Gabby was a paramedic. She did that everyday. Every time she answered an emergency call she was putting her life on the line. It just took me a long time to remember that. Gabby loved what she did, and she was good at it, too."

"Have you forgiven her?"

"Yes. I understand why she did it. She didn't run inside to be a martyr or a hero. She didn't know the tower was going to come down on top of her. She was just doing her job. Fate stepped in and changed her world and mine. And a lot of other people's lives as well."

"Everything you have been saying sure sounds to me like you are coming to grips with losing Gabby."

"I came to grips with losing her when they gave me her watch. I knew she was gone. I didn't need any pieces of her to bury to know I had lost something very special."

"Then why are we here, Paris? Why was it so hard for you to come down here and look at this place? You wear a little bit of Gabby with you all the time. That broken watch you wear is like a poster of the World Trade Center debris. You didn't have to take a taxi ride down here to Ground Zero. You have a screaming image of that terrible day right there on a chain around your neck." Sloan took a breath and started again in a more compassionate voice. "Don't you want to let go of her and move on with your life? Can't you let us have a life together now?" Sloan hated to be so blunt, but she felt the time was right.

Paris shook her head slowly, tears welling up in her eyes.

"I can't, Sloan. I love you, but I just can't." Tears rolled down Paris's face as she spoke. "I thought I could. I really wanted us to be together, but something happened. Don't ask me what. But something told me I couldn't stay with you. I had to come back to New York."

"In your letter you said the same thing. You said you were going to New York. But Paris, you didn't say you were going home—just going to New York. This isn't your home. Not anymore. Banyon is. It always has been, since your first summer at your grandmother's house. What happened? What changed your mind so suddenly? Tell me what it is, and I'll fix it."

Paris shrugged her shoulders.

"It was after the house fire, wasn't it?" Sloan offered. "I know you were scared. I know you were watching your house burn and thinking I was still trapped inside. It must have been terrible for you. It must have been like the hell you experienced with Gabby."

Paris went to the corner to wait for the light to change. Sloan followed.

"That's it, isn't it?" Sloan grabbed Paris by the arm. "I put you through hell all over again."

Paris pulled away and started across the street. Sloan was right behind her, dodging the other pedestrians to keep up. When they stepped onto the sidewalk Paris turned and stared daggers at her.

"Yes, it was terrible. Yes, it was hell for me. And why shouldn't it be. I thought I was losing the person I loved."

"But you didn't lose me. I keep telling you that."

"You don't understand," Paris snapped and started up the street with long strides.

"Gabby can't break your heart again, can she?" Sloan declared. "She's the safe one."

Paris stopped in her tracks but didn't turn around.

"That's why you wear her watch. That's why you haven't said good-bye to her. You don't want to give her up." Sloan continued, her words piercing Paris like a thousand needles. "You hang on to Gabriella Buttichi because she can't hurt you anymore. You don't say good-bye because that would mean you are single again. You'd have to put your heart out there again. And that scares the hell out of you. You are afraid of someone else being taken away. That's a lousy way to live. A damn lousy way to live."

Paris reached for Gabby's watch and clutched it protectively. She turned to Sloan, her face stained with tears.

"I told you, there are no guarantees in life, Paris. You just have to take a chance," Sloan added.

"Forgive me if I hurt you," Paris offered then started up the street.

Sloan caught up with her, and they walked silently for blocks, watching the traffic and the people rush by.

"Do you need to get a cab?" Sloan asked as they crossed Chambers Street.

"No. I need to walk," Paris replied, her eyes finally clear and tear-free.

Sloan fought the impulse to apologize to Paris for speaking so bluntly. She didn't mean to hurt her feelings, and she certainly didn't want to drive her further away, but she knew Paris needed to confront her demons head on.

"Let's take the subway," Paris said, heading for the stairs to the Eighth Street station.

They melded into the crowd on the platform then flowed into the open doors of the subway car. Paris grabbed a strap and hooked her foot around the pole to steady herself as the train pulled away with a lurch. Sloan held on with both hands, swaying back and forth as the car rolled along the rails. She gritted her teeth and swallowed hard as the train clattered noisily over the rough sections, the lights blinking at the intermittent electrical connection. Paris and the other New Yorkers seemed immune and indifferent to the sights, smells and sounds of the subway. When Paris and Sloan reached street level Sloan took a deep breath, relieved at once again seeing daylight.

"Thank goodness. Sun," she muttered.

"Country girl," Paris said with a chuckle, the emotional strain of the morning finally fading.

232

"City girl," Sloan replied with a soft smile. "Come on. I'll buy you lunch at that deli we went to last night. And I promise I won't talk about Gabby anymore."

They ate a quiet lunch then walked through a wing of the Metropolitan Museum of Art acting like typical tourists ogling and pointing at the paintings and sculptures. Sloan fought the occasional urge to add something else to her remarks about Gabby and Paris's difficulty in giving her up. Paris moved through the day with quiet reserve. Her laughs were restrained and her smiles were small, as if showing any kind of emotion would crack the protective coating she had wrapped around herself. They stopped to listen to a street band playing jazz then headed for Paris's apartment. It was getting dark and they were both exhausted after a long day.

"What time is your plane tomorrow?" Paris asked as she unlocked her apartment.

"Early. James couldn't find any flights at a decent hour on such short notice. And I have some buyers coming by after dinner to pick up their orders."

"What time should I set the alarm?"

"You don't have to get up with me unless you are going to the hospital at five o'clock."

"I don't go back to work until next week. I wasn't ready yet. Bill is still handling things for me." Paris sounded a little ashamed of her admission.

"Good. You deserve some time off. Don't feel guilty about it."

"You want anything? Milk, juice, coke, sandwich?" Paris asked, heading for the kitchen.

"No thanks," Sloan replied, leaning on the doorjamb. She studied Paris as she busied herself to avoid talking about their relationship. Sloan didn't want to keep nagging at Paris, but she had to try one more time to get through to her.

"I remember what I used to say when you were leaving your grandmother's house at the end of the summer. Do you?"

"I'm not sure. What?" Paris asked.

233

"I'd knock on the back door and ask if Paris was coming back to play with me again."

"Yes. I remember."

Sloan tapped her knuckles on the door jamb.

"Is Paris coming back to play with me again?" she asked, a look of hopeful desperation on her face.

Paris looked away. She went to the sink and washed her hands. Sloan came to her and touched Paris's hair gently, tears filling Sloan's eyes so she could barely see.

"You aren't coming back, are you?" she asked in a whisper.

Paris looked down and didn't reply. Sloan swallowed hard. She kissed Paris on the cheek and walked out of the kitchen.

When the alarm clock sounded Sloan was already up and dressed, ready to leave. Paris came out of the bedroom, pulling her robe around her.

"Good morning," Paris said, surprised at Sloan's early rising.

"Good morning."

"I didn't hear you get up. I'm sorry."

"I got up around midnight and came out here on the couch. I didn't want to wake you."

"Were you going to leave without saying good-bye?" Paris asked. She immediately knew she had that coming from the sudden way she had left Banyon. "It'll just take me a few minutes to get dressed. Why don't you call a cab while I get ready. The number is by the phone in the kitchen." She rushed into the bedroom to get dressed.

"Paris," Sloan called. "I already called a cab. You don't need to go with me."

"Sure I do," Paris replied, looking back to her with a wrinkled brow.

Sloan shook her head and picked up her bag.

"Don't come," she said softly.

"Sloan, why?" Paris walked back to her, searching Sloan's eyes for clarification.

Sloan kissed her softly then went to the front door. Paris's eyes were wide with bewilderment.

"Take care of yourself, Paris. Please." Sloan went through the door and closed it behind her. She leaned against the door, fighting back the tears and the urge to beg Paris to go with her, if not to Banyon at least to the airport. But she knew that would only prolong the pain. Finally she started up the hall for the elevator and never looked back.

CHAPTER 23

Sloan pulled into her driveway and turned off the engine. She leaned forward and rested her forehead against the steering wheel. She was tired. But more than the physical fatigue, she was emotionally drained as well. The long flight from New York to Chicago and the connection down to Springfield had left her numb. She had spent both flights staring out the window, questioning if she had said the right things to Paris. Had she said enough? Had she said too much? Had she let Paris know how much she loved her and how much she wanted to help? Had she overstepped her bounds when it came to Paris's relationship with Gabby? Should she have thrown away her return ticket and stayed longer? Should she have demanded Paris come back to Banyon with her? Sloan sat up and laughed out loud at the idea she could have demanded Paris do anything she didn't want to do. The thought that Paris would never again set foot in Banyon or into her life terrified Sloan right down to her core, making her hands sweat and her stomach turn.

Sloan placed her suitcase on the porch and went to the shop. She wasn't ready to go inside an empty house. She unlocked the shop door and snapped on the light over the workbench. The first thing she noticed was Paris's smiling face in the photograph taken at the barbecue that was taped to the bulletin board. She brushed the dust from it and traced the outline of Paris's features. The piece of driftwood Paris had thought should be made into a headboard still sat on the pedestal. Sloan ran her hand along the smooth surface of the wood, remembering how Paris had caressed it with such tender strokes. She mentally sketched a design for a headboard. It would be graceful with delicate details, she imagined. The bed would be king size, with a footboard of her most polished wood and most elegant graining. It would be the most beautiful bed she had ever made and it would be for Paris. It would be for her new house, whenever she rebuilt it—if she rebuilt it. Sloan heaved a deep sigh. She leaned against the workbench and waited for the buyers to arrive, but her heart wasn't in it.

For the rest of the week, Sloan finished projects, delivered and shipped orders and thought about Paris. She shopped, ran errands, paid bills and thought about Paris. She fought the urge to call her daily. After four days of not hearing from her, she telephoned Paris's apartment only to be greeted by her answering machine. Sloan assumed she had returned to work, once again submerged in the complex professional world of a big city doctor. After another two days with no word from her, Sloan decided she had wrestled with the uncertainty of how Paris was doing long enough and telephoned her office.

"Doctors DeMont, Hayes and Corelli. May I help you?" the receptionist said.

"Hello. Is Doctor DeMont there?"

"Yes, she is. She's over in the hospital right now, but she'll be back in the office in about an hour. Can I make an appointment for you or are you having an emergency? Are you having chest pains?" the receptionist asked seriously.

Sloan wanted to blurt out yes, she was having chest pain. Paris was breaking her heart by not returning her calls.

"No, I'm fine. I'm calling from Missouri. I just wanted to talk with her for a few minutes."

"I'm afraid Doctor DeMont is very busy today. Can I help you with something? Do you need a physician referral?" she continued.

"No. That's okay. I'll call back later." Sloan wanted to ask her how Paris was. How did she look? Was she her old self again? Was she ever coming back to her? "Thanks anyway." She hung up without leaving her name.

The next morning she tried again to catch Paris at home. And again Paris's answering machine picked up.

"You have reached Paris. Leave your name and number. I'll get back with you."

"Hi sweetheart. I love you. I just wanted to let you know that, again. Call me, please," Sloan said with as much compassion as she could muster. Sloan stood holding the receiver long after the answering machine peeped at the end of the recording. "Please, Paris. I need to talk to you," she whispered desperately then hung up. She hesitated then reached for the redial button to try a different approach. Maybe Paris would respond better if she begged her to return her call. Or perhaps a demanding phone message would work. Sloan replaced the telephone on the cradle just before it started to ring. She couldn't do that to Paris. As much as she wanted to reach out and talk to Paris, she couldn't beg, and she couldn't demand her to do it. She had to let Paris call when she was ready. Not a minute before. As much as it was killing Sloan, she had to let Paris decide what was right for her.

Just as Sloan turned her back on the telephone, it rang. Sloan was so startled she dropped the receiver as she reached for it.

"Hello," she said, anxiously scrambling to answer it.

"Hi, daughter," Charlie said. "You okay?"

"Hi, Dad. Yeah, I'm okay. Sorry, I just dropped the phone."

"So I gathered. You busy?"

"Not really. What do you need?" Sloan asked, trying to hide her concern for Paris.

"We could use your help for a few minutes if you can get away.

I'm replacing the track lighting display, and we sure could use another pair of hands."

"No problem. I'll be there in a few minutes," Sloan replied, grateful to have something to take her mind off Paris, if only for a little while.

Sloan headed for town. It was a hot summer day, and the humidity was making the air thick and sticky. She pushed the wing window wide open so a bit of wind blew across her face. By the time she got to the edge of town, she wished she had taken the car and ridden comfortably in the air conditioning. Sweat was dripping down her back and perspiration was soaking her hair by the time she passed the grocery store and turned down the street in front of Doctor Cameron's clinic. She screeched to a stop, partially blocking the street when she saw Paris's BMW sitting in the corner of the clinic's parking lot with a *For Sale* sign on the windshield. The color drained from Sloan's face, and her mouth dropped. This meant only one thing. Paris wasn't coming back. Sloan pulled into the parking lot and parked behind the sports car. Her heart was in her throat as she opened the door to the sports car and looked in. She pressed her hand into the back of the driver's seat. The tan leather was warm and soft, like Paris's skin. She climbed in and sat quietly, her hands folded in her lap. She took a deep breath, taking in the fading scent of Paris's cologne. Remnants of Paris screamed at her from every corner of the car. The stir stick from the latte they had shared was tucked behind the visor. A map of southwest Missouri was in the map pocket on the door. One of Paris's nearly spent Raging Red lipsticks was in the console along with one of her hair clips. Sloan slipped the nearly empty lipstick into her pocket as if rescuing some small part of Paris. The thought that this lipstick had once touched Paris's lips somehow made it worth keeping. A thousand conflicting images raced across her mind. The one that screamed at her the loudest was that Paris told Seth to put the car up for sale because she wasn't coming back to get it. Sloan slammed her hand against the steering wheel. Then she grabbed it in both hands and shook it for all she was worth.

"Why Paris?" she cried out in frustration. "Why? Why won't

you come back to me? This is your home. This is where you belong." She leaned back against the headrest and heaved a heavy sigh. "I love you, Paris. That's all there is," she whispered.

"Nice car, isn't it?" Seth said as he looked in the driver's window. "You going to buy Paris's car, Sloan?"

"Hi, Seth. No. Too much car for me. No place to haul my furniture."

"Pretty snazzy though," he said looking it over.

"So Paris called you about selling it?" Sloan suggested curiously.

"Actually, no. She sent me an e-mail. Said to go ahead and sell it. Said she wouldn't need it anymore. She said she'd contact me in a few days about the title." He used his handkerchief to brush some dust off the hood. "Had three lookers already today. Folks around here don't see BMW sports cars like this very often. Pete Lindel wanted it real bad until he checked how much the insurance would be. He's had a few too many speeding tickets to afford this car." Seth laughed and shoved his hands in his pockets. "How's Paris doing? Back at work, I guess," he offered.

Sloan didn't want to admit she had no idea or that it had been nearly a week since she last saw or spoke to her.

"I haven't talked to her today, but I guess she's okay," she replied, trying to sound well-informed. "I better get going. Dad is waiting on me to help fix a display." She climbed out and closed the door, allowing her hand to remain for a moment on the door handle Paris had once touched.

"Let me know if you hear from Paris," Seth called as she started her truck. "Tell her hi for me."

"I will," she replied and pulled out of the parking lot, leaving Seth to ogle over the car.

She helped Charlie with the display then stopped for a cheeseburger but had little appetite. It was nearly dark by the time she pulled in her drive. With the time difference she decided it was too late to call Paris. She hurried in the house and checked her answering machine, but it was empty. An aching loneliness followed her

240

to bed and throughout the next two days. She worked long hours in the shop trying to block out the emptiness that gnawed at her.

On Sunday she loaded her truck and trailer with orders to be delivered—rustic and log-framed table and chair sets, plant stands, picture frames, settees, light fixtures, side tables and turned bowls. She looked forward to the three-day trip through Branson, Eureka Springs, Harrison, Fayetteville and Little Rock then back home through Jonesboro. It was always a beautiful drive through the hills and valleys of rural Missouri and Arkansas, one she had hoped to share with Paris. Now she wanted it to take her mind off Paris or at least the telephone that refused to ring. Sloan left another message on Paris's answering machine before heading out Monday morning. She spent the first hour of the ride trying to come up with a better message for next time. The semantics of how to word it became a game for Sloan. She practiced all the possibilities out loud. After exhausting the variables for sixty miles, she screamed out the window.

"Why the fuck don't you call me?" She laughed. "Better not use that one."

Sloan delivered the furniture to her distributors in each city and picked up items to be repaired. One pair of log-framed kitchen chairs needed to be reassembled when the buyer neglected to tie them securely to the top of the car and they rolled off, bounced along the pavement and down an embankment. Surprisingly, the damage was minor and easily fixed. Customer stupidity was not covered in Sloan's guarantee, but she was happy to oblige since the accident demonstrated the durability of her craftsmanship.

She pulled into her drive just before sunset. She was hungry and tired. She wanted a shower, a meal and a good night's sleep. But she needed some fresh air, a walk in the pasture to calm her nerves and her worry about Paris. She headed down her pasture and slipped through the trees to the opening in the fence that led to Paris's property. She stepped onto Paris's pasture and headed for the pond. She climbed the bridge and gazed across the water. The pungent, smoky smell of the charred wood still lingered in the air.

241

She knew it would continue to hang in the air until the debris was hauled away or buried. She glanced up the hill to where the house once stood. It seemed so strange not to see the tall windows and gingerbread trim fill the spaces between the trees. She noticed an SUV parked next to the barn. Perhaps the insurance company had finally made arrangements to have the lot cleared. She hoped so. She hoped whoever it was up there was sizing up the mess and making plans to clear it away.

"How do you like my new car?" Paris's voice came floating toward her from the island.

Sloan snapped her head around. Paris was sitting under the willow tree, her eyes bright and shining.

"Hello," Sloan replied with a dumbfounded stare. Her heart had raced to her throat and was pounding furiously.

"Seems like we always meet here beneath the willow tree," Paris declared fondly.

Sloan continued to stare as if she was cemented to the spot.

"I left you messages," Sloan stated. "Why didn't you . . . what are you . . ." She stammered, unable to make a complete sentence for all the emotions racing through her brain.

"Yes?" Paris said as she smiled across at her.

"Why didn't you call?" Sloan asked, finally able to speak.

"I'm sorry. I know I should have, but I have been very busy." Paris climbed to her feet and walked through the willow branches to meet Sloan at the bottom of the bridge.

"Too busy to say hello?" Sloan asked.

"Forgive me."

Sloan narrowed her eyes critically. "I'm glad you came back, but why are you here?" she asked.

"I have some unfinished business in Banyon."

"I should be madder than hell at you. First you leave without even a good-bye then you refuse to return my calls," Sloan scolded.

"I know. I know. I realize that now. It was no way for me to treat you. I did a lot of thinking and soul searching after you left New York."

Sloan was half afraid Paris had only returned to say good-bye in person.

"What unfinished business? You aren't selling out are you?" Sloan's forehead wrinkled with concern.

"Not Maybelline, or what's left of her. I could never sell all this." Paris looked back at the huge tree and smiled affectionately. "I'm selling other things but not my farm. How could I sell my pond and my willow tree? I have too many memories to ever sell it."

Paris took Sloan's hand and led her over the bridge. They strolled up the slope arm in arm. "So, you like my new car?"

"SUVs are more practical than a sports car, that's for sure." Sloan was more concerned about Paris's motive for returning to Banyon than her new car. She worried this was another short visit to finish paperwork and deliver the title for the BMW.

"Seth said Jeep Cherokees are what every country doctor is driving this year. He said an SUV is an absolute necessity if you have to drive in the snow."

"Yeah, it has four-wheel drive. Do you get much snow in Manhattan?"

"Some. I ride the subway on snowy days."

"Then why bother with a SUV?"

"Because there's no subway in Banyon." Paris raised her eyebrows and watched Sloan's expression.

Sloan's brain went into overload.

"Oh my God!" she gasped. Her eyes widened, and a grin slowly pulled across her face.

"As a country doctor, I'll have to drive in the winter. Seth said I won't have much snow, but you can never be too careful," Paris offered. "My new SUV also comes with a camping package."

She draped her arms around Sloan's shoulders and looked deep into her eyes. Paris had a happy look about her. Her eyes sparkled, and her face beamed with contentment.

"We country girls just love to go camping," Paris said, her smile growing as tears began to well up in Sloan's eyes. "I sold my practice to Bill Hays. He has wanted it for years. And I bought Seth's

243

clinic. I also put Gabby's watch in my drawer. I don't need to wear it anymore. I have someone very special in my life, someone I love deeply. And I want to be with her now and always." She looked softly into Sloan's eyes. "Would you know any place I might stay while I rebuild my house? It might be a long stay. A very long stay."

About the Author

Kenna White lives in a small town nestled in southern Missouri where she enjoys her writing, traveling, making dollhouse miniatures and life's simpler pleasures. After living from the Rocky Mountains to New England, she is once again back where bare feet, faded jeans and lazy streams fill her life.